RECONCILIATION

Shaun Francis

I dedicate this book to my parents and all those who lost their lives during the Troubles.

Contents

RECONCILIATION

Chapter One

1996

He drives his car through country lanes as dark clouds descend over the rolling hills, small loughs, and drumlins of South Armagh. Hedges run parallel along the road, making the early morning light inconspicuous. Farms run from field to field, saddling the border, many of them passed down from generation to generation, producing a bond here as unbreakable as tungsten metal.

He lights a cigarette and takes a long drag as smoke billows into his piercing blue eyes. He has nerves, but these are suppressed. He has always been externally unemotional, but this is deceptive, as a lot is going on within. Still waters run deep, as they say.

A road sign lies ahead. It reads Crossmaglen, and he indicates left.

He drives past the town square and its row of Victorian buildings where the pub is its shrine. He looks at a British Army observation post dominating the area. It is known as 'the Dalek,' a reference from *Dr Who* because it resembles an oversized robot. It possesses no redeeming features and looks like a space centre among agricultural land.

He drives to a brow of a hill and into a farmyard where

a man with cherubic features is waiting for him by a cattle shed. The young man is standing by another car that was driven from the Republic the night before. He gets out with the cigarette now down to a filter and flicks it to the ground.

The cherubic-looking man greets him. 'All set?'

The young man nods, and they swap cars, and he drives on.

***

Father McKenzie closes his book on the catechism and puts it back on the shelf. He can see the church out of his cottage window with its whitewashed exterior and spire of grey slates cutting into the sky. He has baptised the town's babies, officiated their weddings and buried their dead. He is a reassuring figure, especially to women, once young and now middle-aged, the vulnerable ones, going through a crisis of faith or in their marriage. He is always there for them, but his calling to God isn't always compatible with his proclivity for the opposite sex, yet his vows always succumb to his desires.

He looks at the leather-bound books on the shelf. He has eclectic tastes ranging from history books to the classics, many of which he considers masterpieces. His housekeeper keeps the shelves and the rest of the cottage clean and tidy. She is one of his favourites. Their affair has been on and off for a decade now. She sometimes cleans for him in a revealing maid's outfit. However, she isn't one to miss out and likes him to wear his vestments, where she has a penchant for the texture of the chasuble on her stocking thighs.

Father McKenzie's love for women is only surpassed by his love for his country. He wants it to be as one. It is in his daily prayer, and if it is God's will to continue the struggle, then so be it. He will fight with his comrades until it's achieved.

He looks out of the window and sees a car pull up. It is the one he has been waiting for. He walks down the hall, picks up a mortice key from the key tray, and walks out of the door. The man with piercing blue eyes gets out of his car and walks up to him.

'Come this way,' the priest says.

He opens a large arched wooden and ironwork door with the mortice key, and they step inside. They bless themselves at the font, and the young man looks up at the protruding nave embodying the heavens. Stained-glass windows are adorned in the colours of red and blue, showing a distraught Virgin Mary agonising over her loss. He walks up the aisle, passes columns of mosaic images of Christ suffering his crucifixion, and believes in its salvation.

Father McKenzie walks up the aisle and places his hands on the brass lectern. It is in the shape of an eagle with outstretched wings.

The young man stands in the aisle as he speaks.

'Dear Lord, may the son of God be at the shoulder of this man and give him the strength to succeed in his mission today. The calling of God and country will be with him. Amen.'

The young man makes a sign of the cross, and Father McKenzie nods. 'God be with you.'

The young man walks to the first pew before kneeling for a few moments. He puts on a pair of black leather gloves and looks down at a bundle covered by a white cloth. He lifts it up and unwraps it to reveal a Barrett M90 rifle. He covers it up and walks down the aisle with it.

He walks out of the church and through the cemetery, passing many headstones made of marble, granite, and fieldstone where family names have faded through time, but their presence has not.

He walks to a three-foot-high platform where a new gravestone of a Celtic cross is being erected. He unwraps and rests the rifle on the platform and looks through its telescopic sight as rain begins to spit on him.

He looks down at two British soldiers at a checkpoint. One of them is down on his haunches by a stone wall, and he grips his L85 rifle with purpose. He looks noticeably young in his uniform, wearing an MK 6 helmet, khaki green camouflage smock, trousers, and black boots. He is in his teens, and his face looks like it has yet to be introduced to a razor. The other soldier is older but not by much, in his early twenties. He moves with a confident swagger that suggests he has more experience in combat and life.

He stops a vehicle and asks the driver to get out. The driver looks at him with scorn and reluctantly steps out of his car. When the driver is asked for his driving licence, the soldier checks it. He scrutinises the inside of the front and back seats and asks him where he's going. He tells him he is on his way to work, and the soldier is making him late. The older soldier politely asks him to open the boot. The driver gives him a look of contempt which the soldier is used to, and opens it. The soldier inspects it. There's a spare tyre, a car jack, and a toolbox. He is satisfied and hands him back his driving licence and waves him on.

They have been on tour in Crossmaglen, XMG to soldiers, for four months with only a respite for four of these days, but a relentless rota of patrol doesn't dishearten their youthful enthusiasm, even when it's not welcome. The tension here is palpable. It is hostile yet underhand. They are a threat, not just in a martial sense, but to their way of life. Suspicion fills every corner, making its inhabitants insouciant to the carnage around them, and it hums with the raw energy of hate.

The man's eye is ingrained to the scope, and the rain now falling won't separate it. He puts his index finger on the trigger.

'Hey, Stevie!' The older soldier calls out in his distinct Scottish brogue. 'When we finish in this shit'ole I'll take you on a lad's night out in Larkhall. The lasses there will make everything stand to attention!'

The teenage soldier looks at him and smiles.

He pulls the trigger.

The bullet hits the young soldier, and his hands grab hold of his neck, dropping his rifle to the ground. His eyes bulge in shock, and he drops down sideways from the wall to the tarmac. Blood pours through his fingers like lava, and he coughs up blood that spatters to the ground. It streams down the road and mixes with the rain, turning the puddles pale red before congregating in a pothole.

'Stevie!'

The older soldier runs towards him and fires at where he thinks the shot came from, but there is no return fire, so he crouches down beside his mate and holds him.

'Hold on!' he says as he holds his head up. 'I'll get help... jis... jist hold on, pal!'

The teenage soldier's eyes roll back, and his blood-filled mouth gurgles. The complexion of his face goes from flushed to ashen, and his bloody hands let go of his neck.

'Hold on, Stevie, hold on!'

The older soldier holds him as his body jolts.

'Come on, Stevie!'

He jolts again.

Then it stops.

The young man gives Father McKenzie the rifle, gets into his car, and drives away. The priest carries it back to the church, into the vestry, and opens an underground vault. He picks up a torch, switches it on, and walks down the staircase, where he enters a six-foot-high arched brick tunnel. He looks at the outline of his lithe shadow and walks several feet into the vault until he gets to the end, shining his torch on the tomb of Father Thomas McGowan, the first priest of the parish. He places his torch vertically on top of the tomb, emitting a beam of light into the ceiling. He places the wrapped rifle next to it, picks up the torch, displaying his tenebrous figure, and walks back.

He heads back to his cottage and walks into the lounge. Looking at his record collection, he removes a shiny black record from its sleeve. He places it on the player, and the arm drops to the outer edge of the vinyl. It plays Vivaldi's L'inverno *(Winter) First movement.*

He watches police cars speed up as the unsuppressed trills of the violins form a wall of sound. Armed police officers leave their cars, run to the cemetery, and a tall man walks up to the cottage door and rings the bell.

Father McKenzie turns the music down and answers it.

'Hello,' he says in his deep, mellifluous voice. 'I'm Superintendent Craig Nowell.'

The priest motions with his hand. 'Come in,' he says. 'What is going on, Superintendent?'

Nowell steps into the hallway.

'There's been a shooting. A British soldier has been killed, and according to another soldier, shots were fired from this area.'

They walk into the lounge, and Nowell removes his hat to reveal a head of raven hair.

'Did you see anyone?'

Father McKenzie lifts the head off the record player and stops it. 'No, no one.'

'Have you been here all day?'

'Yes, I have. I've been writing my sermon.'

Nowell looks out of the window. 'Is your church open?'

'Aye.'

Nowell nods. 'May I take a look?'

'Certainly.'

He leads the Superintendent out, and they walk to the church door, and he opens it, blessing himself as Nowell looks on. Nowell walks up the aisle, and his footfalls resound, with the priest following closely behind before he stops at the altar and looks back at the pews.

'What time do you have mass?'

'We have one at ten o'clock.'

'How many parishioners will there be?'

'It will be half full.'

'Are they regulars?'

'Yes.'

'Locals?'

'Yes.'

'Good. They may know something.'

A constable comes into the church and walks up the aisle.

'Sir, we have cordoned off the cemetery.'

'Any cartridges found?'

'No, sir.'

'All right, keep looking.'

'What type of gun was used, Superintendent?'

'It could be a Barrett rifle. They can fire rounds at three times the speed of sound from over a mile away. So, this is a perfect spot.'

'On hallowed ground?'

'These men don't respect it.' He steps down from the altar. 'I will need a statement from you. Can my officers take one now?'

'At the police station?'

'No, we can do it here, in your cottage.'

'That'll be no problem, Superintendent.'

2

Father McKenzie lifts the carpet cover of the boot and places the wrapped rifle and cartridges in it. He avoids the checkpoints of South Armagh and all the border south of the province and heads west. He isn't stopped or challenged at any time.

Frank O'Daniels watches a fishing boat weigh anchor under a moonless Donegal sky, and his men push their dinghies out as the sea laps around their legs. They slide in them like dolphins navigating the sea, start the outboard engines, and speed out to meet the boat, bouncing up and down on the ever-increasing waves. When they get to its port side, men hand down wooden boxes and ferry them back to the shore, where they are hauled out.

The supplies have been transferred from a Libyan vessel onto boats off the Maltese coast under the radar of prying eyes. He has been waiting for this shipment for months. It is one of the biggest he has had, and it will help maintain the war against the Brits for the foreseeable future.

Father McKenzie walks down the shore and pulls the collar of his raincoat up to protect himself against the cruel wind. He nearly slips on the wet surface as he plants one foot firmly in front of the other.

'If it's not Christ himself! How are you, Father?'

'I'm very well, Frank. How are you?'

'I'm not too bad now, Father. I'm much better now we have this,' he said, looking out to the dinghies.

'What have you got there?'

'Ten tons of arms,' he replied.

'What type?'

'One hundred AK-47s, Taurus automatic pistols, Glocks, RPG 7 anti-tank rocket launchers and good ol' Semtex.'

'Where are they heading?'

'The same place as your gun.'

One man carries one end of the box, and the other carries the other end. Another man stands in the back of the truck and pushes them in with his foot.

'I want to congratulate you on what you are doing for our boys.'

'It's all down to them. They planned it.'

'Don't be so modest, Father.'

O'Daniels takes out a hip flask and drinks from it.

'Do you want a wee dram, Father?'

'No, thank you.'

'Oh, well,' he says and swallows some more.

'Do you have the gun, Father?'

'Yes, it's in the car.'

'Well, if you will do the honours.'

Father McKenzie heads back to his car, blowing on his numb fingers as he goes, hoping it will restore them back to normal. He opens the boot, picks up the rifle, and heads back to the beach.

'Ah, in a white altar cloth,' Frank laughs. 'Has it been blessed, Father?'

'No, we don't normally bless synthetics.'

'Too true, Father!' He laughs. 'Ciaran, come here a minute!'

Ciaran helps the driver slide a box into the truck, then jumps down and runs to Frank.

'Take this and put it in the truck.'

'No bother, Frank,' he says, taking the rifle from Father McKenzie.

'Where did he drive the car to?' Father McKenzie asks.

'He went over the border to a place near Dundalk, then it's being taken to Mayo where it will be crushed.'

'That's good news.'

The truck starts up and moves out, winding its way up the curving hill. The men drive in the opposite direction but will meet at the same destination. The two left behind watch them go and stand in the darkness of night.

'The Army Council will have to continue the war now.'

'I hope you're right, Father. I hope they will.'

Chapter Two

One month earlier.

Sosaidh pulls up her green tartan patterned skirt and zips it up at the side. She mouths the lyrics to *Jagged Little Pill* playing on her CD player with a blue backlight. When it gets to the chorus, she bellows with carefree abandon. No one is in the house except her, her parents had early starts, and her sister is at her university digs.

After switching the music off, she puts on her school blazer and brushes it down. She ambles downstairs into the kitchen, opens the fridge and takes out a cheese sandwich she made last night. She also takes out two small cartons of orange juice and puts them in her bag.

She closes the front door and double locks it. Her da says you can't be too careful, but everyone knows everyone else here. She could flush the toilet, and they would know it was her.

The morning dew covers the grass, and the pavement has a dark-grey sombre tinge. She makes her way to the bus stop when she notices a car. It slowly follows her from across the street, so she walks across to meet it and gets in.

'Michael, you shouldn't be this close to my house. My parents might see you.'

'I know, but I missed you,' he replies.

'Well, I'm glad you're here.'

Her blue-green eyes smile, and he reflects it.

'What's your first lesson?'

'Biology.'

'You're not dissecting a pig, are you?'

'No, a cow! I've got Miss O'Reilly, and she is one, so she is!'

'You could take a sickie.'

'I can't. I've got an important maths test this afternoon.'

'Can I pick you up at the same place?'

'Michael!' she says, blushing.

'What?'

'You know what!'

'Can I?'

'Aye, you know you can, but I have to be home by seven.'

He smiles. 'You will be.'

She has one of those days where everything seems to go right, no matter what she tries. She feels as high as a balloon ride over the fairy chimneys of the Cappadocia. She correctly answers every question the teacher asks and doesn't perceive herself to be a failure if she gets one wrong, but she gets nothing wrong. She doesn't feel self-conscious even though she's pretty, but there are prettier girls in her year, but today, if they make snide comments, she will brush them aside and swat them like a fly.

She walks past the main building of the upper school and notices her reflection in the window. She looks good. Her hair shines, her eyes are seductive, and her lips blend perfectly with her face. He makes her look and feel this way, but moreover, she is this way now.

She keeps on checking the time on every clock at every lesson she's in. Mid-morning becomes lunch, and lunch becomes early afternoon. She can't wait to finish and fantasises about him, even when she's doing her test, which she sails through. She stares at the clock, trying to spur the minute hand to get to twenty past, but it obdurately resists, and, in the end, she is forced to count the seconds.

When the lesson ends, her teacher gives the class a homework assignment, and she waits as he says the last word of his sentence before she hurries out of the classroom, through the corridor and down the steps before anyone else. She takes long strides at a rapid pace and walks along her route, as arranged, where he is waiting.

'Hi.'

'Hi,' she replies and kisses him.

'That was worth waiting for.'

'It was,' she says.

'So, what's the story? How did your test go?'

'It went well, so it did.'

'When will you get your result?'

'Next week.'

'Well, that's not too bad,' he says. 'Shall I stop off and get some fish and chips?'

'Aye, that will be grand but don't park too close to the shop.'

'Don't you want to be seen with me?'

'You know why.'

'I'm just having you on.'

'Away with you!'

She laughs.

He parks up and walks to the shop, which is five minutes away and she sits and waits.

They met through her da. They are on the same amateur football team together, although her da is coming to the end of his playing days. She attends the matches and loves watching him play. She finds it seductive, watching him skidding in the mud and battling other players. What is more desirable is the secret between them. The look he gives her when he scores, the knowing glances they give each other when he gets close to the touchline. It makes her quiver just knowing what's under his kit.

He opens the back door and puts the bag of fish and chips on the back seat.

'Your da was in the shop.'

'What!'

'Just kidding.'

She hits his shoulder, and he starts the engine.

They get back to his house, and he puts the takeaway in the kitchen. He takes her waist and kisses her, and they stand there holding onto each other before he stops and steers her to his bedroom.

By the bed, she can feel his hardness on her tartan skirt. She should have brought a spare pair of underwear, but she isn't thinking about that now. She is thinking about him. She lets him take her, she wants him to take her, and he takes her to anywhere she wants to go.

They lay on the bed, and he buries his head in between her thighs. He flicks his tongue on her, and she moans with pleasure, inspiring him to hear more. He moistens her as she does with him, and she grabs his hair like she's pulling a heavy load. He rubs in between her legs with his tip, it is swollen and receptive, and she lets out a sound he hasn't heard before. He explores her body, licking her nipples and underarms, where she lets out a gentle laugh. He rises until they are head-to-head, and they kiss, mouths wide open, long and loving, until he enters her, and she tenderly bites his neck. His erection is pulsating and esurient. He slowly puts himself in and out of her. Her cheeks flush, and her neck and breasts souse in their sweat. He slides it back into her and thrusts until his breathing becomes heavy. She grips him and digs her nails into his saturated back, and moans until her mind can't take it anymore.

He lies on her when they finish, then moves his body to her side. They lay there holding each other's exultant bodies and are fulfilled knowing the purity of their fluids is transferred to the other. She squeezes him and lets out a content sound, nuzzling her nose under his chin as he runs his hand along the arch of her back.

'Why do you make me feel so good?'

'Because you make me feel the same way,' he replies.

She lifts her head, and her bright eyes urge him to kiss her lips. Their lips softly meet and refuse to unattach themselves for some time.

He strokes her hair and looks into her eyes. 'Are you hungry?'

'I am now.'

He gets up, and she watches his lean muscular buttocks walk out the door. She lies there serenely and feels older than her years.

He comes back with fish and chips on plates and sets them in the middle of the bed.

'I heated them up.'

'Grand,' she replies with her head sunk into the pillow.

'Come on, before it gets cold. I've got plastic forks.'

She sits up. 'Oh, you do know how to spoil a girl!'

She forks two chips, and he starts on the batter of the fish.

'I love salty chips,' she said.

'Aye, they do the best chips in Armagh.'

'Michael?'

'Aye.'

'Why me?'

'What do you mean?'

'So many girls like you. I hear them talk when you play football. Why did you choose me?'

'How can anyone say why they choose someone? It's instinct. It's something I can't explain.'

'I'm sixteen.'

'Seventeen in November.'

'Aye, I am sixteen going on seventeen!' she sings to the tune of the *Sound of Music* song. 'I just wonder why that's all,' she adds.

'I only see you. I don't see them.'

She leaves the fork stuck in the chip. 'Really?'

'Aye, really. And I waited until you reached the age before I asked you out. It was seven months of hell.'

'I knew you would.'

'You did?'

'Aye, you were building up to it.'

'Well, I was nineteen. Now I'm twenty!' He sings, trying to mock her voice.

She laughs and picks up a chip.

2

Olivia Doherty is engrossed in handstands. She takes a run, stops for a second, and balances on the palms of her hands before tumbling on her back.

Michael walks into the garden and watches her. He is fourteen years her senior, a big age gap. Their mother had many miscarriages before she came along, but she told them both that they took all the strength from the ones left behind.

She takes a run again and holds her stance before falling to the ground. Michael is amused and likes her tenacity.

She sees him and runs up to him. 'Michael!'

'How you doing, kiddo?'

'Michael! Look at this!'

Olivia tries another handstand.

'Hey, not bad!' he says with encouragement.

She runs around effusively and giggles to herself.

Auntie Bernie comes out of the back door. She is thin with elfin features, the type of woman to busy themselves, jumping up to do this or that, never staying in one place for long, and she's as sharp as a squirrel and just as quick.

She puts down a tray of tea and goes back in before coming out with a tray of scones, soda bread, pots of jam and butter, the rich and creamy kind. It's like she's expecting to feed the five thousand. Michael looks at the big feed and doesn't have the appetite for it, but he knows he'll have to eat something just to appease her, so he obediently tucks in and lets her spoil him. Michael knows it gives her pleasure to run around for others, so he sits back and lets her.

'Watch yourself there, wee girl. I don't want to be running up to the hospital with you tonight!'

He wants to laugh at Olivia as Auntie Bernie's words fall on deaf ears.

'How's she been?'

Auntie Bernie butters two scones in rapid succession. 'Ah, she's been grand most of the time. She's a skittery wee thing when she wants to be, but you can't stay cross with her for too long.'

'Every day's an adventure, I suppose,' he said. 'Thanks for looking after her while I was away.'

'No problem, no problem at all.'

'Does she need anything?'

She thinks. 'A pair of shoes for school, she scuffed the ones she has down to the toes. Oh, and dresses as well.'

'I don't like dresses!' Olivia yells.

'Never you mind!'

He takes out his wallet and gives her a wad of money.

'Will this see you through for now?' He asks, handing it to her.

'Aye, it will surely,' she replies, stuffing the money into her pocket.

'Take some for yourself, Auntie, but don't be spending it on the men.'

'What do I want to be spending it on those feckers for!'

The phone rings in the lounge. 'Bath time later, Olivia!'

'It's all right, Auntie, I'm fine!'

She tuts. 'You're not!' she says before rushing off to answer the phone.

Olivia runs up to him, and she holds on to his waist wanting to be pampered. 'Have you come to take me home?'

He strokes her hair and picks some grass out of it. 'No, Auntie Bernie will be looking after you tonight.'

'Oh! Can you stay too!'

'I've got to go somewhere.'

'Where?'

'Just out.'

She lets go of him and runs around in a circle. 'Can I come?'

'Not tonight. Besides, you won't be able to carry me home.'

'I'll try!'

'I'm sure you would.'

She stops running around. 'Auntie Bernie is so annoying!'

'You be a good girl for her, okay.'

'Do I have to have a bath tonight?'

'Aye.'

'I can have one tomorrow!'

'You've been running around all day.' He points down. 'Look at your knees.'

She lifts her leg and looks at the grass stains and dirt

on her knee, so she licks her hand and wipes it off.

'Come here,' he said disapprovingly.

She runs at speed, and he scoops her up in his arms.

She stretches her arms out. 'Michael, look how high I can reach! All the way to mummy!'

'That's fantastic!'

'Can you reach the sky?'

'No, I don't think I can.'

She looks at him with pity and expands her arms as far as she can. 'Don't worry, I'll do it for you.'

3

The day is unseasonably warm, and they are grateful for it as they have devised their rendezvous with careful planning. She told her parents she is on a sleepover at her friends, and he booked the hotel. He picks her up at the scheduled place, and now they can have more than just stolen hours. For the first time, they can spend the night together.

Portrush sits on the North Antrim peninsula, and the amusement park overlooks the sea. The cirrus clouds are high in the blue sky, and the forecast is good weather for the morning. The ocean is still, and seagulls mew as they fly down to pick up scraps of food on the ground. Michael buys Sosaidh candy floss. She has a sweet tooth. He doesn't. In fact, he doesn't eat sweets and prefers fruit. She takes a bite of the strawberry-flavoured floss and looks up at the big dipper.

'Shall we have a go?' he asks.

'I don't know, it looks fast.'

'It's meant to be fast!'

'Aye, okay,' she replies with a nervous titter.

She eats some more candy floss and bins it.

They sit on the ride as it slowly makes its way to the top.

'This is the best bit, the anticipation,' he says.

'I know, but it's the scariest!'

They reach the peak, and the pit of her stomach turns. She closes her eyes while he keeps his open. It's a similar feeling to when an airplane takes off, and her feet seem to rise to her stomach. The roller coaster dips down at such speed it takes her breath away. She looks at him, laughing as it does. It zooms into a loop, and he feels like he's in flight, like a newborn bird just learning the art. She finds it scary yet exhilarating, but she wishes she had eaten the candy floss after and not before. As the ride slows and halts to a stop, he starts to laugh.

'What?' she asks.

'You're having a bad hair day!'

They get off, and she tries to get her fine auburn hair back to its original look and mostly succeeds. He takes her hand, and they kiss and go on a Dodgems ride. They get in a blue pole-mounted car, and Sosaidh drives. He always drives her around, so now she says it's her turn. She lets rip and clatters into a car where two young boys sit. When she hits them from behind, they laugh and then immediately try to get their own back, but she moves away, and they crash into another car where two teenage boys reside. The boys don't take too kindly to their prang and crash into them multiple times until the young boys are just trapped in the corner and are being pulverised to the point of submission. Sosaidh sees their plight and helps them out, colliding with the teenage boys and giving the young boys a chance to break free. Michael watches this, and it's a side he hasn't seen in her before. Determination and persistence. No matter how often they are thumped, she goes back and enters the fray.

Sosaidh goes a little further than most and has certainly made an enemy out of the teenage boys. She circles them again and gets the last bump in before the ride ends. The teenage boys get off and give her a stare that is as unfriendly as a predator on its prey. Michael stares back. It only lasts seconds, but it's enough for them to skulk away, dejected and defeated.

'Well, you showed them,' he said.

'Aye, I did. I didn't like the way they were tormenting those boys. It just seemed unfair, so I let them have it.'

'In more ways than one. I thought they were going to wet themselves.'

'Aye, I taught them to swim before they could walk!'

He laughs at her edginess and finds it enticing. It is appealing when he gets to know a new element of her. She is a woman of many layers, not a girl but a young woman, a fully-fledged one who is more than a match for any man.

'Do you want to go in the arcade?'

'Aye, why not.'

He puts in ten pence into the middle slot of the tipping point machine. The ten pence push some to the verge, but only one falls. She puts in one on the left, then two more and an avalanche of coins fall down. She picks them up and counts three pounds thirty worth of coins.

He gives up and goes on a kung fu game where he's scored on kicks and punches, with the flying kick being the highest score. She watches and incites him to take the flying kick at every other move, which he does and is awarded a high points percentage, finishing third on the leader board. Someone has put their name in as 'Teenage Kicks.' They are number one, and he hopes it's not those two boys from earlier.

They play other games, like a driving game called 'Pole Position,' before they leave. He steps outside the arcade and lights up a cigarette.

'I feel like a tin man with all these coins jangling in my

pocket.'

'You'll look good when you go sliver,' she says.

'Silver?'

'Aye, it will suit you when your hair goes grey.'

'I'm not for grey hairs just yet!'

'But you'll look distinguished.'

'Really?'

He takes one more draw of his cigarette, then drops it and stubs it out with his foot. He takes her hand again.

'I never want to let you out of my sight.'

'You'll be sick of the sight of me as time goes on.'

'Sosaidh, I never will.'

She gets on her tiptoes to raise herself higher than her five feet two inches and kisses him. They hug each other, and she puts her warm nose under his chin. He lets her snuggle into him and wrap herself around him. He smells the scent of her hair and rubs his chin from her nose to her hair. He is normally self-conscious about public displays of affection, but she takes them away.

They saunter down to the beach. The sun's rays make the sand appear like a surface of tiny, crystallised nuggets of gold. Children run towards the water without a care in the world, and Michael has the same feeling. Being with her makes him feel that he is at one with the world. He doesn't owe it anything, and nor will he ask. It's all here in front of him.

They get to the sand and take off their shoes and socks. Boys play football, and the ball goes over their heads to Michael, and he can't resist. He flicks it up before kicking it in the air, and he doesn't move from his spot. It comes down, and he whacks it again, then waits. The boys stand there watching. He whacks it again, still not moving from his spot, and it comes down, and he catches it, still in the same position. He throws it back to them, and they immediately start practising, but they can only do one then they have to run for the second.

'How did you do that?' Sosaidh asks.

'The same way you bashed those boys about. It's committed concentration.'

'Aye, we're both stubborn, so we are, but do you think we're alike?'

'In some ways.'

'What ways?'

'I think we want the same things, and if a couple does, then there's no reason why they shouldn't stay together.'

'What about opposites attract?'

'I only think that can be sustained if a person believes they are lacking in something and find it in the other.'

'So, they feel protected?'

'Aye, I guess so. But we're not opposites, far from it.'

'I know,' she replies.

He puts his arm over her slender shoulders. 'Come on, let's get out of here.'

He drives down Dunluce Road, and they take in the scenic views. He drives so fast that the wind howls through the open windows. Sosaidh unbuckles herself, puts her head out the window, and lets out a caterwaul of joyous sounds. Her hair blows back, and he can see her soft temples, bright blue-green eyes, delicate nose, and full lips. Her nipples and flat naval flash at him through her chiffon blouse as it blows in all directions. He laughs at her spontaneity and holds her leg, thinking she will fall out and be flung into the sea. The breeze gusts into her eyes, and her lashes feel like they are touching her forehead. She keeps her eyes open until they can't take the wind anymore, then closes them to let it feel her until she finally sits back on her seat and re-buckles.

'Wow! That was amazing!' she says, trying to catch her breath.

'Did you like it?'

'Aye! It's difficult to convey in words, but it makes me feel like me.'

'You look like you!'

'I mean the person I want to be.'

'You can be anything you want to be, Sosaidh.'

'I can, can't I?'

'And you will.'

'We will!' she said as she puts her head out of the window again.

He takes his hand off the gear stick, places it on her knee and surveys her as she lets the wind pass through her.

'Whoo-hoo!' she cries.

He presses down on the accelerator, and the car speeds along, going faster at every turn.

'Oh, Jesus, this is great!' she yells.

He lets her enjoy the trip, and he's enjoying himself

through her. He can be serious to the point of being mistaken as being moody, but her sunny disposition enhances his mood and makes him feel less guarded.

'Sosaidh!'

'What?'

He looks at smoke emitting from under the car's bodywork. The car starts to slow, and he releases his foot off the gas as the malfunctioning light glows on the instrument panel. A plume of white vapour trails behind, forcing other cars to overtake as he slows down to a halt.

Sosaidh sits back down in her seat.

'It's overheated,' he says.

She starts to laugh. 'Oh, God! It was fun, though!'

He turns up the heating fan to full.

'What are you doing that for?' she asks.

'It helps keep the coolant at a normal temperature.'

They get out of the car and stand by the side of the road.

A car slows near them. 'Do you need any help?' The man asks.

'No, we should be all right, so we will. Thanks for the offer,' Michael says.

'Okay, take care.'

'Aye, thanks.'

He waits for ten minutes to let the car settle.

'Can you pass me your Peckham Spring,' he says, alluding to an *Only Fools and Horses* episode where street trader Del Boy sells tap water as bottled ones.

'My water? This is expensive stuff!'

She opens the car and hands it to him.

'It's a waste of money. Do you know it spells naïve backwards?'

She giggles. 'It's lucky I brought more, naïve or not.'

He opens the hood, and it smoulders so he looks at the engine to see if there's any damage.

'That's good, the radiator hasn't cracked, and everything else looks fine.'

'What was the problem then?'

'Taking the old girl to her limits, that was the problem.'

'It's this young girl's fault for egging you on!'

'It's no bother. I'll put some water in the coolant and that will sort it out for now.'

He gives the car several minutes before he starts the ignition. It works to his relief, and they continue their drive through the coastal route of the north.

They walk up to the interlocking basalt columns of the Giant's Causeway. The Atlantic Ocean flows serenely around it, and waves drift up harmoniously to the shore. Clouds have formed, although the sun is trying to break through and sporadically achieves it, giving the coast a magical quality.

Small pools of water sit on some of the rocks. He steps on one and takes her hand. The hexagonal columns are like a disconnected staircase that's been half-built. He jovially hops to the top, and she jumps onto the next rock. He reaches out his hand to her, and she steps up to him, looking down from the summit and out to the sea.

A northern fulmar with a forty-four-inch wingspan soars up with the rising air current and over their heads. They watch its solid neck and bull-headed appearance swarm down, then up over the top of the rocks and disappear into the horizon.

He impishly skips down, and she joins in, both in hysterics until they reach the bottom. He picks her up, and she elevates her feet off the ground, and he spins her around. She has butterflies in her stomach and feels like she's floating with her heart in his. She trusts him not to let her fall and does so implicitly. She is open to him, and as the delicate hours pass, they show more of themselves to each other.

Like the many steps of the Causeway, they will have many years in each other's hands. He doesn't know a time without her. It is like nothing existed before, as in the terms anno domino (AD) and before Christ (BC), his first year began when she appeared.

'I love being here alone with you,' she says.

'Aye, it's the only time we can relax.'

'It's as good as 'Cross'.'

'Na, Crossmaglen is the best. We've got Slieve Gullion.'

'A great place to bring up children in,' she says with a smile.

'Aye. We could have a football team!'

'You have them then!'

'I wish I could. They'd be worth a fortune!'

'I'd like to have a career first. You know I want to be a nurse.'

'Aye, and you will. We'll work something out.'

'What about you? You need something more stable, Michael. I worry about our future.'

'You don't need to.'

He puts his arm over her shoulder, and she puts hers around his waist.

'None of this will last forever. One day the conflict will end, and we'll have the life we want,' he said.

'Aye, I think it will end, so it will. It's just when.'

She squeezes her soft hand on his, and he loves it when she does it. He is not used to such things; he has never had a proper girlfriend, and his mother was not demonstrative. Even though he knew she loved him, it just wasn't her way, but with Sosaidh, it's different. She exhibits love without any hidden guise. Is it her youth or her personality? He cannot tell, but it's probably a combination of both. She lost her virginity to him, to someone she loves, most people lose it out of peer pressure or through a drunken mistake, but she did it for all the right reasons.

He points up at the green and rock-strewn hills on the littoral edge of the water and hopes their love will achieve such heights. A northern fulmar, hopefully, the same one, flies above them, with squids between its grey-yellow beak and heads to those hills.

She has her eyes fixed on the hills and looks at the bird descend to nourish its family. He takes out a box from his pocket. He took it out of the glove compartment when they got out of the car.

'Sosaidh.'

'Yes?'

'I have something for you.'

She looks at him with the box.

He hands her the box. 'It's just my way of saying how much you mean to me.'

She opens it and looks at the gold heart-shaped earrings. 'Oh, Michael, they're beautiful.' She gives them back. 'Hold them for a minute while I take these ones off.'

She gently twists the earring back and forth and pulls it out. She takes the heart-shaped ones and positions her thumb and forefinger on one hand to grasp and hold it against the hole in her ear. She positions it correctly and delicately pushes it through the hole until they're each in all the way and pivots them slightly until they are secure.

'How do they look?'

Michael doesn't say anything and pulls her towards him. He kisses her lightly, feeling the outline of her lips. She responds to it and closes her eyes. The world heritage site seems to disappear and transfer them into their own world. It is one where no time and no people exist, only the seeds of their love. She feels the butterflies returning, letting her rise above into the clouds. He feels her and wants to secure it. He wants to give her his might, his will, and his vulnerability. He wants her to take it all and knows she can have it all.

They finally let go of each other, and he looks into her eyes, ones as green as the hills and as blue as the sea.

They walk to the wishing chair, a formation of rocks in the configuration of a barrel back chair. They wait behind other couples, some with families. A hubbub of different accents, English, American and Australian, reverberate. They stand there for fifteen minutes until it's their turn. He asks a couple behind him if they wouldn't mind taking a picture. The couple is Australian. The man has a warm and rich Aussie accent and obliges. Michael sits down, Sosaidh sits on his lap, and the man takes the picture. They smile and their wishes are captured.

4

Craig Nowell steps out of his car with a briefcase in hand and enters the building. He walks up steep stairs that creak as he puts his big feet on each step. He opens the door, and it squeaks at the hinges as he enters a dimly lit snooker hall. The place is deserted except for a young man at the bar. Nowell walks resolutely over to him.

'Jim,' Nowell says.

'Sir,' Jim replies.

Nowell looks around. 'Where is he?'

'Takin' a piss.'

Nowell looks at him disapprovingly. 'So, are you lot still surveying this area?' he asks with a hint of sarcasm.

'We are.'

An older man with a well-worn face comes in, grinning like a Cheshire cat. 'How are you, Craig?'

'Ferguson.'

Nowell shakes his hand, although he has the urge to wash it afterwards as he doesn't like the nicotine stains on Ferguson's fingers.

'Take a seat and rest yourself. Do you wanna drink?'

'No,' Nowell replies.

They both move over to a table and sit down, Ferguson coldly looks at Jim, and he promptly walks out. He takes out a packet of Benson & Hedges, lights up, then retrohale, much to Nowell's displeasure.

'I've got concerns,' Nowell says.

'About what?'

'The strategy.'

'What about it?'

'Sectarian killings. It won't change the landscape. We must look at another way.'

Ferguson sighs. 'It's not a scorched earth policy, Nowell. What do you want us to do? When they are murdering our people, we must strike back. There is no alternative. It's always been this way.'

'I understand that, but you need to go for the snake's head first, the big hitters.'

'Adams and McGuinness are out of the question, besides Belfast wouldn't sanction it. Too much money and too many men.' Ferguson shakes his head. 'It can't be done.'

'You only need one man to kill a President. We need symbolic acts so we can beat them at their game,' Nowell says convincingly.

'One man too many. What we need to do is fight their base.'

'Killing a Taig in front of his children isn't doing that. It's playing right into their bleeding hearts.'

'That was a one-off. He participated in Republican fundraising.'

'He was shot in front of a four-year-old!' Nowell replies indignantly.

'You know it's the intention,' Ferguson retorts.

'It's irresponsible, and it draws attention away from what we're trying to achieve.'

Ferguson sits back in his chair and regains his smile.

'Forget the PR. Trust us.'

Nowell looks at him closely for a moment and places his briefcase on the table and opens it. He takes out an A4 brown manilla envelope and pushes it towards him. Ferguson opens it. It contains all sorts of intelligence paraphernalia, including aerial shots, documents, maps, and mugshots.

Ferguson examines them carefully. 'South Armagh?'

'Correct.'

Ferguson stubs his cigarette out and lights another. He looks at one of the mugshots. It's the cherubic man. 'So, what do you have on him?'

'He's John Donnelly, aged twenty, been in the Provisionals since the age of sixteen. The pictures were taken this year when they were arrested for a mortar attack on the barracks in Forkhill. They were released when we couldn't find any evidence on them, but we believe they carried out the one in Bessbrook this month.'

Ferguson looks at the other mugshot. 'And this one?'

'Michael Doherty, also twenty, has been in the Provisionals for a couple of years. It's hard to find out about them. You know what it's like down there but from our intelligence in Belfast they are the prime suspects for those attacks.'

'They look like good poster boys for them,' he observes. 'Donnelly looks like a chubby Sean Penn and this fella looks like James Dean with Frank Sinatra's eyes.'

'How will you get to them?'

'I have word Donnelly will be arrested in the next twenty-four hours. I can get to him tonight. I know all his haunts.'

'Even the names of the women he screws!'

A thin smile breaks indiscernibly across his lips. 'That too.'

Ferguson gives him a rictus grin and his face looks like a bulldog chewing a wasp. 'I'll contact Belfast, they'll be happy.'

Nowell doesn't return the smile and declares darkly. 'There's no happy endings in life, Ferguson.'

He closes his briefcase and leaves.

5

O'Neil's bar was built during the partition. A neon shamrock is above the door, and pictures of local brewers enhance the plain brickwork of the walls. Its main bar is made from oak wood which runs along the length of the room. Brown leather upholstered stools are placed a foot or so apart, and polished brass pumps gleam with all the beers of your choice.

Michael walks in and sees Donnelly propping up the bar. He is a couple of inches shorter than Michael's five-ten, but he's stocky and a dirty fighter. Michael has seen him win many fights and knows it's best not to mess with his temper.

'Bout ye? Here's a pint for you.'

'Grand,' Michael said.

'Why the face?'

'I just went up to see me ma.'

'Ah, she was a good woman, so she was.'

'Aye, taken by a disease she didn't deserve.'

'Aye. How's Olivia doing? Is she liking school?'

'She's getting on fine. She's got the brains for it.'

Donnelly points to his face. 'Just like her uncle Johnny!'

'I wouldn't go that far!'

'It can't be easy for her, not with your ma's passing.'

'No, but luckily, she's too young to understand. Da killed himself with the drink, but ma...'

'I know. I'm here for her too.'

'Cheers,' he replies and drinks his pint down to a half.

'Is everything okay with us?'

'No problems. We just need to keep a low profile. They've got nothing on us,' Donnelly replies confidently.

Michael nods and drinks most of his pint.

'Another?'

'Then I'll never get out!'

Michael puts his glass down and begins to leave.

'Don't be late tonight! I have some of the most beautiful specimens you'll ever see!'

'And they're at your do!'

'Fuck off!' Donnelly retorts.

Michael walks out and gets into his car. He is happy with his life. He fills it with his Republican activities, which take up his daily living as much as Sosaidh now takes up his nocturnal ones. He feels at the core of everything. South Armagh revolves around him. It is a meteoric rise. He is the up-and-coming kid, and his life is going at a rapid pace. He is living for today. If he has money one day and none the next, he always finds a way of filling his pockets with cash. He robs for the organisation and enjoys doing it. He does not have a legitimate job, nor does he pay taxes, and from the time he left school, hitherto, it is like he doesn't exist.

He lives with Olivia with a wardrobe full of clothes for when he needs them, and when he doesn't, he lives off the charity of the movement. No day is the same. He doesn't wake up to a nine-to-five job, get home in the evening, have his dinner and watch TV until he goes to bed at eleven. That is for men with no ambition. He wakes up wanting to end the day in the last place in the world he thought he would be.

6

Birthday banners are strewn across the lounge area of O'Neil's. A large crowd of people congregate at the bar, enjoying the craic. Children play and chase each other around a maze of bodies as their mothers remonstrate with them.

A four-piece band plays rock and roll and country music. They are one of the best groups in the country, and through people he knows, Donnelly gets them for one night only. Women clap and cheer them on, dancing and swaying to the music. Couples dance, and men spin the women around and then grasp their hands before spinning them around again.

Donnelly stands at the centre of the bar and has his arms wrapped around two young women. He holds court as people pay him their respects. They know who he is.

'Mickey!'

'Johnny!' Michael shouts mockingly. 'Many happy returns!'

He lets go of the women and gives Michael a bear hug. The women take a keen interest in Michael's good looks, and one of them blushes when he looks at her with his come-to-bed eyes.

Sosaidh serves behind the bar under the supervision of the owner, Paul O'Neil. She likes the cash-in-hand money but not the attention, especially from men old enough to be her Grandaddy gawking at her breasts.

Donnelly ushers Sosaidh over, and he asks her to pull his friend a pint. She picks up a tulip glass and places it at a forty-five-degree angle under the tap. She pours it to three-quarters full, then raises the glass vertically and lets it settle before topping it up to the brim with a sideways figure of eight.

She gives it to Michael, and he looks at the shamrock design on the white head, and she gives him a coquettish smile. They agreed not to be too obvious, but it's easier said than done. They have an irrational fear of being caught. They are preoccupied with other's prolonged stares and snap of heads every time they talk to each other.

Donnelly wraps his arms around the two girls again, although they are more captivated by Michael's presence than his and are demurely vying for his attention.

'Did you hear about that wee bastard, Noel?'

'No. Is he still around?'

'Aye, the wee fecker is!'

'What about him?'

'He was in here last night trying to sell a pair of cowboy boots.'

'Any good?'

'Aye, for once they were. He said he got them on a trip to Texas, but he hasn't been outside of Ireland!'

'So, what's the problem?'

'The wee shit was trying to sell them to me, but I wasn't interested.'

'Why?'

'Because they were the wrong fucking sizes! American size eight and ten! But get this! He waited 'til that idiot Danny came in and got him steamin' before trying to sell them. He's a ten, but he only fucking bought the pair!'

'As long as he doesn't wear the other one, he'll be all right!'

The two women laugh at Michael's quip, although he's unconcerned. He's not going there. Sosaidh has style and poise and is well-read, and above all, she is the one.

Donnelly lets go of the women's waists and whispers in Michael's ear. 'I'll take the blonde one.'

Michael pretends to look interested.

'If youse ladies will excuse me,' Donnelly says.

He goes off to the restroom, and Michael drinks his Guinness then follows. He doesn't want to ask what work they do, nor is he interested in discussing the merits of boy bands. Besides, he drank three cups of tea when he popped in to see Auntie Bernie, so he feels the need.

Donnelly stands at the urinal, emptying a pint full of his bladder, and Michael walks in and stands at the next one.

'Mickey, that blonde one has got a lovely tight wee arse!'

'At her age, I would hope so. You can have both if you want. It's no skin off my nose. It's your birthday.'

Donnelly gives him a disbelieving look. 'What the fuck's a matter with you? That brunette would take you in the cubicle right now!'

'Ah, well.'

'Have you got a fucking headache or something?' Donnelly zips up. 'Every man has his vice, and every woman has her price!'

He walks over to the basin, splashes some water on

his mousy hair, and then combs it back with his fingers. They have grown up together, but Michael doesn't feel the need to confide his deepest thoughts to him. He zips up and washes his hands.

Donnelly moves his head at different angles and styles his hair with the water. 'Something's up with you. I can read you like a book. I know you better than you know yourself.'

Michael dries his hands and thinks you'll never know me.

Several blasts of gunfire come from outside. Michael and Donnelly stand there looking at each other. Michael moves to the door and opens it an inch or two. The bar is in chaos. People are running in different directions, falling over each other, jumping over and under tables and shielding their loved ones. High-pitched screams of women and children reverberate around the room as two masked men with assault rifles fire into the melee.

A bullet grazes the head of a young girl of about seven. She falls to the floor and is momentarily dazed. Blood pours from her face as she tries to sit up. They fire a hail of bullets. Michael wants to get to them, but Donnelly pulls him back when holes fill the restroom door.

Sosaidh crouches down and grabs the receiver of the wall-mounted phone. Paul O'Neil sits below it, his mouth agape from a blast to his chest. She looks at her shaking hand, tries to keep the phone still, and dials the three digits.

'Emergency, what service do you require, fire, police or ambulance?'

'There's a shooting at O'Neil's bar in Crossmaglen. Yes... gunmen... they're here shooting people. We need help!'

'Are they there now?'

'Aye, they're here now. Can't you hear them?'

'Yes, I can hear them. Just stay on the line. I have called for the police and ambulances. A rapid response team will be with you soon. Just stay on the line with me.'

Splinters of wood bustle into the air as a bullet whizzes past her, and masonry falls onto the bar as shots hit the ceiling. Dust falls onto her hair, getting into her eyes, and she wipes off the irritants.

'We'll be with you as soon as we...'

She is cut off as bullets shatter the phone, leaving wires flickering and fizzing over her head. The young girl gets up, runs under the bar flap, and into Sosaidh's arms. Blood trickles down her temple, and a deluge of tears runs down to her jowls.

'My mummy! My mummy's out there. Please help me get to my mummy!'

Sosaidh puts her finger to the girl's lips. 'I will. You just need to be quiet. I'll take you to her soon. You just need to be quiet until then, okay,' she whispers.

Sosaidh takes her, and they huddle down under the bar.

The girl whimpers. 'Oh, Mummy.'

The bar flap opens, and a man with a black balaclava covering his head stands over them. He points his gun at her, and she looks at him with terrified eyes and prays. 'Our father, who art in heaven...'

She doesn't get to the next verse, and the girl lets out

a frantic scream.

The man steps out and pushes open the men's toilet door with the muzzle of his gun. He walks to the first cubicle, where the door is closed. He sees the other cubicle doors are open, so he fires at the closed one, and as he does, Michael runs at him from behind the last cubicle. Michael grabs the gun and wrestles it out of his hands. Donnelly jumps on him, and the man falls back against the door. Michael tries to fire the gun, but it jams, and the man kicks Donnelly off and takes out a Glock from his jacket pocket. He gets to his feet, and they both point their guns at each other, and he steps back and opens the door.

Michael chases after him and fires, hitting him in the shoulder. Donnelly and other men run towards them, throwing bottles and pint glasses, hitting one on the head. A man runs towards the other gunman with a bass drum from the stage, and the armed man shoots, and he falls back with the drum lying on his stomach. Michael shoots the other gunman in his side as glass smashes all around them, and men still try to get to them as they make a hasty retreat out of the door.

A car is waiting outside, and the driver sees they are in trouble and fires out of the car window. The man with the injured shoulder fires several rounds. As the other man jumps in the front passenger seat, he fires again, then jumps in the back as it speeds off. Michael fires, shattering the back window until the car disappears down the road.

He and the others step back into the bar.

Donnelly looks at the gun. 'It's a Shipyard special.'

'Aye, deadly,' said Michael.

'You need to wipe your prints off.'

Michael doesn't hear him and looks at the bodies. Some are piled up, forming a mountain of heads and limbs. Others just lay on tables and chairs. Blood drips down the walls like a slaughterhouse in an abattoir. He looks over the bar but can only see Paul O'Neil, so he goes to the ladies' to see if Sosaidh is there. He looks in all the cubicles where one woman sits on the toilet with her head in her hands. He walks back out to the bar, searching for her and getting more anxious by the minute.

'Mickey, we have to go!' Donnelly implores.

'You go. I'll stay here.'

'What for!'

He hears a whine from under the bar and casts his eyes over it, and he sees two heads, so he walks around and through the opening. It's like he's walking in slow motion, and he stops. She is here, and he collapses down next to her, pressing his forehead on hers like he wants them to be joined together. Her eyes are open, and her petrified stare remains. He lifts her head up and touches the gaping hole in her cheek. He can't believe they shot her there. Her face doesn't belong to her anymore, it's been replaced by a twisted and haunted one, and her eyes stare into a place they did not want to go. His agony is so pronounced that no noise comes from him. He only hears the girl weeping next to him, and he holds out his hand to her, but she doesn't look at him and trembles with fear.

Donnelly's feet crunch over broken glass. 'Jesus, Mickey!'

Michael doesn't know what to say in response, and his thoughts are as fragmented as the cracked glass.

'Mickey, we have to get out of here!'

'I can't leave her,' he said, distraught. He then looks at the girl. 'And this girl has to find her ma.'

Donnelly looks at the dead woman near the stage and knows it's her mother. He looks back at Michael and shakes his head. Michael strokes Sosaidh's hair, then touches her ear lobe and wipes the blood off the earrings he bought her.

'Mickey, we've got to go!'

'You go.'

'Wait there!'

Donnelly walks over to one of the women he was holding earlier and takes her by the elbow.

'Huh, what are you doing?'

He walks her over to the bar and stands her next to the girl. 'You see this girl, stay with her!'

She begins to sob as Donnelly positions her with the young girl.

'Mickey!'

'I'll stay,' he whispers.

'She's dead. You can't do anything for her.'

He kisses her disfigured face. Donnelly can see her molar teeth through the hole, and he looks away.

'We have to go. Otherwise, we'll get lifted!'

'No, no...' Michael replies.

Donnelly squats down next to him and clasps his head like a vice. 'We'll find out who did this. We'll find them, believe me! But to do it, we need to go!'

Michael sighs deeply and delicately lets go of her like she's a priceless work of art. He kisses her forehead and rests her head on the floor. He gets to his feet and stumbles, and Donnelly holds him as he steadies himself. He looks at her, fighting the tears, and Donnelly tries to comfort him but can only pat his shoulder in condolence. They step on debris and through injured bodies, as well as perished ones. As they get to the entrance, the young girl sees her mother and starts screaming. She is incandescent with rage, and the woman tries to hold her but breaks free and runs to Michael.

She grips him so tightly the whiteness of her knuckles show. Michael holds the back of her head as it shakes with the rhythm of a newborn puppy.

'It's okay, darlin',' Michael says soothingly.

Donnelly clutches Michael's jacket and pulls him away.

'We'll take her,' Michael says.

'To where?!'

'To her grannies.'

'Away and fuck!'

'She's Danny McGowan's kid. He was one of ours before he got it in the head last year.'

Donnelly faces him and tries to read if he's serious or not, but Michael conveys an expression a poker player, playing his last hand.

'WE'RE TAKING HER,' Michael enunciates.

Donnelly sees his warm blue eyes change to ones that are solemn and almost cold. His face constricts and his eyebrows narrow the brow of his face. He doesn't blink and his large almond-shaped eyes stare at him fiercely. Donnelly just lets out a deep sigh as Michael takes the girl's hand and leads her to the door.

Donnelly steps in front of them and kicks the door open, then looks out. No one is there, so he runs to his car, opens the door, and starts the ignition. He tells Michael and the girl to get in, but Michael hesitates and looks back. The sound of whooping sirens can be heard in the distance, so he opens the passenger door, pushes his reluctant friend and the girl in, puts his foot on the accelerator, and spins away.

CHAPTER THREE

2016

Olivia is outside the dome-shaped building of the Waterfront Hall. She takes out her iPhone from her Gucci handbag, a bag she couldn't resist buying yesterday and taps it.

'Hi, Jan, yes, I've just arrived. Have you booked the one o'clock meeting for Monday? Oh, grand… okay, wish me luck!'

The main hall is full of hundreds of businesspeople. They have come from all over the UK and some even from North America.

The chairperson steps up to the podium. 'I hope you've had a pleasant morning,' she says. 'And have enjoyed all the facilities the Waterfront has to offer.'

Olivia stands on the sidelines and clutches her speech. She looks up at the plafond of oblique patterns and spotlights shining out of it. It accentuates modernity, and she is the vanguard of this new aspiration. She holds the speech and knows this is the most important to date, she just needs to put on a good show, and they'll like it.

'I would now like to present our next speaker of the morning, Olivia Doherty.'

The audience applauds, and she walks onto the large wooden stage.

'Thank you, everyone. My name is Olivia Doherty, and I'm the creator of *youthalliance.com*. We are an organisation dedicated to providing education and vocational training for our future, Northern Ireland's sixteen to twenty-four-year-olds. We have grown seventy per cent since our conception two years ago, which suggests an expanding and successful body to do business with.'

She shows the audience a film about her business. She continues to speak for the next twenty minutes using a PowerPoint presentation. She knows this is her calling and wants to mix her passion for cross-community integration with business expertise.

After her speech, she mingles with others in the reception and talks with different groups of people, promoting her credentials and enthusiastically trying to convince them to finance her.

A tall young man enters the group and listens. She gives him a sidelong glance; he has dark hair and light brown Mediterranean eyes, and she can feel his presence even when she's not looking at him. She keeps on talking, but her thoughts are of him. She is slightly embarrassed by this and feels her cheeks getting hot like she's some lovesick teenager, but she lets the sensation take her as anything else is self-denial.

He waits for her to finish and then takes two glasses of orange juice from a waiter and hands one to her.

'I thought you might need one?'

'Thanks,' she says and takes the glass.

'I'm Simon.'

'Olivia.'

'I was impressed with your presentation, Olivia. You must have put a lot of work into it.'

'I always do my homework.'

'It shows. I'm sure you'll get support for it even from these money merchants.'

'I hope so.'

He looks at his watch. A Rolex, she notes.

'Look, I'm just going to get some lunch. Would you like to join me?'

'Well...'

'I'm buying.' He smiles. 'Well, I'm not really. The company is.'

'All right, go on then, I might as well get something out of you greedy money merchants!'

They get one of the last tables in the restaurant and order. As they chat, they find the conservation rolls without interruption.

'How's your meal?'

'It's fine. How about yours?'

'It's good,' he replies. 'So, how long have you been a vegetarian?'

'Since the age of nine. I don't eat anything with eyes!'

He watches her blue eyes light up, which changes her expression and makes it softer. She has high cheekbones, and her complexion is like porcelain due to the lack of Ulster sun.

'So, how did your company come about?'

'I just saw an opening for it. Belfast is rapidly changing, especially its infrastructure, but sometimes it doesn't focus on the things that really matter. Its community. We need to focus on that more.'

'And lost opportunities.'

'Aye, definitely, there's been many of those.'

'I think you're a crusader, and that's a rarity these days.'

'Maybe,' she replies, brushing her long straight dark brown hair back.

He looks out of the window. 'God, we can't even get away from it here.'

She looks out and sees people with opposing flags and not the ones you usually associate with the six counties. Men and women, young and old, stand on opposing sides, one with Union flags and the other with a circle of twelve, five-pointed yellow stars on an azure background.

'Times are changing,' she says.

'Aye, they are. Have you voted yet?'

'Aye, first thing.'

'Snap!'

'I'm a Remainer,' she declares.

'Me too, although I won't tell my parents that.'

'Why? Won't they approve?'

'No. Staunch leavers, I'm afraid. What about your parents?'

'They're no longer with us.'

'Oh, I'm sorry to hear that.'

'Thank you,' she says. 'We need to stay integrated with Europe and each other. It's the only way we'll survive.'

He nods. 'I like what you're doing, Olivia. Most people here are more concerned about financial incentives.'

Olivia picks up her glass of water. 'Like you?'

'That's a low blow! There's much more to this shy and humble man than meets the eye, you know!'

'Shy! You?'

'Okay, you've got me there!' He laughs. 'You are doing things that people our age lose track of, you know, the social issues.'

'I suppose that's from my rebellious student days wanting to uproot things.'

'It could be. Where did you study?'

'Coleraine.'

'The coastline up there is beautiful.'

'It is, surely.'

'I studied Law at Queens.'

She raises her eyebrows. 'Queens. My, my,' she says teasingly.

'It's not that impressive. I dropped out after a year.'

'Why?'

'I concluded that justice is a loaded question.'

'I suppose you're right, but indecision can be a bad thing.'

'I know but I'm happy with where I am now. Anyway,

I've decided I would like to see you again.'

'You don't waste time, do you! Well, I haven't decided on you yet, the jury's still out on that one.'

'Juries! Don't talk to me about juries!'

She senses that he really wants to get to know her, and she doesn't feel inhibited and talks to him freely, much to her surprise, and she even enjoys the playful flirting.

He reaches inside his blazer pocket and produces his wallet. 'Here's my card. If you ever want to negotiate any further business.'

She takes out a card from her handbag. 'I'll return in kind then.' She places her card in his hand. 'If you have any ideas, feel free to send them my way.'

He flashes a smile and reveals a perfect set of white teeth. 'I will,' he replies.

When the conference is over, they talk at length outside the hall. People pass by without them noticing until they realise they're the last ones there. They just don't want the day to end so he thinks of the next best thing.

'Do you want to go for a drink?'

'Yes, that would be nice,' she says.

2

Michael leans nonchalantly on the bonnet of his car and looks at his phone. He is in his fortieth year, and despite having a lean athletic body, it feels rumpled and used, a lot of it due to insomnia. He's waiting for Olivia outside St. John's Roman Catholic School and although he doesn't particularly like these talks, she tells him they are good for him. He works for her and does these talks to support her but doesn't always feel they are worth doing.

Olivia parks up, and he knows she will jump out as she is always on the move.

'Hi,' she says as she approaches him.

'How are you doing?' he asks.

'I'm grand, and you?'

'I'm okay. I haven't seen you for a while, just texts.'

'Sorry, I've had a lot of work on,' she replies as she hands him some documents.

Michael looks at them. 'What's this?'

'They're just some notes about the place, protocols, etcetera.'

'Okay,' he said. 'I went up to Mummy's and didn't see any flowers from you? It's the anniversary, you know.'

'I'm sorry, I've been so busy. Don't worry, I'll be up there this week.'

He looks at her and knows she will.

'Shall we go in then?'

'All right.'

'Michael, you're not still nervous about these talks, are you? You're a dab hand at it now,' she says, waving him in. 'Come on, you'll be fine.'

'Is this what it's come to, my little sister acting the big girl and telling me what to do?'

'Women are in charge now!'

'Oh, you think so.'

'Aye, especially this one!' she laughs, and she takes him by the arm.

The school hall holds hundreds of children, and it's quite a daunting prospect for Michael as he views this with Olivia from the back of the hall. He looks at the green fire exit sign in the middle and thinks it would be the best place to go.

The children sit chatting, messing around and nudging each other. They have no knowledge of what went on then, only what their parents have told them or from images they've seen on *YouTube*. They are oblivious to it, it doesn't enter their minds, and it can't compete with social media or the rites of passage in their lives.

The children hush as a young female teacher stands in front of them. Michael knows this is his cue and makes his way up to the front.

'Today,' she tells them with authority. 'We have a man who will speak to us about past events in our history. I hope you will listen attentively to what he has to say. So, may I introduce Michael Doherty?'

'Hello, my name is Michael Doherty, and I'm currently a youth worker at my sister's organisation, Youth Alliance. It hasn't always been this way, though, because I was in another organisation that fought for your independence. The one which begins with an *I*.'

'The RA!' a schoolboy shouts out to the laughter of others.

'Quiet!' the female teacher remonstrates.

'Aye, that's the one,' Michael replies, and the schoolboy's riposte calms his nerves. 'I was convicted of shooting a British soldier, a soldier I saw as an unwanted alien force on our land. I served time, and I'm here talking to you today to explain how things were then, and if you have any questions, I'll answer them as best as I can.'

Olivia smiles at a middle-aged blonde woman standing at the far corner of the hall. She wears dark glasses because she doesn't want him to recognise her, although it's been some years now. She doesn't respond to Olivia's smile and looks back at him stone-faced.

Once the talk finishes, Michael and Olivia meet up in the car park.

'Did you see the kids' faces? They really took in everything you said.'

'Even if it was too green?'

'I don't think that will ever change!'

'It's getting easier.'

'Good.' She smiles. 'What are you doing tonight?'

'Why?'

'If you're passing my way, can you give me a lift to the Odyssey?'

'What time?'

'Seven-thirty.'

'Aye, no problem.'

He opens his car door. 'Don't forget about your Ma now.'

'I won't,' she says. 'Thanks.'

He drives off into the distance, and Olivia waves him off. She then turns around, and an attractive older woman walks towards her. She takes off her glasses and puts them in a case.

'Thanks for coming, Martha.'

'I debated over it,' she says with a well-pronounced home counties accent.

'I just wanted you to hear for yourself what Michael has to say.'

'I heard… I heard that he still believes in the cause.'

Olivia looks at her sympathetically and feels torn between protecting her brother and showing her compassion.

'He's changing.'

'Has anything changed?' Martha says doubtfully.

'Yes, so much has changed here.'

'But remains the same.'

'Just give me an opportunity to let him speak with you. I'll arrange it.'

'I want to, but for what purpose?'

'So, he can recognise things and understand. Just talk. That's all I ask,' she pleads.

'I don't think so, Olivia.'

'Please... for me.'

Martha looks pensive. 'Can we visit Crossmaglen?'

'Crossmaglen?'

'Yes, I want to see where my son died.'

'Are you sure?'

'Yes, I'm sure.'

3

They stand in the heart of the town. Nothing has changed, the layout of the square is as it was, and the pub and shops are the same. It's like nothing took place here. The only difference is the absence of the observation tower, the Borucki post, which dominated the sky for twenty-three years.

'Are you okay?' Olivia asks.

'Yes.'

'This is the main square.'

Martha looks around. 'I expected it to be bigger.'

'It's not a big place. The army observation post used to be over there,' Olivia explains, pointing to the area.

'It was a bad place, wasn't it? The British called this place Bandit Country.'

'Yes, it had a bad reputation.'

She looks at Olivia. 'I'm glad you were too young for all of that.'

'Me too.'

'I would like to see where it happened,' she says.

'All right. It's a mile or so down this road.'

They drive out of the square and down Cullaville Road, which leads onto Old Road. Rolling green hills surround them, and the bucolic scenery makes it look like the most peaceful of places. Olivia stops halfway between Crossmaglen and the townland of Cullaville, which bestrides the border, and they get out and look around.

'Is this the place?'

'Yes, this is the place,' Olivia replies.

Martha looks at the masonry-assembled stone wall and walks towards it. She looks at it like she's looking at her son and pictures him here. She was told the last thing he did was smile, and it has stayed with her, for better or worse. She thinks of all the things she has missed, of him becoming a husband, a father, and an officer. She will never attend his wedding or see his children, for these are things she hungers for that never were. She stands there for many minutes without moving until her teardrops fall on the wall.

Olivia walks over to her and rubs the top of her back. She stands there with her, and her stomach feels queasy. Her brother did this, and she can't appraise her own sentiment, let alone Martha's. She hands her a tissue, and she takes it, wiping her eyes. They stand there mutely until Martha can coalesce and collect herself.

'Why here?'

'Michael told me that army watchtowers had blind spots and could only surveil a small percentage of the terrain in certain weather.'

'Is that the church?'

'Yes.'

'The hill leading to it is quite high.'

'Yes, it is.'

Speaking rhetorically. 'It has a deceptive beauty.'

Olivia lets her take it in. She doesn't want to take away any of her thoughts.

'When Stephen was born, I sat there all night just looking at him...' she says as she looks at the church. 'I didn't sleep. I thought about my life and how it had led to this point.'

Olivia imagines her lying there staring at her baby. She envisions her feelings and how powerful the bond was, one encapsulated by love and protection.

'I just couldn't move my eyes away from him. It felt like a laser beam of love going into him. I couldn't process the maelstrom of feelings. I only knew they would never evaporate and would always leave a permanent imprint on me.'

Olivia observes her and knows her mind is in another place where she feels comfort.

After a minute, Martha looks back at her and takes out an envelope from her jacket pocket. 'It's for him.'

Chapter Four

Michael hits the brakes and narrowly avoids a group of young women as they run across the road in their tight, short skirts and high heels.

'That was close!' Olivia said.

The young women titter and wave, acknowledging their mistake, apologising to him in their own private sign language.

'I hope you two don't end up like that.'

'Erin will!'

'I hope so!' Erin declares.

'I hope not! I don't want to be standing over you with your head in the toilet!'

'You won't be. You'll be with Simon.'

'Who?' Michael asks.

Olivia looks at him. 'Oh, it's just someone I'm seeing,' she says coyly. 'It's early days yet.'

'Okay. As long as he treats you well, that's the main thing.'

'He does.'

Michael smiles. 'Just looking out for you, kiddo.'

'What are you doing tonight, Michael? Are you on the prowl too?'

'No, Erin, Belfast women are too high maintenance for me. Whatever happened to a bag of chips and a Babycham?'

'We ladies like to be treated well,' Olivia says.

'Why don't you come out with us tonight, Michael?'

'Thanks for the offer, Erin, but I wouldn't get a word in edgeways!'

'Really!'

'I don't think I'll survive a night out with you lushes, anyway.'

Michael stops the car, and Erin gets out, saying her goodbyes. Olivia sits there, and he watches her open her handbag.

'No payment. I'm rich enough,' he jokes.

Olivia takes out an envelope from her handbag. 'I want you to read this. It's important.'

***

When Michael was five, he asked his mother why he couldn't play with the other boys and girls who didn't go to the same school or church as him. She explains to him it is because of the colours.

She tells him green is a colour you see all over Ireland, it is a tranquil colour, and it represents us. He asked what tranquil meant, and she described it as calming and reassuring, like his blanket.

'My blanket?'

'Aye, your blanket. You like it, surely; it brings you

comfort, so it does. You fall asleep covered in your blanket, don't you, wee man?'

'Aye, Mummy, I do.'

'Well, that's what it means to us,' she said.

'So, what about orange?'

'Well, orange is something that you don't see here. Orange was brought over here like the sun.'

'The sun?'

'Aye, the sun. We rarely see the sun here. We only see green because when it rains, as it often does, it's because it's crying for our land, and that's why there is so much of it.'

'You're right, Mummy. I see green all the time.'

'But orange...'

'What about it?' he asked as he jumped on her lap.

'It burns, so it doesn't belong here. You've been burned before, haven't you? Remember when you threw your jumper into nanny's fire to get more heat.'

'I remember!'

'Well, when you tried to get it out, you burned your fingers.'

Michael looks at his fingers and blows on them.

'I put your hand in cold water, didn't I?'

'Aye, you did, Mummy.'

'Well, rain is water, isn't it? And it made your hand better, but the flames were orange, and they burned you.'

He looks at her with his big blue eyes. 'So, that's why

I can't play with them?'

'Aye, because you'll be burned and burning scars for life.'

'Forever and ever, you mean?'

'Aye.'

'I don't want that, do I, Mummy!'

'And that's why you are green, and they are orange.'

He considered this for a moment, and she picked up his blanket and softly rubbed it on his face. He felt its softness and began to understand.

***

Michael puts his car keys on the table and sits down in his sparsely furnished lounge. He unfolds a white envelope on the table, there is no name on it and it is creased in the middle. He sits down and irons it out, picks it up and opens it.

> 'Mr. Doherty. You may wonder why I have written this letter, given the circumstances. Well, to tell the truth, I have asked myself the same question a thousand times. I have seen your face, and you mine, but what lies in your make-up is open to conjecture...'

Michael looks up and then back at the letter.

> 'Nineteen ninety-six was the year I lost my son, Stephen, and every day that passes is a step closer to him...'

He reads it to the end and then throws it on the table. He rubs his temples and his head pounds, and beads of sweat form on his brow. He gets up and paces his apartment like a Formula One driver doing circuit laps. He walks back to the letter and reads it again, but this time he takes it in, and it hurts.

He sits in a daze and wants to know how his sister has become involved. He thinks of phoning her but knows he won't get an answer. He goes into the bathroom, washes his hands, and thinks about every sentence as he does before foaming his hands again until they are raw.

He reads the letter eight times, and each perusal is more intense than the last. He tries to sleep in the night, but his dreams intrude.

He dreams of his mother; she is tending crops on an allotment. She grows root vegetables and potatoes. She carries a young Olivia in her arms and sits her down while she cultivates the crops. He watches her talk to other women; they all have their own individual plots, yet they grow the same vegetables. He is never on the same tract as her, and if he moves closer, she immediately jumps to another plot. The women help each other collect the vegetables and are animated and loquacious as they do it.

He watches his mother work, and she turns and looks at him, and finally, he's on the same plot as her. She points down to the soil and looks at him again. He moves closer and looks down to where she points. He starts to dig the soil with his hands. He looks up, but his mother is gone. He digs with his bare hands until he comes across a white cloth. He opens the cloth, and a rifle is wrapped inside. He picks it up, and it drips with blood.

No one is in the allotment now, just him and the rifle. The blood from the rifle turns the soil red, and he stands there stuck in it. He hears inhuman sounds, like hyenas, and turns around, and his mother, Olivia, and the other women are all pointing and screaming at him as he sinks into the earth.

He wakes up soaked in worrying sweat. His mind rushes with the most horrifying images, and he spends the morning brooding and feels like he's one of the living dead. The dream taunts him, and he can't channel his morose thoughts. All he can do is try to keep them at bay.

2

Olivia looks out of her office window at the aluminium iceberg-shaped structure of the Titanic Centre. She is proud to say she has built up her business, with the help of government subsidies, into a thriving company. She has networked and turned Youth Alliance into the province's foremost educational and vocational training organisation. She looks at the sun shining over the city and sees a bright future ahead.

The door swings open behind her, and she jumps out of her daydream. Michael walks up to her desk and throws the envelope like a frisbee onto it. She looks at it and needs no explanation of its content.

He points at the envelope. 'What's this about, Olivia?!'

'Michael.'

'What the hell is going on!'

She sits down, but he opts to stand. Even if he was offered an invitation to sit, he would see it as an insult, and she doesn't offer, knowing it would be one.

'Martha contacted me...'

'Martha! So, you're on first-name terms now!'

'She contacted me three months ago. We exchanged numbers and talked. I just wanted her to understand the situation better. I tried to explain it all to her, but in the end, I wasn't the one to do it.'

'Why did you do it?'

'I just wanted to tell her what a good person you are.'

'Do you think she'll believe it!'

'I just wanted to tell her.'

'I can speak for myself!'

'I know, that's why I think it's time, Michael.'

He gives her a baffled look. 'Time for what?'

'Time to talk. For you to end this.'

'End what?'

'You're suffering. I see it, even if you don't. I know when your eyes are smiling and when they're not.'

She sits forward and lowers her tone. 'It's time to talk to her and tell her what happened.'

'I can't do that, Olivia.'

She stands up. 'Why? I know it's in you. It's something left unsaid that wants to speak.'

'What is done, is done. I can't change that for her or anyone,' he says consolatory.

She moves around from the front of the desk and stands directly in front of him. 'You can. People change. Times change.'

'Not this.'

'Exactly this. If you don't talk to her while she's here, you'll regret it.'

'She's here?'

'Aye, she's here. She was at St. John's yesterday; I've seen her every day, and she's here for a few more.'

'Olivia, I know you have the best intentions, but the past is the past.'

'It isn't for you; I know it isn't.'

Chapter Five

Michael drinks his coffee and waits. He is early. He's always been punctual and hates being late, but he wishes he were today. He feels like he's waiting to go to an exam at school or for the most important job interview of his life.

He watches people rush around Great Victoria Street, going about their normal day, taking their lunch breaks or going out shopping. He strokes his stubble, and it feels like sandpaper on his fingertips. He's had three hours of interrupted sleep, but the coffee keeps him alert. More than that, he's wired. He's on his third latte, and it's beginning to lose its sweet milky taste.

He looks at a father take his daughter's hand as they come out of a shop. She takes it but only as leverage to swing and howl with laughter as she does it. It reminds him of Olivia when she was her age, and just as he holds that thought, he sees the familiar face of his sister.

Olivia walks across a pedestrian crossing with a woman in her fifties beside her. The woman holds the strap of her handbag tightly as the wind blows her blonde hair across her face. She is here, and she is real, and she is the woman whose life he changed irrevocably.

Olivia opens the door of the café and walks in with her. The wind follows them, and its coldness blows through the door and cuts through him like a knife. July in Belfast can be like March in Moscow. He can feel the palms of his hands sweat, so he wipes them on the knees of his jeans, and the disparity of temperatures on his body unsettles him.

'Hi Michael,' Olivia says.

He stands up to greet her, and she kisses him on the cheek.

'This is Martha.'

He swallows his heartbeat. 'Hello.'

'Hello,' Martha replies.

He looks at her face, it's serious and anxious, and he sees from the dark circles under her eyes that she hasn't slept either.

'What would you like to drink, Martha?' Olivia asks.

'Tea, please.'

'Michael?'

'I'm fine.'

Olivia goes over to the counter, and Martha sits down opposite him and places her handbag on the inside of the chair, and brushes something off her shoulder. He thinks it must be microscopic because he cannot see anything there.

He looks at her closely. She is younger than her years but has faint wrinkles on her forehead and around her eyes which are as blue as his yet more expressive. She has an aquiline nose that is slightly too big for her delicate features, it has an arch in the middle and doesn't quite go with her precise countenance, but he can tell that she takes time maintaining her good looks, her makeup is exact, and the colours match her complexion, not too bold and not too conservative.

She looks at him fleetingly as her eyes zoom around the room. He has soulful, translucent blue eyes, which are knowing and profound, and when she looks at them, she feels like he can read her mind. His dark brown hair is swept back, and his sideburns are neatly trimmed to give him an appearance that wouldn't look out of place in the nineteen-fifties.

The silence makes him uncomfortable as conversations flow around them. Normally, he is devoid of such unease, but this situation is alien to him. He can feel his heart pounding and stealthily tries to inhale and exhale at a normal pace. She is now brushing something off her skirt, and he feels he has to say something, but his innate reticence prevents it, and he wishes he stayed in bed. He looks over to the counter where Olivia is being served and can't wait for her to return. He watches her for what seems like an eternity. She pays contactless with her card and makes her way back with the tray.

'Here you go. Tea for you, Martha.'

Martha takes the cup and saucer.

Olivia flashes a smile. 'Okay, grand. I'm going back to the office now, so you know where I am if you need me.'

He watches her intently as she opens the door and walks out, and he wishes he was going with her. He looks back at Martha and observes her pouring tea and milk into the cup. He tries to grab the words he needs with an imaginary hand and put a sentence in his mouth, but none are forthcoming.

He clears his throat. 'Erm... well....' He thinks she's

going to speak, so he leaves an opening for her. 'You first.'

'No, go on,' she replies.

'Did you have a good journey?'

'Yes.'

'Kent is a fair bit away.'

'Yes, it's quite far.'

'I was born down near the border myself...' he says before pausing.

She doesn't say anything and raises her eyebrows to indicate for him to continue.

'Oscar Wilde said the Irish are the greatest talkers since the Greeks, but today?'

'If an informer didn't give you up, would you have owned up to it?'

Michael is startled by her candour, and it affects his train of thought, but he tries to remain calm.

'Well, I didn't at first, but once I was released, I believed the truth should come out. As for the informer, he wasn't in our brigade. He was from the south, believe it or not.'

'So, you might not have admitted it?'

'I don't know. I don't know what to say to you.'

'I just want to know why?'

'Why?' He sighs. 'Why is a complex word here.'

'Do you think you were released too soon?'

'It was under the agreement, nothing to do with me.'

'How do you feel about it?'

'Feel?' He shrugs. 'I didn't ask for it.'

'Stephen would have been thirty-eight this month.'

He puts his hands under the table.

'You don't have any family, do you?'

'No,'

'Children?'

'No. Just Olivia.'

'She's doing well in life.'

'Aye, she is.'

'She urged me to come here today. I wanted answers, but I didn't know if I wanted to meet you to get them.'

'I don't want to be here either,' he admits. 'I don't know what you want or if I can give you anything?'

She regards him through narrow eyes. 'You know Stephen was my only child.'

'I know. But it was a war, and casualties were part of it.'

'He was innocent.'

'And so were fourteen people shot dead at a peaceful demo.'

'My government doesn't speak for me.'

'You vote, don't you? That makes you part of the establishment.'

'Don't talk to me about the establishment. It took me two weeks to get Stephen's body back.'

'I didn't choose this as a career. It chose me.'

'But when you kill a person, a part of you must die

too?'

Her comment rankles him, and he shakes his head. 'You have to look at the bigger picture.'

She looks bemused and frowns. 'What picture?'

'All the things that took place before. All the injustices.'

She glares at him. 'Well, now you're just blurring it.'

He puts his hands on the table. 'I'm trying to give you something. Look, there's a long history here, and people have even longer memories.'

'That's the wrong mentality.'

'We didn't create this situation, youse did.'

'How dare you? You can't blame us when you were killing innocent people.'

'No one's innocent.'

'My son was.'

'He was a British soldier.'

'He was just a boy!'

A young couple at the next table looks at her, they are surprised by her outburst, but she gives them a deathly stare and embarrassed, they return to their conversation.

She picks up her cup and sips her tea, giving herself time to regain her composure.

'It was a difficult time... difficult to get out of. Your boy was just caught up in it.'

'He was needlessly killed. You gave him no warning.'

'You had a shoot-to-kill policy too. We got no warning

from youse.'

'I can't say whether that was right or wrong, but those were the times we lived in.'

'Exactly! That's what I'm trying to tell you.'

'Are you saying it was a mistake?'

'I'm saying the British were to blame for many of their own deaths.'

She looks away, and her eyes dart around the room. Michael sits back uneasily in his chair and feels spent. He just can't seem to clarify what he wants to say.

'I have a thousand questions to ask, but they're all disjointed in my mind. We're just getting nowhere with this.'

'I'm trying,' he replies.

She stands up suddenly. 'I have to go.'

'Already?'

'Yes.'

'How long are you here for?'

'I fly back in the morning. I don't want to stay here a minute longer.'

'That's a shame.' He rose to his feet. 'Look, maybe we can talk some more,' he said. 'In the future,' he adds.

She doesn't answer.

'Okay, it was good to meet you.'

He automatically extends his hands, then halfway through, thinks better of it. She notices this and does not reciprocate and picks up her handbag.

2

She thinks about heading back to her hotel and decides against it. She just needs to walk and reflect. She makes her way out of the bustling centre and onto Grosvenor Road before turning left into the working-class haven in the west of town.

She ventures into a road where Irish Tricolours hover above her on their lampposts. Green, white, and orange colours are neatly painted on the curbs as if a dignitary is set to visit any day soon, but what surprises her the most is how close the differing neighbourhoods are to each other, and it makes this road even more entrenched.

A six-metre-high iron fence known as the peace walls run along the street, separating each community like the imaginary 'iron curtain' separating East from West. The fence is painted green with a higher tensile fence to stop petrol bombs or bricks from being thrown over to the other side, but the green paint is camouflaged by the consummate artwork of murals displaying a broad canvas of people from Frederick Douglass to Mandela to represent their oppression.

An open-top bus drives by, and the tour guide points out the significance of the wall and its concept. She feels anger at this and how this place has become a tourist attraction with no care for the slaughter they've caused. As she passes, she looks at people, talking in their funny accents and joking around. They always seem up for that, as if everything is a joke to them. What isn't a joke is they all support the killing of her son, even the young ones with no memory of it, and she feels disgust and pity in equal measure.

She continues to a junction and stops to look at a

picture of a young man smiling on the side of a building. His chestnut hair flows down to his shoulders. It's Bobby Sands, and underneath is a quote from his starving mind. She reads it.

'*Our revenge will be the laughter of our children...*'

How ironic, she thinks, and it confirms to her that they believe it because it's drummed into them at an early age and never disputed. She takes in the whole area, the environs, and feels hemmed in by it as it's sealed shut from any outside interference, so after an hour of walking, she's ready to go.

Olivia has not done much in the hour she left them. She stares vacantly at her computer screen, thinking about what is being said. She hopes it is going well, but it might not be. She cannot tell. She wanted them to meet in her office, but Martha vetoed the idea. She wanted the meeting to be in public. He is a murderer, she asserted. Olivia recoils at this as he has never been given this appellation by the people he knows, but that's just it. The people he knows have no problem with what he did, whereas outsiders like Martha will call a spade a spade.

She logs off and swipes her phone. She has received no messages from either of them. No news is good news, but a woman's intuition says the contrary, and she is full of disquiet, so she leaves her office and takes the short walk into the city centre.

She stands on the opposite side of the road but can only see him through the window and not her. She gives it a few minutes, but she doesn't appear, so she walks to the café and heads inside.

She stands over him. 'Hi.'

'Hi.'

'Is Martha here?'

He looks down furtively. 'No.'

'What happened?'

'She didn't want to hear me out.'

'Because?'

'Because she's already made up her mind and I can't change it. She doesn't want to see me for who I am. She only wants to see me for what I did.'

'But she will.'

'She wouldn't let me catch my breath; she bombarded me with accusations rather than questions. I couldn't get her to listen, and she couldn't get me to talk.'

She thought that here in the safety of a coffee shop, they would be able to address things, and he would feel secure in his own domain, but she doesn't really understand the monumental task he faces.

She looks at him and says in a soft voice. 'You've had this inside you for a long time, and you need to let it out. It doesn't need to be hidden. You may not want to tell me, but you should feel obliged to tell her.'

He scratches the stubble on his chin and looks directly at her. 'I don't know if I can tell her everything, and I know she'll want that.'

'You have to, Michael. Now is the time.'

'I just think I'll be giving a part of me up.'

'But it will be a part that you don't want.'

The Europa Hotel stands in the city centre. It opened

in 1971, the year the first British soldier was killed during the conflict. It has the distinction of being the most bombed hotel in Europe, thirty-six times during that timescale. Still, due to extensive renovations, it now has a majestic look which hosts VIPs and presidents.

Martha walks slowly between the bollards and through its revolving gold-plated doors. She looks around the reception. The receptionist gives information about the city to an American couple who listen and answer back in their distinctive New York accents that lack consonants at the end of the words. She passes them, sees the open bar, walks in, and sits down on a bar chair. The bartender welcomes her, and she orders a John Daly. The young man serves her, and she knocks back its sweet grain taste. She orders another and ruminates over her conversation with him, going over every minute detail, every word, verbatim, trying to understand his motives for her son's murder. She thinks if she used this word, this tone, would he have been more forthcoming?

She orders again and throws it back.

She wants to scream and flail her arms but instead sits there in silent despair, staring into space.

'Another, please.'

The barmen cast a look of concern only for her to give him her cold stare, so he acquiesces and replies. 'Coming up.'

'Martha.'

She half turns and sees Olivia.

'Oh, hello.'

'I've been looking for you. Where did you go?'

'Oh, I've been sightseeing your most famous... I mean notorious roads.' She gestures. 'Join me.'

'Are you all right?'

'Yes, I'm fine.' she said reassuringly. 'Would you like a drink?'

'Okay, I'll have a white wine, please.'

'Barman. White wine if you please.'

Olivia sits down. 'I've just talked to Michael.'

'So, you know how it went.'

'I just wanted to ask you that?'

Martha gazes at her. 'I wish you never persuaded me. I got nothing from your brother. He was so matter of fact; it was like he was telling me his shopping list.'

Olivia doesn't want to patronise her and tries to carefully manage the situation. 'You just need to keep at it.'

'What for? There's no point.'

'It's important for both of you.'

She ponders this for a moment. 'What will it lead to, Olivia? You assured me he was ready to talk, but from what I've just experienced, he isn't ready for anything,' she said bluntly.

Olivia tries to be as positive as possible. Every negative Martha produces she will counter with a positive. Every excuse she makes not to continue, she will push ahead.

'It'll lead to an understanding, so it will. He'll hear your side, and you'll hear his.'

'If you were there today, you'd see that it won't lead anywhere.'

'But you have only just met. I know he has more to say.'

'Then why didn't he say it?'

'Because he doesn't know how.'

Martha puts one foot on the floor and spreads her hands out. 'I was there in front of him, and he still couldn't say why!'

'It takes time... he'll take time... time to let out the things he has to say.'

Martha sits back on the stool and looks at the bottles on the wall of the bar for what seems an inordinate amount of time. Olivia lets her contemplate and doesn't disturb her.

'I would like to think you're right,' she concedes.

'We both want this. That's why you contacted me, and it's why I brought you together.' She puts her hand on her shoulder. 'Look, I'll talk to him again, and we can set up another meeting. I don't think you should leave it like this. We have all worked to make this happen. I want to do it for him, but most of all, I want it for you.'

Martha is non-committal. 'We'll see,' she said with a faint smile.

Chapter Six

Olivia and Simon step inside a high-speed lift at the entrance hall. The estate agent is giving them an overview of the apartment block as they head up to the top.

'As you can see, it has a stunning panoramic view of the city.'

They look out, and the water looks like a mirror with white clouds reflecting from it.

She sees them looking at the river. 'The Lagan is a key amenity. You can use it to walk along or cycle,' she said. 'Do you cycle?'

'I don't, but Simon does.'

'Aye, I've got a bike, but I use it more for cross-country.'

'It will be ideal for here, too; it's facilitated for that use. Basically, it's bike friendly. You can ride for twenty-one miles of traffic-free pleasure.'

'That sounds great,' Simon says.

'I might get a bike now!' Olivia says.

'You should. There are many young couples here that ride together, especially at the weekends.'

'I bet they do,' Simon says.

Olivia wants to laugh at the innuendo and just about keeps a straight face, which is lost on the estate agent's pitch. She just stays in work mode and continues to show them the best views.

They step out of the lift into the hall, and the estate agent gives them the keys.

'Go ahead, open it.'

Simon hands the key to Olivia, and she opens the door.

They step inside, and Olivia loves its smell. It's the smell of new beginnings, and she loves the thought of it. A starting point to organise her life around until another inception is born.

The apartment is sleek with an abundance of space, and they walk on laminated flooring.

'It's authentic wood made right here in Belfast,' the estate agent says.

They both look down on it, and Olivia can see herself walking barefoot on it.

'The kitchen is fully equipped and with contemporary interiors. What more can you ask for?' she proudly declares. 'And here,' she says as she opens the doors to the balcony. 'It offers views of the quay and beyond.'

They step out onto it.

'They are like fully fledged living spaces of their own,' the agent says.

The light air drifts up to Olivia's face, and she has goosebumps. 'Look, I can see my office from here!'

'Oh, aye, you can,' Simon says.

'Well, what more can you ask for?' the agent asks.

2

Michael orders another pint and waits for Olivia. He thinks about his meeting with Martha and how he could have said things, but he has an inbuilt defence mechanism and doesn't know how to express himself. The magnitude of the whole thing curtailed any success. How could he apologise to her? What good would it do? How can he say sorry for something as devastating as that? He just can't.

Ten minutes pass before Olivia walks in with a tall, dark, good-looking fella. Michael can see what she sees in him, but he can also see what he sees in her, as his sister is a traditional Celtic beauty.

'Hi Michael,' Olivia says, kissing him on the cheek. 'Started already, I see.'

'Well, I didn't know how long it would take you to apply your makeup.'

'Michael, this is Simon.'

He holds out his hand. 'Hi, Simon, good to meet you.'

Simon shakes his hand. 'You too, Michael.'

'What would youse like to drink?' he asks.

'A Babycham!' she replies.

'What?' Simon says, looking surprised.

'Oh, nothing. I'll have a white wine.'

'Simon?'

'I'll have a bottle of Bud, thanks.'

'So, you're in advertising?' Michael asks.

'That's right.'

'Hard work?'

'It can be. You know, there's always pressure to get results.'

'Sure, there must be.'

'How's your job going? Olivia tells me you're great with the kids.'

'I try my best.'

'Don't be modest! He's fantastic! They hold on to his every word.'

'It sounds like you are doing a lot of good, Michael?'

'Aye, I think it's important for future generations to understand.'

'Aye, they need to understand so it doesn't happen again,' Simon says.

Olivia looks around, finds an empty table, and claims it. Michael watches them together and sees they have a natural rapport. It could just be their honeymoon period or something more substantial, something that's just meant to be. Soulmates, as it's often called. He does not feel that with anyone because his life is just too complex.

He and Simon talk about superficial, non-threatening things like football. Simon tells him of his love for Manchester United, and Michael, in jest, ridicules him by saying he's a glory hunter for supporting them.

Simon gets more drinks in, and it gives Michael the opportunity of being alone with his sister.

'How am I doing?'

'Grand,' Olivia replies.

'Is it serious?'

'Aye, it's serious,' she replies.

'Well, who am I to say,' Michael says.

'Exactly.'

'Okay.'

'We've moved in together,' she reveals.

'Really.'

At that moment, Simon returns with the drinks.

'Thanks, babe,' Olivia says.

'Cheers, Michael,' Simon says, holding up his bottle of bud.

'Slainte,' Michael says, raising his pint.

'So, where are youse two living now?'

Simon looks knowingly at Olivia. 'By the Lagan.'

'Affordable?'

'We can afford it, so it's fine,' Simon replies.

Michael nods.

'Problem?' Simon asks.

'It's just I don't know too much about you, Simon. I know you're a different religion, which doesn't exactly sit comfortably with our background...'

'Yours,' Olivia intercedes.

'Ours,' Michael counters.

'Look, I know who you are and what you've been through, but I can look beyond that. I hope you can too.'

Michael wants to give him the benefit of the doubt, but old habits die hard, so he does it for her sake.

'All right,' he says.

She winks at him, and he winks back in recognition.

3

Olivia types at speed on her laptop while watching TV. A husband chases his wife in the woods with a knife. She stops typing as the husband chases his wife to a tree and slashes the back of her blouse.

Simon walks into the room with a towel wrapped around his waist.

'Do you want a glass of wine?'

She's absorbed by the drama and doesn't answer.

'Olivia!'

She looks at him. 'Oh, sorry.' She said, still glued to the TV. 'Wow! She made it!'

The wife runs to a road and flags down a passing car, much to her husband's fury.

'Well, do you?'

'Aye, it's wine o'clock. White, please.'

'Okay.'

She thinks the ending will be good when the series finally reaches its conclusion. The credits roll, and the next episode countdown appears in the bottom right-hand corner. She picks up the remote control and pauses it, then closes her laptop as she feels she has done enough for today.

Simon walks back wearing a dressing gown and holding two glasses of wine. Olivia thanks him, walks out to their apartment's balcony, and looks at the quiet stillness of the river.

'It's beautiful, isn't it.'

'Aye, we're lucky, aren't we... I'm lucky.'

Olivia smiles and touches his chest.

The breeze feels good on her face. She puts her glass down on the table and looks at him.

'Our so many months anniversary is coming up,' she says amusingly.

'Right?'

'I just thought it's about time I met your parents, don't you?'

'Well...'

'You know about my family.'

'Aye, you've been very open.'

'Exactly, I'm an open book, but when it comes to your family, you seem to close up.'

'I'm sorry. I don't mean to be this way. It's just meeting Michael has brought extra complications.'

'But you have accepted it.'

'Sure, although other men would have run a mile!'

'I know. I've been so open with you because you are the one. I just want you to be open with me.'

'I will,' he puts his arms around her. 'You are the one too... always.'

They embrace with a soft lingering kiss, and she takes his hand and leads him to the bedroom.

Chapter Seven

The black iron gates open, and Simon drives into the driveway. The tyres drive over the pristine, newly laid gravel, and it only accentuates Olivia's multitude of senses. She looks at the palatial white mansion with its period-style detail. It has a Georgian-style entrance with side lights, traditional sliding sash windows with feature panelling and deep sills.

'Are you okay?' Simon asks.

She is astounded. 'I didn't realise your parents had a place like this!'

'I told you they were well off.'

'Aye, but this is a bit more than that!'

They walk up to the mansion and through the white pillars leading to the door. Simon rings the doorbell, and much to Olivia's astonishment, a maid answers and welcomes them in. She steps inside, and they walk along a solid oak flooring, in a hall where the walls are adorned with beautiful artwork from distinguished painters.

Simon insists he opens the drawing-room door instead of the maid, as he knows it would be too ostentatious. He lets Olivia go in first, and she is greeted by a stylish brunette with stately elegance standing by a mahogany surround fireplace with a tiled inset.

'Hello, Son.'

'Hello, Mum,' he replied. 'Mum, this is Olivia.'

'Hello, Olivia, it's good to meet you,' she smiles. 'Please, sit down. I'm glad you're here. Simon has kept you a closely guarded secret.'

They both sit on a brown leather Cromwell sofa, and he joins his fingers with hers and his thumb caresses her little finger.

'It's good to be here. You have such a beautiful home, Mrs...'

'Call me Elizabeth. Thank you. We love it too. It's Georgian. A lot of the décor dates from that period too. I'll show you the grounds later, but first, let's have some tea.'

Elizabeth presses a buzzer on the wall, and Olivia doesn't know whether to laugh or have reverence.

'How's the apartment, Olivia?'

'It's great. It overlooks the river, and the rooms are spacious and modern.'

'It sounds nice. You must be proud of your achievements.'

'Yes, I suppose I am.'

'See what a good university education can do for you, Simon.'

'I know. Thanks for the reminder!'

Elizabeth smiles at Olivia. 'Simon has done well in his chosen profession too. We're proud of him.'

The maid walks in with a tray of tea and places it on the table.

'Thank you, Lena.'

'You're welcome,' she replies as she leaves the room.

'She's an excellent worker, and her English is better than some of the Indigenous population. Tea or coffee, Olivia?'

'Coffee, please. White, no sugar.'

Elizabeth pours the coffee, and as she does, a tall man walks into the lounge wearing a police uniform. Olivia can't believe her eyes. She thinks it must be an illusion or a mirage and feels a bombardment of beats from her heart, with each one vibrating from her chest to her head.

'Sorry darling. Apologies for being late. I was held up at work,' he said.

'Hello, Son,' he said before turning his dark brown, almost black eyes on her. 'And you must be Olivia?'

Olivia's mouth feels like it's dropped down to the floor until she finally manages to speak. 'Yes, I am.'

The tall, dark figure smiles at her, but his eyes don't corroborate with his mouth, and his lips remain fixed. She can see where Simon gets his good looks and standing from, although he doesn't give off any of his warm energy.

She doesn't look at Simon because of the displeasure she feels towards him for not letting her know in advance. She lets go of his hand and just listens to his father talk about the house and its history, like it's a monologue, until, what feels like an age, they finish their tea and go outside.

The lawn is cut to perfection and looks pristine in the sunshine. The garden is full of herbaceous borders, and oriental poppies form a small section as they come out of the conservatory. Olivia and Simon walk down to a large pond with giant floating lilies. Her anger is overtaken by her shock. She feels discombobulated. He tries to hold her hand, but she rejects it and watches the lilies float along.

'I'm sorry.'

'Why didn't you tell me? When you said your surname was Nowell, I didn't think you were the son of Craig Nowell!'

'I didn't tell you for that reason. What would you have done knowing I was the son of the chief constable?'

'I don't know!'

'You do know, you would have run for the hills! Look, I'm sorry it happened this way, but our families couldn't be more different.' He faces her and puts his hands on her shoulders. 'Once you told me about Michael, I didn't know how to tell you.'

'You should have told me. You should have trusted me. Don't you trust me?'

'You know I do. I'm besotted with you, so the more difficult it got, the harder it was to tell you.'

'Right, good, because I'm with you because I want to be with you because I love you. You should have trusted me and told me.'

'I just didn't know how to tell you.'

'You are telling me!'

He puts her hands into his. 'We'll just have to keep our cards close to our chest until they accept the situation. They think it's just a fling, and it'll be over any time soon. I know you're mad at me, but what would you have done in my predicament?'

She watches a lily gently touch another and examines his words. 'All right, but no more secrets.'

'There won't be.'

***

Nowell walks into the conservatory and sits down next to his wife. He's changed out of his uniform into a collarless neck shirt and beige chinos. He looks at the couple embracing and imagines what conversation they are having.

Simon is his only child. Elizabeth had complications at birth and was unable to give him another. An only child is a precious commodity. He doesn't possess an heir with a spare. If he loses Simon, he can't be replaced. Nowell knows only too well that his son is headstrong and difficult to sway, so he and his wife have agreed to take a relaxed approach. When Simon told them about the relationship, he believed it was a novelty for his son and would soon fade. They sent him to private Presbyterian schools and colleges in the hope he would never stray from his roots. He looks at the couple and knows they are not cut from the same cloth, and he feels like a Southern gentleman whose daughter has brought a black man to the family home. Miscegenation is an anathema to him, but this is worse. He wonders why Simon is doing it. Is it the excitement of the sex? His fears fascinate him even when he doesn't want to think of it.

He lets them continue their animated conversation, and then he approaches.

'I hope I'm not intruding?'

'No, it's all right,' Simon replies.

Nowell looks around. 'Do you like the grounds?'

'Yes, who wouldn't,' Olivia says.

'My dad likes to show the place off.'

'Ambition is important to a man.'

'And a woman,' she replies.

'Of course,' he says in recognition.

'I'll get us a drink,' Simon says.

She doesn't really want to be left alone and glares at him, and he mirrors her expression. 'I won't be long,' he reassures her.

'It's a nice pond, isn't it, Olivia?'

'Aye, it's amazing.'

Nowell walks onto the pond's wooden decking bridge, and he asks her to follow. She gingerly steps onto it and walks behind him until they stop in the middle.

'There's a lot of flora and fauna. The stones there are the perfect habitat for amphibians and insects. We have a great variety of birds here. Honeybees too. You see the sloping stones? Well, the bees can drink the water from there without falling in.'

'It sounds great for the environment.'

'It is. I believe in conserving things, and this country is the most beautiful in Europe, so we need to protect it.'

'I couldn't agree more. Europe needs to be an innovator when it comes to the environment.'

'Yes, especially us British.'

'I believe it's up to an individual to choose who they are,' she remarks.

He doesn't respond to it and changes the subject. 'So, how's your environment in Laganside?'

'It's grand. We love it. The view is breathtaking.'

'I know, it's a nice area, and it sounds like a real commitment?'

'Yes, it is. We just clicked straight away. Sometimes it can happen like that.'

'You mean it's happened before?'

'No. I mean, everything fell into place.'

He nods. 'That's good. I'm sorry for asking these questions, but my son doesn't always confide in me on matters of the heart.'

'I know he isn't always open, but he has his reasons,' she said, thinking of the obvious one.

'He hasn't talked about you before, and we only found out about your existence last week. So, you can see how difficult it is to adjust.'

'I do. And we all need to adapt to new circumstances.'

'I just want him to have the best start.'

'I can tell, and he has that,' she said, looking around.

'I just have those fatherly instincts. I want him to be successful. You can understand that, can't you?'

'Yes, we both want the same thing.'

'That's all I want to hear, Olivia.'

Simon walks towards them with some drinks.

'Here he is,' Nowell says.

Simon hands Olivia a drink. 'There you go.'

Olivia takes it. 'Thank you.'

'We were just talking about you, Son.'

'And?'

'It's good to see you're happy. Olivia is a genuinely nice young woman.'

'She is,' Simon replies.

Chapter Eight

Michael walks through a crowd of young people. They are dancing with their hands in the air, trying to get noticed. Some movements are rhythmic, and some are robotic, but they are all out for an enjoyable time. Ubiquitous flat screens play music videos to each tune. The flashing strobe lighting makes him blink every time it hits him as he weaves in and out like a slalom skier through the masses.

'Mickey!'

Donnelly is standing with a group of women in their early twenties. He hasn't changed, physically or temperamentally. He is his own law. He can be a friend for life or an enemy for eternity.

'How are you doin'?'

'Grand, yourself?'

'Can we go somewhere?' Michael asks.

'Sure. Step into my office. I'll be back, girls!'

Donnelly's office is spacious with a large desk, an Apple laptop, flat screens, CCTV monitors and a drinks cabinet. The dance music follows them and thumps inside, but it's bearable.

'Do you like the sounds?'

'What do you think?' he says in a negative tone. 'Give me Nirvana any day.'

Donnelly walks to the drinks cabinet. 'Those days are gone. You've got to get with it. Get with the grooves.'

Donnelly opens a bottle of the black stuff and gives it to him. Michael pours it at an angle and watches the dark liquid flow down the side of the glass, then he allows the stout surge to settle until the white head forms at the top.

'What's up?' Donnelly asks.

'Not much, just keeping busy.'

'Come on, tell me!'

'It's Olivia. She's got a new man. I'm just acting the protective brother.'

'It'll most probably be one of many. She's a good-looking girl.'

'Aye.'

'Are you happy doing that stuff for her?'

'It's been good. Good to get things out in the open.'

'Yeah, but once the novelty wears off, you can always come here and work for me.'

'It's not always legal, though.'

'What is?' Donnelly points at the CCTV monitors. 'Look at them. They're happy. It's all they know. Not like us and what we went through.'

'We paid the price, though.'

'And we made it!' He gestures his hand around the room. 'I'm building something here, and I want you to be a part of it.'

'I'm doing fine, so I am.'

'Well, the offer's there.' He signals. 'Take a seat.'

'Do you miss those days?' Michael asks.

'Aye, some of it was the unknown, like we didn't know what would happen from one day to the next. We were invincible!'

'It's because we were so young. We didn't think about the consequences. We just did it. Things were so different then. I felt different.'

'A leopard never changes its spots,' Donnelly says.

Michael tries to smile but can't because he doesn't know how to feel anymore. He looks at the screens and the young people enjoying themselves and feels it's past him by. At their age, he was doing something completely different. He was part of history and thought he was making a difference, far more than any youngster today, but he lost a lot more. He eschewed his own well-being for the greater good. He had to hide his fragility behind the cause and project a tough persona, and in doing so, he lost part of himself in the process and feels it's never been reclaimed.

2

Nowell sits by the fireplace in his drawing room, and gentle orange flames lick each other as they rise. He reads by a lamp, and the dim light gives the new pages of his book a jaundiced look. He's an avid reader of military history. The book is on the battle of Stalingrad and how the whole German Sixth Army was wiped out by the Soviets in close-quarters combat. He is nearly finished and reads that out of ninety-one thousand Germans captured, only five thousand would return to see the fatherland again.

He puts the book down and pinches his tired eyes. He picks up his glass of scotch and drinks a leisurely mouthful when Elizabeth walks in.

She walks up to him and puts her hand on his shoulder. 'What are you reading?'

He puts down his glass and holds the book up for her to see.

'Haven't you read enough of those already?'

'I can never read enough.'

'Well, don't be too late.'

'I won't.'

He peers into the fire.

'What are you thinking?' she asks.

'Oh, different things.'

'Such as?'

'Simon's new relationship, it's just taken me by surprise.'

'I know, when he told me of her faith, it was a surprise to me too, but we can't stop him. He's his own man now.'

'I know that very well. It's just never happened in our families before, we've been here for hundreds of years, and it's never been broken.'

She squeezes his shoulder. 'He may change his mind. It might just be a passing phase, and he'll realise how difficult it is to venture outside of his kind.'

'I don't think he recognises that; he seems too wrapped up in her to acknowledge it.'

'Maybe you can talk to him and find out what he plans to do?'

'Yes, I'll have to try and discover what he wants.'

She kisses him on the cheek. 'I'm going to bed now. Night.'

He taps her hand. 'Night, darling. I'll be up soon.'

When she leaves, he picks up the glass and circulates the melting ice in a clockwise motion and looks at it deeply.

The Police Service of Northern Ireland was redesigned on the recommendation of the Patton report in 2001. It set out a series of changes by remodelling the organisation's structure. The restyling was symbolic, and the first part of the change was its name from the Royal Ulster Constabulary to the more integrated-sounding Police Service of Northern Ireland or the fashionable acronym PSNI.

The new police service is more accountable than its previous incarnation, and through a police ombudsman, an independent and impartial entity, which deals with complaints and corruption, it's under more scrutiny.

Its most visible change is its Britishness. Its Royal prefix was omitted, the union flag doesn't fly outside of stations, and a new service emblem was created to denote Irish and British traditions. St. Patrick's Saltire and the Shamrock were incorporated into a once distinctively ethnic organisation.

The main reconstruction is the recruitment of Catholics which Patton identified as being crucial to the public's acceptance of a once discriminatory force. He endorsed a fifty-fifty split between religions for it to be fully received by its population, although through sceptical reluctance, it still hasn't come to pass.

Nowell is pleased that it hasn't as he discerns his kind are being eradicated in every walk of life. So, to do it with one that his people dominated is unethical because the new recruit's families were the enemy.

Nowell walks into the police service of Northern Ireland Headquarters and takes the lift to the top floor. He steps out, and a police constable stands to attention at his very presence. He barely acknowledges him and walks into his office.

He walks over to his desk and looks out of the window. Two constables, a male and a female, talk to each other. They are both from the other religion, the one so desperately needed to show that everything has improved here and that there is no more prejudicial policing.

He sits down at his desk and boots up his computer. Windows starts, and he puts in his password. He gets a screen up and watches a video on how to become a recruit. It tells the story of a young woman from the West of the city who is going through the application process. She is a smart, attractive young woman who says she has always wanted to join but believes she wouldn't be wanted because of her background. She easily passes the assessments and is clearly capable, but Nowell is left with a distinct loathing of her. He is uncomfortable with the presentation and abhors pietistic preaching.

He looks out of the window again and knows the young woman in the video is the one standing there talking. He sees her as performative and as superficial as the presentation. He thinks maybe it's his age or just this youth's spoilt upbringing. Corporal punishment in schools is abolished, National Service is abolished, and the Royal Ulster Constabulary is abolished to make way for these hybrids with their narcissistic sense of entitlement.

He watches the young woman walk, similar to his son's choice of mate's walk. He assures himself that he is the best father and knows he hasn't made any errors, yet his son has, and his biggest flaw is her. He is all for reproduction, and she is an attractive young woman, but her looks aren't the issue. It's her kind. He cannot promote a gene pool which goes against everything he stands for.

He goes on the Northern Ireland database, and types in her name—Olivia Doherty. He sees she has no criminal record or spent convictions, and this doesn't surprise him. He then types in her next of kin and clicks the mouse. A name comes up—Michael Doherty.

He has a criminal conviction, and Nowell recognises the name.

Chapter Nine

Martha's alarm goes off at seven like it does every morning. She's been awake since six thirty-eight when she first checked the time. She turns it off and lies back on her side, looking at the curtain and the brightness of dawn. She gets out of bed, and her body aches, especially her shoulder. She rubs it, thinking her fingers will miraculously heal it. She goes to the bathroom, sits on the toilet, and feels the warm water drain from her before mindlessly putting on her dressing gown and slippers. She makes her way down the stairs, holding on to the bannister, not quite feeling awake, and walks into the kitchen to put the kettle on. She opens the blinds and peers out at the first burst of the sun coming through. She turns on the kettle and drops a tea bag into the cup before pouring the boiling water. She does this to modulate the amount of milk to put in, whether it be a dash or more. She opts for three dashes, stirs it to the right colour, a chestnut brown, and waits a minute before sipping. She loves the first cuppa in the morning as it somehow tastes better than all the rest.

The *Times* newspaper hurtles its way through the letterbox and onto the doormat, and she thinks of her dog Benji and when he used to devour it by charging the door when the paperboy put the folded newspaper through it. Ultimately, she had to put a letterbox guard up, especially for the Sunday supplements with which he had a field day. He left her three years ago when old age took over his once energetic body. She knew something was wrong when his appetite decreased, and she had no choice but to put him to sleep. She thought about getting another dog, but there was no dog like Benji. He was the best.

She drinks her tea and reads the paper. She sits down at her Walton dining table with a brown grain pattern and trapezium steel legs. The headlines are about Brexit. She voted to leave as she doesn't believe the UK benefits from a German and French-led institution.

Once she reads the paper, she goes into the bathroom and brushes her teeth with an electric toothbrush. She then takes a shower, washes her hair with her favourite toiletry she bought from QVC, and showers her body down. She gets out after ten minutes and dries herself, then takes some cream from the bathroom cabinet and massages it into her shoulder, hoping it'll help with the inflammation.

She's had issues with her shoulder for a few years. Her GP told her it was rheumatoid arthritis and its hereditary. Her mother had it. She had hip replacements, too, which eventually made her immobile, although she lived to the advanced age of ninety. She used to take her mother out shopping or to a garden centre; they were both horticulturists, and she got her love of gardening from her.

Martha's mother was a history teacher and worked at a local school. Her father was an accountant and worked for a broker in London. Her mother was a great letter writer, like her, and she constantly wrote to her twin sister in Toronto, whom she missed. She first met her aunt when she was four and, at first, she thought it was her mother but in different clothes. It scared her, and she cried, as she didn't know which one was which, and she only recognised her when her mother comforted her, and she could smell her distinctive fragrance.

Her mother gave her a love of words. Although she taught history, she loved literature and introduced her to Dickens, the Brontë sisters, Shakespeare, and Virginia Woolf. She would spend hours reading, lost in the stories. Although she found Dickens over-sentimental, she marvelled at his genius for prose. She didn't have to think about what she would study; it would always be an English degree, and then she would complete her teacher's training. She enjoys teaching, and although she had to take an extended absence when she lost Stephen, she has returned to it part-time. She writes recreationally, but mostly she reads, especially stories of loss, the ones that speak to her.

She makes her second cup of tea of the day and opens the kitchen door. The birds sing and tweet, and she smells the summer breeze with its scent of nectar and closes her eyes. She feels like she is momentarily in a different world, a world where everything is full of love, and this feeling enters her stomach and rises to her chest. She opens her eyes again and thinks of her parents. They gave her and her older sister a great childhood and a foundation in academia. Her sister went into accountancy like her father and married well, and she now lives in a town house in Kensington and Chelsea with her husband, a banker, and their three children, although they have all flown the nest to go on to bigger and better things.

Her parents were married for fifty-seven years until her father died aged eighty-two, but their youngest daughter was only married for nineteen.

She met her husband through her father as they worked for the same company and got on well, in no small part than their love for cricket. They played in a local team together; her father was an accomplished batsman, and her husband was a fine fast bowler. They also loved watching Kent play at the St Lawrence ground in Canterbury.

She particularly remembers them winning the county championship the year Stephen was born. She hitherto had never seen her father drunk, much to her mother's displeasure, but he was a jovial one. It was a year she fondly remembers, and it was her happiest.

She and her husband were both natives of Kent, although her husband is a Man of Kent, because he was born east of the River Medway, as opposed to her family, being born to the west, making her father a Kentish man and her a Kentish maid, respectively.

They met when her family threw a garden party one spring day on the Easter bank holiday. She stood there talking to her sister when he approached. His hair was quite long for an accountant but just the right length to get away with in his conventional profession. His brown hair shined in the sun, which she liked, but his smile was even brighter. He charmed her, and when she looks back, it was with a superficial charm, not a deep, dark, brooding one that she longed for and so admired in Emily Brontë's Heathcliff. He told her everything a young woman wanted to hear, and she fell for him. Her family admired him, and her mother would talk about him constantly as if she was the one he was going to marry. He also came from a reputable upper-middle-class family. They were a family of academics; his father was a headmaster at a grammar school, and his mother was a head librarian at a university.

When they all met for dinner at her parent's house, it was like a contract was being signed, this was the deal, and this would be her life. At the time, she didn't feel it, but now she's in no doubt. It was the spirit of the times, her parent's generation passing the baton on to hers, but only in the understanding, she would maintain the status quo.

The marriage was good for several years, even when she developed endometriosis and required a hysterectomy. He got a promotion, and she worked contently as a teacher. They bought a three-bedroom house in the heart of Kent near her parents and owned an apartment in the city. They went on holidays abroad to places like Canada, to visit her aunt, and to countries like the United States, France, and Italy. As Stephen grew, he enjoyed them more and more, but as time went on, she noticed a change in her husband. He became more distant, taciturn, and less involved in the family unit. She would ask what was wrong, and he would reply, 'Nothing's wrong. I'm fine.' This became his mantra, and he would diplomatically dismiss her concerns. She suspected an affair but could prove nothing, although she didn't delve into it too much or didn't want to as she was wrapped up in bringing up her son, and he became the source of her solace.

She couldn't tell if Stephen's death was a spark for her divorce or whether it was inevitable. She was so consumed with her own agony that she never thought to understand her husband's. He became a bystander in her breakdown and couldn't help her because she didn't want him to. She needed and wanted the anguish. It told her she was grieving, and it was what she needed to do.

It wasn't her husband who left the relationship. It was her. She instigated it with rows, some petty and some considerable. Recriminations for his dalliances, real or not. She was so absorbed that the marriage didn't matter as it had died with her son.

The decree nisi came eight months after Stephen died. Her ex-husband remarried, and his wife conveniently bore him two children. It didn't matter to her; she was imperious about it. All she wanted was solitude. She didn't think anyone knew what she was going through. She had counselling, and it succoured her in some ways but not in the way she wanted the truth, and to seek the truth, she needed to understand why it happened. She wanted answers. Why would someone kill her son? Who were they? What motivated them to commit such a callous act?

She knew his killer and his name. When she first saw him, he stood before her like an apparition. It was too unreal to be real. She thought he didn't look like a killer. She could see Stephen in him, a youthful innocence, much to her revulsion. She didn't want to associate him with her son, but she did, in looks as well as in his youth.

She hoped she would never see him again and he would spend the rest of his life in one of those eight concrete blocks shaped in the form of the capital letter H. As time went on, she thought the H must stand for hell, hell on earth, and these men were trapped in a hermetic structure devoid of humanity, including their own. It was what she wanted, but she wasn't getting any closer to the truth until one day, she reached this point.

2

The day starts like any other, but this day her sister visits with her granddaughter, who is in her early teens and an expert in social media. Martha wonders why she can't read or listen to the radio, indulge herself in the arts and learn from it, but that's how she lives. Through this form of communication, it is both a revelation and a curse. It is also addictive. She notices her attention span is limited. She just scrolls for hours, mostly at nothing, looking up at the right time to engage back in the conversation. It is mechanical and, most of all, damaging to her one-to-one interactions. Martha doesn't utilise social media, although she likes to use it for internet shopping and other things, but she isn't engrossed in it until now.

She sits next to her great-niece, who vacuously scrolls on her phone. When she asks her what site she's on, she replies.

'Instagram, of course.'

She tells her she also uses Facebook but explains that older people use it more. Martha laughs and asks does she mean her?

'Yes, by and large,' she replies.

She asks Martha why she doesn't use it, and she says she has no need to use it.

'I can just use it to keep in touch with people, family, friends... anyone. You can see how people are doing and join groups, etcetera.'

Martha doesn't really see the point. She says she's fine in her own company and community, walking in her neighbourhood and is satisfied with that. Martha's great-niece gives her a puzzled look and asks flippantly, hasn't she heard of globalisation? She asks Martha to get her phone and tells her to go to the App Store and download Facebook. Martha says she doesn't need to, so her great-niece takes her phone and talks her through it step by step, how to save her password, upload pictures and post.

'Right, I'm going to be your first friend.'

'Okay,' she replies.

'Tap on friend request, that's it, there you go, you have your first friend. Easy, isn't it?'

'Yes, it seems to be.'

'You never know who you'll meet on Facebook, Aunt Martha. Sometimes it changes lives.'

When they leave, Martha empties the dishwasher and throws out the remnants of the shepherd's pie she ate last night. She thinks about what she will eat that night as she is doing it, and homemade soup sounds good to her.

She drives to the local supermarket, a couple of miles away, to get the vegetables and vegetable stock for the soup. She also gets other groceries, like cereal, oat milk, skimmed milk, and tea bags. Martha takes her trolley to the self-service checkout, packs, looks at her overpriced receipt and thinks inflation is biting.

When she gets home, she cuts the vegetables into small pieces, puts the stock in water, adds coconut milk, and leaves it to cook.

She sits down and puts the television on. The regional evening news is showing for the southeast, she watches it for a while before turning it on to the other regional channels, northwest, Points West, and Northern Ireland, and she stays on that region.

A female presenter with a distinctive Belfast accent reads from an autocue about the dissolution of Stormont. She listens to different politicians arguing their points and thinks that's all they seem to do. Why can't they have a calm, constructive debate?

The next item is about a young woman, a successful businesswoman, who has a Youth Alliance business that helps young people with their education and finding jobs. The business is one of the most successful of its kind in the province, but it's not the business that draws her attention. It's her name. Maybe it's just a coincidence, as she's sure her surname is a common one there, but an intuitive feeling draws her in. She looks at her and can see his eyes, but hers are smiling, and they sparkle when she talks.

Once the news item finishes, she opens her desktop and types in youth alliance and reads about Olivia's work and discovers she's won awards for it. She types in Facebook on Google, then types her name, and her face comes up first from a list of Olivia Doherty's. She taps on her picture, and her page opens. She has one hundred and seventy-one friends, but she has one friend she thinks about every day. She thinks about what sort of life he's leading. What does he do for a living? She even thinks of how close they have been to each other in miles. Has he ever been to England? If yes, how close has he been to Kent? Olivia Doherty stands next to him in her picture posts.

She writes: Me and Michael – love you, Bro X

It's him, she thinks. God, it's him!

CHAPTER TEN

She thinks about the moment she saw him again and how meeting him changed her life. She walks out to her garden, enters her shed, and picks up secateurs and gloves. She walks to her rose bush, moves her secateurs at an angle, and makes a sloping cut into the pedicel of the rose. The slant of the cut faces away from her. If she doesn't cut it this way, the rain will cause it to rot. She looks at the cut and is satisfied with it. She walks over to another rose, a Rosa 'Crimson Glory' and smells its damask scent. It's a perfumed scent, and she feels her body relax as a wave of fine chemicals is released. She puts the secateurs on the table and sits down in her gazebo to take it all in. Her garden has become her sanctuary. There isn't a thing out of place or a plant that doesn't belong to another. They all follow a structure and complement each other perfectly. It's her haven, her place of contemplation, of understanding all the complexities of her emotions that the dead of night fails to curb. Sitting here, in her favourite season—summer— makes it all come into focus and gives her a respite from the anguish that haunts her on a nightly basis. She makes sure her days are full so she can keep the torture at bay, but it's the nights, the dread of it even, that she can't fight, but here, she is in her moment, and she looks out at her vast garden and beyond.

She can see her son here. She can see him doing three hundred and sixty degrees on his tricycle, going round and round, making her feel dizzy just watching, and she hears him and his cackle as he does it. It's laughter that never leaves her.

She can see him chasing a blue butterfly around the garden and his fascination when it stops and sits on a leaf. She would tell him to stand still and watch it and, when it moves to observe the splendour of its flight. His eyes would expand, and his mouth would form an 'O' shape as he concentrated on it. When it flew away, his excitement would get the better of him, and he would chase it once again as if he was chasing all his dreams at once.

She looks at the wildflower, augmenting the lush green of the Downs. It makes her feel content, joy mixed with pain. If the pain subsides, so will he, and she can't let go of him. There are too many memories here that she can never let go of. If she does, what is there?

She walks back to her gazebo and sits on its bench, shading herself from the high sun. She opens her notebook and picks up her pen. She writes long-sloping words at a rapid pace, like a stream of consciousness. However, her academic temperament prevents her from leaving commas and semi-colons out. It helps to write down her thoughts, it's not a diary per se, but it helps her offload all her affliction into it, like shedding skin until a new set of anguish returns. She writes, stops, looks out at the hills, and starts writing again. She needs to write these words not to cleanse but to understand and make sense of her thoughts. She knows it helps, and that is all there is. When she feels she has written what she needs to, she closes the book, places her pen on top of it, and lets it rest until the next time she needs it.

She sits there for a time, then goes inside with the notebook in hand and puts it on the kitchen table. She decides to change her shoes and puts her boots on and walk down to the woods.

She walks in between a row of sweet chestnut coppices and listens to nothing but nature breathe life into her. Nothing is man-made here, only nurture. She wanders through the open glade and loves to get lost in it. It doesn't faze her. She isn't afraid of getting lost, as it gives her a sense of purpose to find her way back home again.

She wanders on and has a feeling of being. This is her heaven, her good place from the bad. Twigs crack under her feet, and bunnies run across her path, heading for their holes, and suddenly, she stops.

There it is.

A butterfly flutters in front of her and lands on a flower. It's an Adonis Blue, a male, from its pellucid blue wing topside and one of such beauty it could appear in paradise. She stands there in awe as its colour sparkles in the sun and its wings flop on the flower. The flower sways from side to side, and it's happy to sway with it. She watches it for some time before going over to a tree stump and placing half an orange on it. She observes it as it lands on another flower before landing on the orange, where its proboscis flexes and drinks the sweet citrus. She wishes she had brought her phone to take a photo but feels it's not needed. It's stored in her mind's eye, and she will see this day forever.

She wanders further, mulling over things, searching, and debating with herself. It helps her come to terms with things. She takes in the smell of nectar and slowly blinks as the sensation hits her. All she can feel is his love, and she shakes with emotion. Her head drops to the side in comfort, and she continues. She feels a sense of self here like she can have any emotion or thought, and it's not judged by anyone.

When she gets home, she sits in the garden and thinks about how she feels and what she can do to change things. She can't go on living like this. She has lost so much over the last three decades. Everything she has ever loved has slipped through her fingers, and she has no grip on it. It makes her want to give up, but something pulls her back every time and maintains its lonely equilibrium.

2

She has a clearer mind now, and all the negative pieces of this morning have vanished. She knows how to change things now; she made this decision while walking in the woods, and it isn't a reluctant one. It's one she's sure of. She picks up her phone and dials.

'Hello, Olivia.'

'Oh, hi, Martha!'

Olivia is sitting at her desk, and she's surprised by the call. She normally phones her, not the other way around.

'How are you? Sorry to call. I know you're busy.'

'Yes. It's been a busy day, full of meetings. How about you?'

'I've been gardening.'

'That sounds great. I'd love a garden!'

'I'm sure you'll have one, one day.'

'I hope so.'

'After I finished gardening, I went for a walk, and I thought about the best way to communicate with your brother, and I concluded that the best way is to write to him and get our innermost thoughts out.'

'Yes.'

'So, I would like to correspond with him.'

Olivia doesn't say anything.

'Olivia?'

'I'm here.' There is a pause before she speaks again. 'Are you sure?'

'Yes, I'm sure. It's something I need to do.'

'If you're sure?'

'I am.'

'I agree. I think Michael will find it easier too. You can start again and take it from there.'

'Yes. We didn't get off to the best of starts.'

'Michael thinks so too. He said he wants to speak to you again, but this way is better.'

'Yes, it is.'

'All right, I'll speak to him, and we can arrange things.'

'I'll send the letters to your address, and you can pass them on to him.'

'That's fine. I will.'

'Good. Okay, I won't take up any more of your time.'

'You're not. You can call me anytime.'

'Okay, bye for now.'

She goes back inside, gets some writing paper from her study, sits at her garden table, shaded by the sun, and begins writing. Martha has a lot to get out. She puts it all down in cursive writing, all the things she should have said before it was blocked by a wall between them. There is no wall in this format, only her true emotions, uncensored and unequivocal, and it is the best way to start.

Michael,

Thank you for agreeing to this. This is a better form of communication as it gives us the freedom to explore what we want to say without prejudice. I feel this discourse will suit us as it will make neither of us the aggressor or patronise the other to get our point across.

We are burdened by emotions, but through these letters, we are not burdened by each other. Our face-to-face meeting made us apprehensive and defensive to ever be successful. I don't rule out meeting you again, but to do it, we must start from a solid foundation and build upon it with frankness and trust.

I feel we should engage this way to fully understand the needs of the other, and the only way to do it is not just to get to the truth but to get to the core of the truth...'

When Olivia receives the letter from Martha, she gives it to Michael. When she does, he recalls what it was like reading the first one, but he listens to her explanation and, although sceptical, agrees to try it.

He endeavours but can't compete with the raw emotions and transparency of her prose, but when he receives them, he handles them delicately. His replies are formal, and they never delve into her depths. She sees his letters as superficial and not forthcoming in their explanations. She wants more, not so much in content but in sentiment, one where he gives more of himself by revealing himself and not one where he is projecting a political manifesto.

Martha,

I think this is a good idea. As the way we met didn't allow us to say what we could have said. We don't need rhetorical hostility as it will only cause conflict that neither of us wants. I think it is best to do this in the security of our own homes.

We should do this in stages, firstly, by asking questions, contemplating the answer, and responding to it.

We can, through these letters, elaborate on our answers and reach a conclusion that will satisfy the other. We have the chance to have a serious debate as to why this happened and the antecedent that led to this action.

I can tell you about the conditions I grew up in and give a detailed account of my background. It is a background vastly different from yours. I say this to try and make you understand the social and political standpoint from which I come from. It was a place set apart, even in my own country...'

He finds putting his thoughts into words difficult, whereas she has no such difficulty. If he lets too much out, his guilt overwhelms him. He has made peace with his conscience, and now she wants to excavate it. He has crafted an impregnable boundary and inside is wreckage accumulated from the decisions he made. He doesn't answer them and never feels the need to. He knows they won't disappear or be forgotten, but they are within a circle of magnetic waves, and no one can pass through them.

3

Michael watches a boat sail down the river, and Olivia walks onto her balcony with two cups of tea.

'Thanks,' he said, taking the cup. 'It's quite still here.'

'Aye, I know, and it's fairly quiet.'

Michael looks up and watches a plane fly by.

'Well, for a city, anyway,' she laughs.

'I just want to say thank you for writing to Martha.'

'Thank you?'

'Aye, thank you. I know it's been difficult to do.'

Michael looks at the boat getting smaller by the minute.

'I want to ask you something. It's something I've been working on. It'll be funded by both my company and the educational authorities.'

'What will?'

'A series of talks. About what happened. Talks in front of an older audience, and they'll be in Britain and finish here.'

'What?'

'You and Martha. She wants to meet and talk again; she needs to get more than she's getting.'

'You're joking?' He puts his cup down on the table. 'Without consulting me first?'

'I talked to Martha yesterday, and she has agreed, in principle, to do it. You need to get this out in the open. Burying it inside won't help.'

'I'm not burying it. I'm trying to deal with it. I've talked with her. I've written to her. I can't give her anymore.'

'I think you can, for your own peace of mind. I'll be going with you. I'll arrange the whole trip.'

Michael sighs.

'Martha deserves this. She has waited all these years for an explanation, and you must tell her the truth.'

'I want to, but a force within me is preventing it.'

'It's called pain, Michael. You must let it out, show it to her, not just for yourself but for her, and she'll respond to it.'

Michael is exasperated and feels cornered like he is in a straitjacket. It isn't easy to break free from the shackles and decode an emotion that has lain dormant and release it into an unknown sphere.

'I can't do it without you, Michael.'

'And she's okay with this?'

'Yes, she is. She wants to meet you again. She feels the letters aren't helping as much as she thought, but if you take this time together, you're bound to help her.'

Chapter Eleven

Celtic Park is the home of the Celtic Football Club and is known as paradise by its supporters. Michael and Donnelly are major fans, both of whom have supported them as early as they can remember. The team was the first British club to win the coveted European Cup in nineteen sixty-seven. As they were known, the 'Lisbon Lions' beat the might of Inter Milan in Portugal to lift the prestigious trophy.

Glasgow is a city divided, and its divide is demonstrated most by its teams, Celtic and Rangers. An Irish priest formed the Celtic Football Club to help impoverished Irish Catholic immigrants who flooded the city's east end in the nineteenth century. Rangers got support from the indigenous Protestant population and Irish Protestant immigrants who supported the union and the crown.

The first place the talks are held is in this city.

Michael watches Celtic beat Rangers in an early kick-off. The old firm derby is one of the highlights of Michael's year. Donnelly has come over for the match and is ecstatic, so they decide to go out for a celebratory drink.

Michael chalks his cue and takes the break. Fifteen balls are scattered on the pool table, and a stripe is potted. Donnelly tells him it was a lucky shot, and

Michael acknowledges with a cheeky grin. He pots three more stripes in succession but misses the fourth.

'I'll clear the table now.'

'You wish,' Michael replies.

Donnelly does, but he misses a long shot on the black and leaves Michael with an easy pot into the left-hand middle pocket.

'You lucky bastard!' Donnelly shouts.

'No luck about it. The only ball that matters is the white one.'

Two young local men approach them and ask if they want a game.

'A fiver for each game,' one says.

'A tenner, and you're on,' Donnelly says.

The men put their bottles on the table, and Michael hands one of them his cue. The man chalks and breaks. He doesn't pot, so Donnelly seizes his chance and pots half the balls. The other man takes to the table and pots one of his, only for Michael to clear the table.

After four matches, it's three-one to Michael and Donnelly. Michael feels sorry for them, so gets the drinks in.

'Are you men from Ulster?' one of the men asks.

'Aye,' Michael says.

'Like Georgie Best.'

'Aye,' Donnelly says.

'So, you're United fans?'

'No. We support the Bhoys. Celtic through and

through,' Donnelly declares.

The man swigs his beer and says nothing.

Donnelly clears up on the next frame.

Four-one.

The last game is played in an uneasy atmosphere, like a matador and a bull are circling each other.

Five-one.

'That's fifty you owe us!' Donnelly shouts, rubbing salt into the wound.

'Look, whoever wins the next game wins,' Michael says conciliatory.

'What?' Donnelly questions.

Michael is feeling good about the result of the football match and just wants to give them a chance after such a thrashing. The local men agree, but the match doesn't go their way, and they lose.

'Pay up! Fairs, fair.' Donnelly says.

'We're not going to pay you cheating Fenian bastards!'

Donnelly holds the top of the cue, and Michael knows what's going to happen. He smashes it over the man's head, and wood chip splinters over the table. Blood pours out of his head and trickles down his face. The other man smashes a bottle against the table and comes at Michael, holding the sharded glass like a dagger. Michael kicks it out of his hand and punches him, shattering his nose as it crunches on his fist. The man drops, and Donnelly kicks him in the face. It happens in a flash and is over in the same time span, and Michael knows it's a mess.

He phones Olivia. She has just come back to the hotel

after shopping with Martha and sits on her bed.

'Michael, how could you do this!'

'I didn't do anything.'

'Are you deliberately trying to sabotage this!'

'You know I'm not.'

'Well, you've got a bloody good way of showing it! I can't believe this!'

'The talks will go ahead.'

'God! How could you and Johnny do this?'

'Like I said, we didn't do anything.'

They spend the night locked up, and in hindsight, Michael thinks it wasn't such a good idea to invite Donnelly on this occasion. He just needed someone in his corner because the tension he feels is high, so he just brought him along to ease it.

The next morning the custody sergeant returns their belongings, and they sign a form to say they've received their possessions. Olivia watches them as they do so. She's relieved the two local men haven't pressed charges, most probably because all the witness statements say they started it.

They get into her car, looking dishevelled and worn out, but Olivia is too furious to care. She can see Michael is crestfallen, but she needs to read him the riot act just the same.

'Look, Olivia, none of this is Michael's fault. These men lost a pool game and took exception to it.'

'It was all in self-defence,' Michael adds.

'Exactly.'

'Are you mad! You know we have the first talk this morning!' she shouts.

'Aye, I know,' Michael says.

'He'll get spruced up and be as good as new,' Donnelly reassures her.

Olivia looks at Donnelly in her rearview mirror and shakes her head.

'You could have ended this before it began! What would have happened then?'

'I'll sort it. It will be okay.'

'You better, Michael. I'm relying on you.'

'I'll be there,' he tells her.

2

Michael gets back to the hotel and gets in the shower. He puts the water temperature on lukewarm to wake himself up, although his knuckles still burn as he rinses shampoo out of his hair and the suds drip down his torso. He must be quick, so he shaves at pace by the sink and gets dressed. He receives a text from Donnelly to say he is on his way back home and is glad as he needs to do this without interference. He puts his wallet and phone in his jacket and is ready to go. He's not nervous because he hasn't had time to be, and he just wants to get it over with.

The college is one of those new renovations. It has windows of different colours, purple, blue, and yellow, and cladding has been placed over the bleak grey seventies concrete design to jazz it up.

Olivia and Martha talk between themselves, and he feels separated from the conversation. She is still angry with him, so he understands her distance.

He watches the students walk into the hall. A low volume of chatter descends like the sound of a bee hive. Most of them are attached to their portable devices, like an extension of their arms. Others have headphones on and are in their own worlds. As he has gotten older, they get younger and look like smurfs with cute, almost air-brushed faces. He doesn't know if anything he says today will have an impact. He is sure they are more interested in relationships and having the latest gadgets than listening to something they've never known.

In the hall, the babble stops, and the teacher faces the students.

'Morning, everyone,' he says.

The students return the salutation with a less enthusiastic response. It is a Monday morning; a Friday morning would garner a different reaction.

Michael sits there self-consciously and wants to hide his knuckles when an image comes into his mind. The image is of the black gloves he wore on that fateful day, he tries to get the image out of his mind, but the harder he tries, the more vivid it becomes.

'Today, I have the pleasure of introducing you to two people who have lived through a period of recent British history. May I introduce you to Michael Doherty, a Republican, and Martha, a mother of a British soldier who served in Northern Ireland.'

Michael stands up, feels faint, and tries to hold on to something, but all he does is stagger and falter out of the hall. The teacher stops what he is saying, more shocked than anything else, and watches him walk out.

Martha looks over to Olivia and doesn't know what to say. She hastily follows her brother, not knowing what to do.

He walks down the corridor, stops, faces the wall, and leans his sweaty palms on it.

'Michael, what's going on?'

Olivia is still angry with him, but when she sees his condition, her exasperation turns to concern.

'Michael, are you okay?'

'Just give me a minute.'

The teacher comes down the hall and asks if everything is all right. Olivia can see from the expression on his face that he's perturbed by the situation. Still, she assures the teacher it is, even though she doesn't know herself.

'I just need a moment with my brother.'

'Yes, certainly,' the teacher says.

She puts her hand on his arm. 'Michael, it's okay.'

He starts to get his breathing back to a regular pattern and calms.

'What happened?'

'Something came over me.'

'Are you all right?'

'Aye, I will be in a minute.'

'Okay,' she says. 'Look, we can go if you want to.'

'No, I don't want to let you down.'

'You won't be.'

He stands up to his full height and looks at her. 'Let's go in.'

They both walk back, and he takes his seat. Martha looks at him, but he avoids her gaze. The teacher introduces them again, adding more to the inauguration, then asks Michael why he joined up. Michael gets himself together and answers.

'I grew up in a place that is deeply entrenched in Irish unity. If you can imagine this hall and all the people in it are part of this land, then one person enters the hall and says you are now part of our land, even though they are one and you are hundreds. This is where I'm from, a place apart, where if there was a vote tomorrow, they would embrace Irish unity. This place becomes part of who you are; if you leave it, it never leaves you,' he says.

The teacher asks Martha why her son joined.

'He joined because he always had an interest in the army. My father served in the Second World War, his father in the First World War, and my son became interested in the theatres of war. I knew from the time he reached eight or nine that he would become a soldier. I would buy him toy soldiers or video games on warfare. He loved it and loved life. I knew he would become an officer one day. He wanted to make his way up the ranks and not just go to a military academy like Sandhurst. He was academic, but he was also forthright, and that's what he wanted.'

The teacher asks what his views on Ireland were.

'He thought the Irish had been dealt a bad card. He didn't support reunification, but he did sympathise with their plight in some ways.'

Michael looks at her. She hasn't spoken of this before, and it seems unusual that someone would fight combatants whom he empathised with. He then talks about the structure of the organisation, and that he was in a brigade rather than an active service unit, that's how apart they were from the other counties.

She said that her son's regiment had a reputation over there. They engaged in operations that penetrated the Republicans and disseminated some of them, which made them feared and hated in equal measure.

The teacher asks them if they believe their meeting would change their opinions.

'I'll always be an Irish Republican and will always believe in a thirty-two-county socialist republic. I haven't changed my beliefs and never will. We had Brexit and a Scottish referendum. I believe we should now have an

Irish one.'

'I don't believe that what my son fought against should come to pass. I believe most people over there want to be part of the union, so it's my wish that it stays this way,' she says.

The teacher asks more questions, but they are harmless ones and don't search too deeply. Martha believes it is because of Michael's earlier display, and the teacher is embarrassed and wants to cut the talks short. She has worked in education for a long time and knows its workings. The teacher hasn't even asked the students for their input. What should have been a truly momentous moment for her has become a disappointment.

Once it's finished, they stand in the hall and watch the students make their way out. Martha can't hide her disdain, and Olivia notices this.

'I'm glad you came today. It was an interesting talk. I'm sure it will get better. It is the first one, so there are bound to be teething problems, but I'm sure they can be ironed out. Anyway, it was a pleasure,' the teacher says.

The teacher leaves, and they stand there in the hall, just the three of them. They are despondent and know the teacher's right, although 'teething problems' is a euphemism for a shambles.

Michael picks up his jacket and puts it on.

'How did you do that?' Martha asks.

'Do what?'

She points. 'Your hand.'

'I had a spot of bother.'

'Some men picked a fight with him,' Olivia interjects.

She knows Martha's judgement is sound, so there's no need to tell an untruth.

'Where?'

'In a bar,' Michael replies.

'So that's why you weren't in your room. I knocked for you last night. I wanted to talk things over, but you weren't there. I knocked on two different occasions, and you weren't there. I went downstairs this morning and saw you get out of the car, looking the worse for wear.'

'I was arrested and spent the night in a cell, but it wasn't my fault.'

Martha studies him. 'Thank you for telling the truth because if you hadn't, I would have left, but you're being honest, so I'm going to stay.'

Chapter Twelve

Michael drives from city to city. Sometimes they listen to music, sometimes they talk, mainly superficial conversations, and nearly always initiated by Olivia. It is difficult to extract anything from him at the best of times, and in this situation, he needs to keep things close to his chest. Olivia senses this. She knows him and his silence and feels she is officiating a match between two giant emotions.

The two are distant from each other, like a sensor in a car when it is driving too close to one another. Olivia doesn't know if they will ever find common ground, but her astuteness can cut through any deception with a knife. She knows him and his moral code, especially for family. It has always been there for residents in their border town. The societal doctrine of the rolling hills of South Armagh dictates the bonds of blood, which are just as important as the bonds with land.

He drives down the M1 from the Midlands and into the cityscape of England's capital. Olivia senses this one is more important than the others because it is Martha's base and not theirs, so it has more significance.

They get to the hotel in the heart of Greenwich just after three in the afternoon. They would have got there earlier if it wasn't for the M25 southbound traffic slowing everything down to a trickle. They get there exhausted, so they agree not to eat together and order room service instead before having an early night.

The next morning Michael waits for them in the foyer. He observes the receptionists checking people in and out and porters rushing around with trolleys full of suitcases and is happy he doesn't have a job like that.

One of the lifts opens, and Olivia walks out. She is clear-eyed and looks like she had a good sleep, which is better than he'll ever get.

'Shall we get a bite to eat?' he asks.

'No, let's wait for Martha to come down,' she replies.

'She's normally late. Shall we start, and she can follow,' he said.

He doesn't want to sit there and eat with her in silence this morning.

'All right, I'll give her a knock later.'

He heartily eats a full English as he thinks he'll need his strength for today. Anyway, he loves the smell of sizzled bacon. She eats a poached egg on toast at a more leisurely pace. She slices the yolk through the middle and lets it dribble onto the bread, cutting a triangle of bread with a piece of egg on top and enjoys each bite.

He wonders what Martha will be like today and tries to fathom her state of mind, but he'll just have to see. He and Olivia exchange diverse threads of conversation. They can laugh at things with their wicked sense of humour and they can telepathically synchronise each other's thoughts. Even if they don't see each other for a few days they can reacquaint in a sentence.

He dips a mushroom in her egg and sops up the yolk.

'Hey, you fecker! Your dish has meat in it! You're lucky I don't want anymore!'

She picks up a tissue and dabs her lips.

'I'm nervous about today.'

'Why?' he asks.

'It's her town and not ours, so it just feels different.'

'It shouldn't be. The talks have been quite similar. I don't think it's deviated much?'

'Aye, I get where you coming from, but it just doesn't feel like the others.'

'Let me do the worrying.'

She drinks and then puts her cup down. 'Are you going to tell her about Sosaidh?

'No.'

'Why not?'

'I don't think she should know.'

'But it's significant.'

'I know, but I want her to understand me first.'

Olivia considers this. 'I think you're right, but it's still important. She'll need to know at some point.'

'Aye, but not yet.'

Martha sits on the bed and looks into her mirror. She picks up her mascara and gently flicks her eyelashes with it. She has always been self-conscious of her appearance, but lately, she's just going through the motions like it's a laborious task. She does this and thinks she might miss breakfast as she doesn't feel that hungry.

The door knocks, and she puts her mirror down and answers it.

'Hi, Martha. I just wanted to know if you want anything ordered for breakfast before they close?' Olivia said.

'That's okay. I'll be down in a minute. Come in.'

'Wow! I love your mascara. Dior, isn't it?'

'Yes.'

'It really suits you.'

She sits down and applies her makeup.

'Thank you.'

Olivia walks over to her. 'Martha, I just want to say I'm here for you.'

Martha looks away from the mirror and up at her. 'Yes, I know.'

'That's good,' Olivia said. 'What do you use?'

'I like Dior. And you?'

'Same as you, but I also like Maybelline and glossier.'

Martha puts her mascara in her makeup bag and they both go downstairs.

She chooses porridge with blueberries and Earl Grey tea. Michael has already eaten, so he goes back to his room. Olivia orders a coffee and sits with her, and they talk some more about cosmetics.

Greenwich Park is the oldest enclosed Royal Park. It takes up vast swathes of the borough. It consists of the Meridian Line, where world time is calculated and the

National Maritime Museum, where Britain's seafaring history is revered.

Olivia and Martha walk through the park up to viewpoint hill before stopping at the top to take in the scenic vista of the city. A soft breeze blows off the Thames, which gently drifts to the park. The place feels free from the polluted city and gives the inhabitants a brief respite of tranquillity from the metropolis.

They both sit down next to an old chestnut tree and look around the area.

'The views here are spectacular,' Olivia says. She points. 'There's Canary Wharf and St. Paul's.'

'Yes,' Martha says. 'I'm not an admirer of Canary Wharf, but St. Paul's Cathedral is majestic.'

'Simon would love it here.'

'Yes, he would, especially Canary Wharf. You should bring him here when you're next in town.'

'That's a good idea.'

'Do you come to the city often?'

'I used to, not so much now. I used to come here in the summer and at Christmas. I brought Stephen here when he was young. He loved the festive lights on Oxford Street. We would listen to carol singers, and he would join in. He knew all the words. I would just look at his eyes light up from all the colours and sounds. It was a magical time.'

'I'm sure you cherish those times.'

'Yes, some places have a special place in my heart.'

Martha looks at the families in the park. The day and

place will have a special place in their hearts too. Ones that will linger in their consciousness and give them happiness.

'He doesn't understand grief.'

'He wants to, Martha.'

'No, he doesn't because it will signal his guilt.'

'He feels that already.'

'When?'

'Just because he doesn't show it doesn't mean he doesn't feel it.'

'He doesn't feel, he muses, he interprets, but he doesn't feel.'

'You can't say that when he's trying to navigate it. This is difficult for him too.'

'But where are we going, Olivia?'

'I would like it to bring about some sort of resolution to your lives so you can move on.'

She stares into the distance. 'I don't think I want to continue.'

'Please do, and let's see what today brings.'

Olivia observes her looking at the families. She wonders how she copes with the depths of hurt she endures and wants to help her, and her brother reach some kind of peace.

2

An audience of a hundred people sit before them, history and humanities students with their lecturers. Martha takes a sip of Perrier water and doesn't know if she can sustain any more of this. She looks at Michael sitting with his arms folded like they're burrowed inside him, locked in his own private space, autonomous and detached.

The speaker rises to his feet and introduces the guests to the audience. He explains the background and antecedents leading to the incident. The speaker says he would like to start the proceedings by asking how they felt about meeting for the first time.

Martha takes another sip of water and begins. 'I wanted to know the circumstances of what took place. To know every detail, to have understanding. Because I didn't understand, it made me want to seek the truth. I dehumanised him for so long, but I needed to look into his eyes and see what was happening. It's like starting something new for the first time. On the first day you are overwhelmed by the environment and all the information, it's difficult to process it all but you still want to know everything on the first day and have a feeling of despondency when you don't achieve it.'

Michael looks at the audience for a reaction, and they show none. He tries to listen but feels himself separating from her when she uses the term 'dehumanise' to describe him. He thinks about where they both come from. She hasn't lived where he's lived, seen the things he's seen, or been subjected to the things he has. She just doesn't know.

She speaks for some time before the speaker lets

Michael into the conversation. He picks up his microphone and faces the audience.

'I didn't want to meet Martha, but I had to give her something, some form of explanation. When you're a soldier of war, you don't know or even think about the hurt you inflict. I was targeting British imperialism, not a person. I was going after the oppressors and the whole system, which is what her son represented to me. A British soldier is a prestigious target, and my purpose was to eradicate them from my country.'

Martha interjects. 'I saw our first meeting as a one-off because I thought I was betraying my son by meeting him. I had this fight within myself. Was I doing the right thing? Did he even care about what he had done? I thought the meeting wouldn't bring my son back, so what was the point? In the end, his sister Olivia persuaded me, so I thought, let's press ahead.'

'I had some trepidation about the meeting, but things happened so fast that I didn't really have time to think about it. I thought one meeting would be enough, but that was wishful thinking because we could never be content with that, and I thought we had to meet again to rectify the damage.'

'It was like an iceberg. So much hadn't been said. One, for self-protection and two, because of our completely opposing views. I needed more time to evaluate and determine where to go,' she said.

The speaker asks Martha where she was when she heard the news of her son's death.

'I'm a teacher and was about to go away on a school trip to France. I was packing and looking forward to going away for a few days with the children when two men in uniform or CNOs, casualty notifying officers, came to the door and said they would like to speak to me about my son. I let them in, and they came into the lounge. One of them asked my husband and I to take a seat. My husband did, but I refused and told him to tell us what had happened. He told us that my son had been manning a checkpoint and had been shot and killed by a sniper. I was in disbelief, and my world caved in. I just dropped to the floor; my husband tried to pick me up, but my knees buckled. I couldn't sit or stand. I could only lay on the floor...'

Michael doesn't look at her and avoids looking at the audience in case he's being judged, so he just looks at his microphone.

'I had to see him. I was trying to tell myself he was still alive and they had made a mistake. I didn't know what to do with my emotions. Everything rushed towards me like a freight train. The suitcase I packed for France was now being packed for Belfast. I got the first flight out. As we flew across the sea, I looked at the clouds and felt like I was not on the earth, and everything ceased to be real. When we got there, we went straight to the mortuary. It was an experience that will be engraved forever in my memory. I looked at him lying there and wanted to lay beside him, but I just hugged his body. I thought not only had they murdered my son, but they had also murdered me too. I thought, how will I ever recover from this, and how will I live without him? That's what goes through your mind. How will I live?'

The audience is captivated, and their silence is deafening. Michael shuffles in his chair and feels uneasy hearing this. Martha appears phlegmatic and dignified when addressing the hall. Michael tries to quantify what he has done but knows he can't. It is one step too far for his conscience to bear.

After they have spoken, the speaker asks the audience if they have any questions.

A woman in the audience stands up. She is tall with short black hair, and her fringe is neatly trimmed. She doesn't appear to be nervous. Public speaking isn't taxing for her. It is part of her job. She is dressed in the latest fashion and gives out an aura of hipness among her students, willing to learn new trends and thoughts from them without abandoning her mantra.

'Hello, my name is Claire, and I'm a lecturer from the University of Greenwich.'

Michael thinks it will be another routine question he has heard ten times before. Do you believe in the peace process? What societal changes have happened in the province since Brexit? The normal political and intellectual ones fascinate the intelligentsia, but what he is expecting doesn't happen. Claire stands there and doesn't ask a question. Instead, she speaks.

'In the nineties, my older brother Anthony served in the province. I was studying for my A-levels at college, and all I thought about was Britpop and getting the top grades. Anthony was three years older than me. He was a big strapping lad with the sort of defiant machismo that said no one could touch him, and to me, it looked fine over there as a peace process was taking place. I watched the jubilant scenes of people waving Irish tricolours and congratulating a bookish-looking man with black hair and beard telling everyone he wanted peace, so I was glad knowing that Anthony would soon be home, but it didn't happen that way,' she says.

'The day, I was told, was a haze. My father came into my bedroom, and I thought he was going to tell me to turn down *Wonderwall* which was playing on my stereo, but he didn't. He turned it off instead. He told me that an armoured car my brother was driving drove past makeshift bales of hay, and as it did, an eight-hundred-pound remote-controlled bomb was detonated, and my brother was killed along with three other soldiers. He didn't tell me at the time that only the bottom half of him remained, welded to his seat from the intense heat of the blast.

'I sat there with my knees pressed into my chest, and I started to rock myself, yelling in repetition for what seemed like hours. My mum and dad tried to hold me, but I just shook even more. In the end, they had to call an ambulance, and I was sedated.'

Michael listens intently and presses his microphone into his ribs.

'It took me a long time to come to terms with his death. I isolated myself from friends and family, read and listened to morbid music, ones that fit my mood. My grades began to suffer, so I took a year out to cope with it...' She pauses before going on. 'Forgiveness is a word, they say, that is cathartic. It is a word difficult to use, but an understanding of all the elements that brought about my brother's death is something I look at. I believe, holistically, it is the only way to comprehend it. You must understand the environment in which Michael spent his formative years, and Michael must understand the loss of a son who is part of their being. I, myself, feel the pain more acutely than most. He was my only sibling. He advocated for me through this imperfect world. He closeted me from the evils of life. I hated the people that did this to him for a long time, but I concluded that the deep psychological injury inflicted on me will never heal until I forgive, so I did, and that's what set me free.'

She sits down, and there's a silence before the audience stands up and claps, followed by Martha. Michael looks at Martha in acknowledgement, something he hasn't done before, and he is the last, but not least, to stand.

3

The Cutty Sark has been moored on a permanent dry dock in Greenwich since nineteen fifty-four. She is one of her kind's last tea clipper ships, renowned for her speed, and a monument to a time when Britain ruled the waves.

Michael walks around the ship, looking at its artefacts. He has admiration and condemnation in equal supply, he is aware the British Empire was the largest in world history, but he knows only too well it was at a cost to the people it colonised.

He looks at the long narrow copper hull and thinks it could cut through any country it chose. He walks up to the deck and looks at the abundance of rigging rope, braided and spliced on their pullies. He feels like these ropes, forever in place, with his life and emotions being pulled in this trajectory. Its tensile strength holds whatever nature can throw at it, but it can also snap at any point.

When he's seen enough of the ship, he makes his way down to the high street. The omnipresent red buses meander their way down, stopping regularly at the countless traffic lights. He avoids walking into people as most are attached to their phones. They talk into their mobile watches or just talk with earphones on. He hears every word of their conversations, from what they think of work to what they think of their boyfriends or girlfriends, giving him a montage of their lives in five short minutes.

He strolls around, not going anywhere in particular. He likes to walk and is keenly interested in people, and London has many interesting people.

As he wanders, he comes across Greenwich Market

and saunters into its cobbled square. The stalls are wide and varied, from jewellery, chess sets, and clothes to vegan toiletries. There are also a great variety of food stalls, ranging from Japanese, Korean, and Latin foods, but the best aroma comes from a Caribbean one and it's perfect for his taste buds.

He walks up to a Black man who greets him with a smile.

'How ae yuh? Wat would yuh like?'

Michael looks at the dishes but keeps on coming back to the same one.

'Mi see yuh loekin at di chicken.' The man gets a tray and puts a large spoonful of the chicken dish onto it. 'C'mon, try some!'

'Has it got reggae reggae sauce in it?'

'Only de best! Yuh like reggae?'

'Aye, Bob Marley, Jimmy Cliff, those guys...'

'Yuh got taste... here...' The man gives Michael the plate. 'Jerk shicken, rice, peas, spicy sweet potatoes, and lots of peppers.'

He takes a bite. 'It's fantastic.'

'Yuh, Irish?'

'Aye.'

'Hey man, more Blacks, more Irish, more dogs!'

'A better world.'

'Exactly, brother!'

He serves Michael a full tray, and they talk music and about being Black or Irish in England. The Caribbean man says it's now cool to be Irish or your four-legged friend but not to be Black. He says it with a smile, and Michael doesn't know if he is being serious or not, but he knows there was a time when Black people weren't welcome.

He recalls watching a BBC documentary presented by two journalists, one White and the other Black, working undercover, and their purpose was to find a flat to live in. The Black journalist went first and would answer advertisements of flats to rent, but when he went to enquire, he was told they were taken, then the White journalist would enquire about 'the taken' flats, and they would offer it to him, there and then. So, he believes the man has a point.

He throws his polystyrene tray in one of the many recycle bins and is about to leave when a woman approaches him.

'Hello, Michael, isn't it?'

He turns around. 'Aye, that's right, and you're Claire?'

'Yes. Enjoying the cuisine?'

'Aye, it's amazing!'

'Do you like the town?'

'God no, it's too much of an urban jungle for me.'

'Yes, all concrete charm! Except for the parks.'

'And the noise,' he replies.

'That's London for you.'

'Aye, anyway, what brings you here?'

'I live here for a start, and I just spoke to Martha. She wanted to talk to me.'

'Right.'

'She's in the park now.'

He knows only too well what they talked about. They talked about him; he is certain of it.

'Do you want to go for a coffee somewhere?' she asks.

'Okay.'

They make their way out of the market and find a café and order coffee. Al fresco.

He pays, then sits down and watches the traffic cruise by, cars bibbing at cyclists and cyclists shouting back, if the middle finger can be called shouting.

'I suppose you want to know what Martha and I talked about?'

'I can guess.'

'We talked about loss.'

Michael holds his cup but doesn't pick it up.

'Loss is like a black hole in my chest, and I just work around it, Michael. I put positive things that enhance my life around its periphery. The black hole never goes away, but the positive things impede it, so it doesn't get any bigger.'

'How do you come up with something like that?'

'Therapy. Talking therapy. Talking until I talk it out of my system. Sometimes I just sit there and cry for an hour, sometimes I talk non-stop. That's how I feel. You need therapy too, Michael.'

'Me? I don't think it will help me.'

'It will. It doesn't make you any less of a man. Men

need help too.'

'I'm okay. I just deal with it in my own way.'

'Really? Then you'll never deal with it.'

'I live with it, Claire. I have no choice.'

'There are groups out there to help. Why don't you seek support? There are lots of networks. It'll be good for you. I'll give you the numbers.'

'Why are you being so kind to me? I don't deserve it.'

'Because if I hate it won't set me free, remember. It will destroy me, and I can't let it. I'll blame the terrorist who did it, I'll blame your country for supporting him, and I'll blame Americans for financing him. The blame game is just part of that destruction, and I can't live like that.'

'I can understand that,' he agrees. 'I had to be someone else when I came out of prison. Not a terrorist, not a murderer, but a normal man, a man who must live his life the best way he can.'

'But it was all a deception, and it's time to change it, Michael. You need to confront who you are. Do these talks, talk more to Martha, and go to therapy because if you don't, you'll be the loneliest man alive.'

When she leaves him, her voice resonates. He walks out of the noise and into the park, hoping Martha's still there, and she is, sitting on a bench. She is the only one sitting on it, so he sits down next to her.

'Are you a people watcher?' he asks.

'Yes.'

'Me too.'

'I used to come up to the city a lot, but not so much now. It's a different speed for me these days.'

'Aye. I thought Belfast was busy, but it's just a parochial town compared to this.'

'Do you ever wonder what would have happened to you if you were English?'

'If I were English? No, as John Lennon sang, I had the luck of the Irish.'

'I know the song. It paints the Irish as having a tragic history and wishing they were English. It's not the greatest endorsement of your culture.'

'It's the one I grew up in,' he says.

'One, where they get impressionable young people to do their bidding.'

'Like I said, it's the culture I grew up in, and if I was English, I might sound posh like you.'

Martha lets a slight smile draw on her face before it goes again.

'How do you think today's talk went?'

'I was moved by what Claire had to say. We have the same experience. I spoke to her afterwards, and it helped me because I've been finding this increasingly difficult to cope with.'

'Aye, me too.'

'Really?'

'Aye.'

'You don't show it?'

'You sound like Olivia.'

'It's just I haven't seen a change.'

'I spoke to her too.'

'Who? Claire?'

'Aye. I remember it, the news of her brother. People were celebrating in a pub when I walked in. I wasn't, but many were. He was killed just before...'

'Stephen.' She looks at him. 'You can say his name!' She looks away again and delays a response before adding. 'Yes, he was one of the last.'

'Aye.'

'The peace process was beginning to happen, but there was no peace for me.'

'No, there wasn't.'

'I wish he was here, Michael, and not just a series of memories.'

It's the first time she's said his name, and it makes him feel good. He's happy she is addressing him this way because it makes him feel human.

'I wish it too,' he replies.

He feels himself say it and doesn't prevent it, he's surprised he has, but it's spontaneous, and he means it. She glares at him, trying to grasp if it's real. He did this, all of it. He took her son's life and, in a sense, ruined his own. Her feelings towards him are a dichotomy of loathing and pity.

'How could you have done it, Michael?'

'If the man now could talk to the young man, then it would never have happened.'

'But it did?'

'I know, but it wouldn't happen now.'

'But now isn't then.'

'We can change that. Claire doesn't know who killed her brother, but you know who killed your son. We can make each other understand.'

'But you change the subject when it gets too difficult.

'I want to say things, but something is holding me back.'

'It's you. YOU are holding you back!'

He pinches his Adam's apple. He doesn't know why he's holding back. It's just from years of conditioning, years of fighting with his conscience. He looks at her, and she stares at him. Then he looks back at the people going about their daily routine.

'Do you know what the most hurtful thing is? Is that I'm giving this my all, and you aren't. I have to use all my strength to conquer every emotion I have, and you aren't.'

'I'm trying.'

'You need to change... change completely.'

'Everything I say is lost in translation. I'm saying the words, but they are 'words,' and you don't seem to understand what I'm saying. I want you to understand my whole life and what brought me to the point where you lost your son.'

'I'm listening, but I need a panoramic picture, and you don't want to give it. You only give your interpretation, and that is all you give. I just want you to be transparent and not hide behind your masculinity or cause. The most masculine men are the weakest because they hide their sensitivity behind bravado. It is the ones who open up and show themselves who are the strongest because they're not afraid to. If you can do that, then you're a man I can trust.'

'It's just...'

'It's just nothing! That's all you give! You need to reveal your innermost thoughts to me.'

'If I remember every minute detail, I'll be haunted by it. I know what I am to you, but there is more to me than that. If you look beyond what I did and see me as a human being, then we can get somewhere, but what you say, and your stare says it all.'

'Stare?'

'Aye, it burns a hole in me.'

'Good!'

'Look, I'm like you. I must live with this, day in and day out, but for different reasons. It's not something I want, and I was doing well until...'

'Until I came along?'

'No, I'm not trying to say that, but I am trying to say that you need to give me time.'

Chapter Thirteen

Victoria Square's large glass dome is a mainstay of Belfast city centre, and it dominates the area, and now as the evening falls, it shines even more brightly as it illuminates the sky.

Simon walks under the dome and steps into the best jeweller in the square, and the jeweller welcomes him with a bright smile exhibiting his porcelain teeth. He is a well-groomed young man, his suit is immaculate, and his hair is perfectly coiffured, and more importantly for his profession, his nails are finely manicured.

'I'm looking for a ring.'

'Well, sir, you've come to the right place.'

'I'm looking for something special.'

The young jeweller looks at him knowingly. 'Am I right in saying an engagement ring?'

'Yes.'

'I understand. I won't be a moment, sir.'

He goes through the door behind him, gliding the floor like a ballroom dancer. Simon looks at a Rolex while he waits. It is gold with a perpetual mechanical chronograph, a beautiful piece of work, but it's in the tens of thousands, so it'll have to wait for another time.

Besides, he's wearing one, and this occasion is far more important.

The young jeweller flies back into the room with quick, sharp movements and deftly places a tray full of engagement rings on the counter.

'Here we are, sir. A great selection of engagement rings for you.'

He explains the cut of each stone with effusive hand movements and points to an eye-catching one, the most expensive. Simon thinks this will be a good commission for him.

'This is a beautiful ring. It features a halo design with a beautifully cut centre diamond and smaller diamonds cut to the right and left. You see, there are bees, but this...' He accentuates the centre of the ring. 'This, is the Queen Bee.'

Simon looks at it and thinks it's too ostentatious for him. It looks like a ring Richard Burton would fly to Paris and buy to dazzle Elizabeth Taylor. He lets the jeweller talk some more even though he has already decided. He has only been looking at one ring and has been looking at it since the tray was brought out. It's the only one he wants.

'What about this one?'

'This one, oh yes, this is a beautiful ring. A diamond solitaire with an exquisitely cut diamond...'

'It's perfect.'

'Is that your choice, sir.'

'Yes.'

'I'll just get its case if you can just bear with me,' he

said, leaving in a flash.

Simon sees Olivia in his mind's eye. Her face is as clear as a diamond. He knows what real love is now. It's him and her.

2

The last part of the talks ends in Belfast. There is an uneasy peace between Michael and Martha, much like the city they're in. She stays at the Europa, and he goes back to his empty flat. It feels bare as he leaves his suitcase in the hall because he's had the company of two women who are now the most important in his life. He stretches out on his sofa like a cat and feels like he's ready to sleep, but he needs a shower first. As he thinks of having one, he takes his shoes off, lies down, and closes his eyes.

The next morning, he rises early and has a much-needed shower, washing his hair three times. He makes himself coffee and toast, which he hurriedly eats and texts Olivia. She texts him back to meet her and Martha at the college at nine. He shaves, brushes his teeth, and combs back his hair to look as presentable as possible.

The college is on the outskirts of the city. It's non-denominational, the first one he's ever visited. Olivia chose it for Martha more than him. She doesn't want her to be ill at ease by talking in a Catholic one. It will be difficult enough for her but even more difficult in one with Republican sympathies.

The college was only built three years ago, and from the posters in the corridors, it strives to be innovative and places this above all other virtues. It wants its students to be forward-thinking and stipulates this as part of reaching their full potential.

Olivia has done a lot of business with the college and helps students find jobs to suit their talents. It is a high-achieving one, and the exam results are among the highest in the area.

She welcomes Michael and makes Martha feel welcome by personally showing her around the place. Martha looks at the adolescent faces and can only think of Stephen, but she buries this deep inside.

The hall is full by nine-thirty. Martha talks first, then Michael, and then there are questions from the students. They answer them quite easily, as many have been asked before, so Michael, especially, has his reply formulated in his head.

One student stands up. He is lanky and has a mane of caramel hair as well as a septum piercing which fascinates Michael.

'Hello, my name is Nick. I'll cut to the chase, my da was a loyalist and was involved in sectarian killings, and I just wanted to say a wee bit about this. He was born in Ballymena to a strict Presbyterian family. As a youngster, he would go to Dr Paisley's rallies and quote his words. He lived in a world where your beliefs dictated your actions.

'One night, he followed a man in his twenties to his house. My da watched him go in before knocking on his door. The man's father opened it, and my da pushed him aside. His son was watching TV with his ma. My da pointed a gun at him, and he got up from the sofa with his arms in the air. His father begged for his life and said take him, but not my son and his mother kneeled down beside them. The father refused to get out of the way of his son, his son shouted at him to move, but he wouldn't, so my da shot both of them dead. The mother went into shock and collapsed,' he said.

'My da was in prison with you, Michael, although, for obvious reasons, you never met. I want to say my father regretted what he did, although it was a long process. I just want to tell you the most amazing thing out of all this, is this man,' he points to a young man next to him.

'I'm now friends with him. He is the son of the man my daddy killed, the man I just mentioned, and he came here today to hear you talk and to show you how people can change. We're best friends now, from our shared experience. My da's brother was shot dead, so I know how families can be torn apart, and I'm here to say it's not too late to turn your life around.'

Michael stands outside the college after the talk and watches boys play football on the pitch. The outside left reminds him of how he played. He was quick, a visionary, producing moments of magic with his lethal left foot. He watches the boy go past two players before placing the ball in the right-hand corner of the goal.

'Hello, Michael, I'm Billy, Nick's da.'

He looks at a burly bald man with a Union flag tattoo on his neck. He notices he has the words love and hate branded on the fingers of each hand as he shakes one of them.

'We were in the H-blocks together,' Billy says.

'Aye, we were.'

'Do you wanna walk?'

He looks at his watch. 'Look Billy...'

'Come on.' Signalling him with his hand. 'It'll do you good.'

Billy walks towards the school field, and he follows.

'You met my son. What did you think of what he said?'

'It was powerful, so it was.'

'When did you get to the Maze?' Billy asks.

'I'm sure it was after you.'

'I got there in eighty-one, and you know what happened that year!'

'Aye, ten men died.'

'How about you?'

'Ninety-six. October… Nineteenth of October.'

'It seems to grate on you?'

Michael doesn't give a reply.

'It's okay. I know how you feel. When were you let out?'

'In 2000,' Michael says. 'I was one of the last.'

'I was in the last five, but it didn't surprise me. After what I did, I thought I'll be there for life.'

'We were soldiers. We just followed the orders we were given.'

'Orders, yeah, fuckin' orders, but what about our conscience.'

Michael ignores the comment. 'That's what we signed up to, to pledge our allegiance to our country, like any other soldier.'

'How old were you when you joined?'

'Eighteen,' Michael replies.

'I was seventeen and still a virgin, although my buddies didn't know that. I knew fuck all about the world, just that I hated Taigs. The politics didn't mean a thing.

It was us and them. That's how I saw it, black and white, clear as day.'

'It was nothing but politics for me,' Michael says. 'I read books on Irish history, the famine, Michael Collins... I wanted to go to university, but I got the calling instead.'

'You killed one. I killed fifteen. I was never the same again. I lost what I could have been.' He holds out his arms and turns them the other way. 'I cut my wrists. I'm lucky to be alive, but you're never lucky when you don't want to be here.'

'How do you live?'

'Day by fuckin' day, Michael. It gets better, but it never wants to part with you. I changed after this,' he says, holding one scarred arm out. 'I started to read the scriptures and brought God into my life. I'm a pastor now and hold sermons. I visit schools and colleges, just like you, to talk but most of all to be open about what I did. No brushing things under the carpet, no lies, no embellishments, just the truth, and the truth will heal your soul.'

'I think I'm doing that.'

He stops and lets out an incredulous laugh. 'I think not, my friend, I think not! You're saying what you want to hear, what you tell yourself, because to go to a place you need to be will kill you. Well, so be it. You must die to be reborn. You need to kill the old you to see the truth in the new one. The mother of the soldier you killed is here, but you aren't giving her justice. She will only be satisfied when you part with the lies, and your soul will only be released when you do it.'

3

Olivia opens the oven to look at the vegetable lasagna. The cheese slowly bubbles on top of the pasta, and she's happy with its golden-brown look. Her hair is wet, so she asks Simon to take out the dish while she goes to dry it. He takes it out and puts it on the side to cool. The doorbell rings, and Olivia calls for him to answer it before turning the hair dryer on.

'Hello. You must be Martha?'

'Yes. And you're Simon?'

'Yes. It's good to meet you at last,' he said. 'Come in.'

She steps into the hallway. 'I bought a bottle of white wine as it will go best with the meal.'

He takes it from her. 'Aye, it will surely.'

She follows him into the lounge, and he goes off to open the bottle. She looks around the room. The furniture and décor are brand new. It looks like any apartment in London inhabited by solvent professionals, but she's certain they could get more for their money in Belfast.

'Here you are, Martha,' Simon says, handing her a glass of wine.

'Thank you,' she says as she takes the glass. 'You have a fabulous place.'

'Well, we like it. We intend to buy it as a first home, then get a mortgage on a house and rent this one out.'

'It sounds like a plan.'

'Yes. It'll be tight for the first few years, but Olivia will just have to cut back on the expensive shoes.'

Martha smiles. 'Ah, a woman's downfall.'

'Yes, I suppose you can't have enough shoes.'

Olivia comes out in a dress she bought that day in Victoria Square.

'Hello, Martha,' she says and kisses her cheek. 'Thanks for coming. What's he been saying?'

'It's all good, don't worry,' he says sheepishly.

'I love your dress. The colour really suits you.'

Simon holds her waist. 'It sure does.'

'Thank you. I've been eyeing it up for a while and thought, what the hell! Come on, let's get the dinner dished out,' she says.

He follows her into the kitchen, and Martha sits on the sofa. She thinks they look good together starting out on a new and exciting venture, planning but not knowing what the future has in store, and not knowing is even more exhilarating for a young couple.

The doorbell rings, and from the commotion in the kitchen, she feels the need to answer it, so she opens the door.

'Hello.'

Michael stands there with a couple of bottles of beer.

'Hi. Are you the maître d' for tonight?

'No, I was hoping you are,' she replies.

'No, it's my day off.'

They stand there looking at each other. 'Are you coming in?'

'Aye, thanks.'

He walks into the lounge and places the bottles on the table. He can hear Olivia shouting at Simon to get the plates.

'Are they okay in there?'

'Yes, I think so.'

She walks to the balcony and looks out.

'It's a great place, isn't it,' he says.

'The river is nice. It reminds me of the Thames.'

'But cleaner.'

She puts the glass to her lips and stops. 'Not as stately, though.'

'Fifty-three and a half miles long.'

'Like I said, not as exalted.'

'How long is the Thames?'

'Two hundred and fifteen miles.'

'Okay, but like I said, not as clean.'

'It's cleaner than it was.'

'You are more at home here. I mean than last time we met.'

'We both know why. It was strained because of the exceptional conditions we met. We were both nervous, so it didn't portend for a good meeting.'

'Aye. You're right, but there was never a good time.'

'No. That's true. There wasn't.'

Simon walks in with the steaming dishes and welcomes Michael as he puts their plates on the table. Olivia carries the other two plates and kisses him on the cheek before he sits down. She takes his bottles into the kitchen, and Simon opens one and pours a pint out.

'It smells delicious,' Martha says.

They all sit, and Martha begins to eat as she listens to Michael and Olivia tease each other like siblings do.

'How is it?' Olivia asks.

They are unanimous in their praise. Martha just had a light breakfast, so she's famished and enjoys every bite.

'So, you're a teacher, Martha?' Simon asks.

'Yes, I teach English.'

'You're an avid reader, then?'

'Yes, I am. I like all the classics. My favourite authors are Virginia Woolf, the Brontë sisters, and Flannery O'Connor.'

'I read Woolf at College. She's outstanding,' Olivia says.

'Teaching is one of those occupations that is more than a job. It's a vocation,' Simon says.

'Yes, it is. I'm passionate about it. I take great pride in watching the children grow as people.'

'You must have a great rapport with them,' Olivia comments.

'Yes. I spend a lot of time with them, inside and outside the class.'

'You seem to understand them from what you have told me.'

'I like to think so. I understand them like they are my own children.'

Olivia nods. 'They must go to you when they can't talk to their...' Olivia stops herself from saying the word and feels embarrassed by her obvious faux pas.

'Their parents, you mean?' Martha replies with a smile that understands Olivia's mistake.

'Yes.'

'I treat them like they are my own, Olivia. I still have a maternal instinct. It doesn't end or goes away. You'll have it one day.'

Olivia looks at Simon, and he gives her a wink. 'I hope so,' she replies.

'How do you think the tour went?' Simon asks.

'Tour?' Martha replies with derision.

'Sorry, I didn't intend to say that it's the wrong word to use.'

'It's fine, Simon,' she replies.

'The talks. How do you think it went? Obviously, they must have been difficult for you.'

'Yes, they were, but some of the audience members made it worthwhile. What they had to say had such an impact on me, and it gave me the will to continue.'

Michael sits uneasily and picks up his pint and takes a gulp.

'Yes. What Claire said in London and the young man today. It was so emotional to hear their stories,' Olivia says.

'What happened today?' Simon asks.

'A young man told us about his father. He was a Loyalist. He killed a young Catholic, but now he is best friends with the son of the man his da killed,' Olivia says.

'Aye. I met his father afterwards. He works for the church now. He told me what it's like to live after you've...' he hesitates. 'After you've killed someone. He found God...'

'And what have you found?' Martha interjects.

Michael doesn't answer and sits back in his chair.

'I think Michael is trying to find his way,' Olivia intercedes. 'Have we all finished?'

'Yes. Thank you, Olivia.' Martha replies.

'I've got Eton Mess for dessert.'

'It sounds great,' Simon says. 'I'll give you a hand.'

They pick up the plates and walk into the kitchen. Olivia puts her plates down and puts the palm of her hand on her forehead like she has a temperature. Simon puts his plates down and gives her a hug, and she buries her head on his solid chest.

Michael gets up with his pint and heads to the balcony. Martha watches him from the table. She just doesn't have a filter for him because she doesn't want one. She knows he's an intelligent man. He has a degree with the highest attainment but has something else— perception. She doesn't let those silences fool her. She knows his mind is racing, and how he scrutinises her language and expression is uncanny. He has gotten inside her mind, and she feels exposed. She realises she is at fault, too, as she is doing the same thing by invading and penetrating his brick wall and coaxing him into her web. She manages to get something from him through their letters and can draw him out of his pores. She is succeeding in sieving out the gold from the debris, but he needs to show it and not just write it.

She listens to plates being put into the dishwasher and feels her truculence towards Michael is out of character and has a twinge of regret at her response.

They come out with the desserts and place them on the table, and Michael returns from the balcony.

'I want to apologise for sounding mordacious. I didn't mean it to sound that way,' Martha says.

Olivia stands up and puts her arms around Martha's shoulders. 'We all said things that we didn't mean to say. You are here because I want you here. To me, you're part of the family. That's how I feel about you, so you can say whatever you want.'

Martha places her hands on Olivia's and feels their warmth. Michael doesn't say anything, and in a perverse way, he agrees.

After they have their meal they decide to take a stroll, walking along the river. Simon and Olivia walk ahead with their arms joined together.

'Do you like it here now?' Michael asks.

'Yes, it's growing on me. It's compact for a city. I like the view of the hills on its periphery. All the new buildings, too, it's like it's rebuilding its soul,' Martha replies.

'It's called the Black Mountain, it's spectacular, so it is. And you're right, it feels like a young city now.'

'With old views.'

'I hope not. Look at these two,' Michael says, pointing to his sister and her man.

'They seem made for each other.'

Michael nods, then asks. 'Are you relieved it's over?

'Somewhat. And you?'

'The same.'

'What has been the most difficult?' she asks.

'What hasn't been the most difficult!'

'Was it that hard for you?'

'Aye.'

'I don't want to torture you, Michael. I know you're tortured enough.'

'How?'

'I see it. I know it has a hold on you.'

'You have a hold on me.'

She looks baffled. 'Is that how you see me?'

'I just think it's something you can hit me with no matter what I say or do.'

She stops and lets Olivia and Simon walk further ahead. The streetlights illuminate the water, and it glistens, giving off a magical glow. She looks at it and turns back to him.

'I'm not here for that. I'm here to give my son's eighteen years of life some meaning.'

'I know. I think about it from dawn to dusk.'

'I don't say it to hurt you. I say it to try and understand what the hell I'm doing here, talking to someone who took away the rest of his years!'

He holds out his hand and tries to touch her but

retreats. She stands there with her hands in her coat pockets and looks up. A star sparkles. It's alone and not grouped with the others, like a solitary celestial light in the night sky, and she thinks of him.

Chapter Fourteen

Two oast houses sit on each side of the village green. They are decorative and not the running mills they once were. The green was once used for cricket but is deemed too small and dangerous for the modern cars surrounding it. It's a quaint village in the way all home counties villages are. The front gardens are exquisite, and the village pub originates from the Tudor times.

Michael passed a windmill earlier and thought he might have crossed the continent to the Netherlands. It is a high-earning area and certainly upper middle-class in temperament.

He rubs the back of his neck and wipes his sweat. The weather is warm, and unlike anything, he is used to, and he wishes he wore a t-shirt instead of a long-sleeved top. He is used to the fresh air and the prevalence of bovine scent and not to the sticky vent of this atmosphere.

A ragdoll cat with a cream colourpoint walks down the pavement and stops to look at him before nonchalantly walking on. It walks to the house he has come to visit. He looks at the brass door number, it says number thirteen.

He walks up to the door and rings the bell. It opens.

'Hello,' Michael says.

Martha looks at him. She's astonished, but the English

understated type barely registers on her face.

'How are you?' he adds.

'I'm surprised if that's the word?'

'I just thought the last time we saw each other didn't go so well, and I figured it would be less intimidating here.'

'But this is my house?'

'I know. I was in two minds about coming here. The talks brought everything back, and I wanted to be normal again. It wasn't easy for me.'

'Nor me, but why did you come?'

'Just to talk properly, one-to-one.'

'Olivia is arranging more talks, and you have been corresponding with me. Nine letters now.'

'Aye.'

Michael rubs the back of his neck again, but it doesn't ease him from the heat.

'Maybe I was wrong to come here?'

'Do you have a car?'

'Aye, just over there.'

'Meet me tomorrow at one o'clock in Canterbury. It's about eight miles north of here. I'll be in the King's Arms in the high street.'

'All right.'

2

The pub is a quarter full, which is a blessing as they don't want too many people there. They sit discreetly in the corner, away from the dartboard, which isn't being used.

'How's your wine?' he asks.

'It's fine. How's your orange juice?'

'Expensive.'

'It's unusual for an Irishman not to drink?'

'You know I do, just not when I drive. Anyway, don't believe in stereotypes.'

She smiles, and it's the first time he has seen this expression. He is surprised but pleased to see it there, however brief.

'How's Olivia?'

'She's doing well. Working hard as usual.'

'She texted me the other day but failed to tell me you were coming.'

'She doesn't know.'

'Oh, so you're cagey with her too?'

'No.'

'Just with me?'

'I speak when I have something to say.'

'And you have a voice now?'

'I suppose you could say that, now anyway. When I was released, I had to sign on and you'd be given a start-up grant of about a thousand pounds, but it didn't give me any realistic opportunities.'

'But you do now.'

'I suppose.'

'Something that's never been applicable to me.'

He takes a sip of orange juice and senses criticism from her tone.

He takes a small book out from the inside of his jacket pocket. 'I bought this for you,' he said, handing it to her. 'I used to read a lot, mostly political stuff. I received a history degree inside, but I also like poetry, words like these.'

She looks at the cover. 'Seamus Heaney – *Wintering Out*.'

'It has a lot of meaning, oblique, but it's there.'

'I've read his work. A lot of it is about the North.'

'Aye. It says there is a place of clear water, the first hill in the world, unpopulated in time or place. It's a kind of what if? What if there was no sense of history?'

'Language is important, but history. It stifles you.'

'You can get caught up in it without any escape.'

'History is all you talk about over there.'

'It's shaped us.'

She looks at him deeply. 'You know what happened that day. I want you to tell me what happened. Only you can give me that. When I first met you, the hairs on the back of my neck stood up. It was awful. I felt sick. I had to meet you to look into your eyes and find some sense of humanity. But all you give me is rhetoric, and that's useless to me.'

He doesn't know what to say as self-reproach races through him.

They finish their drinks and walk out of the pub onto the high street. The weather is warm but overcast. A young family walks past them, making their way to the River Stour. Their young daughter runs in circles around her father, who playfully tries to catch her, and she screams with delight every time he does.

'Do you want to go for a short drive?' she asks.

'Where to?'

'To the beginning.'

They walk next to a stone wall and up to the entrance of the cemetery. She walks ahead of him, and he follows with leaden steps. She stops, and he looks at her.

'He's here, isn't he?'

'Yes.'

'I can't,' he says in a whisper.

'Michael, I just want you to understand.' She holds out her hand. 'Please, come with me.'

He looks at her hand, takes it, and feels a sense of connection, a sharing, with a unique contrast of grief and guilt.

The graves consist of kerbed to cremation memorials. Others are like the Victorian ones, lean at precarious angles and look in complete disrepair. There must have been an ongoing recycling of graves to resolve the overpopulated cemeteries by piling one body on top of the other. The decaying state of these monuments is not from their immediate families from years gone by, who lovingly tended to their graves, but from their ancestors who have no physical contact with their family history and thus don't have any concern for them.

He walks further into the churchyard with her and feels a hot sensation run through his body. He lets go of her hand and lets her walk on.

Stephen's grave has a bespoke granite design with a shaped, curled headstone. A bronze cross is carved on its top right side with the insignia of his regiment on its left, but it's his age that he focuses on, although it's always been etched in his mind.

'Come closer,' she asks.

He hesitantly steps forward and stands beside her.

She looks at the grave. 'Stephen was just doing his job.'

'So was I, Martha. Maturity is a wonderful gift, though.'

'I remember saying goodbye to him. I told him one day this would mean something.'

'You're a brave woman.'

'I must be. The man who did this doesn't seem like the man who stands before me now, and that's difficult. I should despise you, Michael, but you were nothing but a boy too.'

'Aye, one full of hate, which is something I no longer have.'

'That's good to hear.'

'You and I can help each other. I know I can help you. I want to help. I want that for you and your son.'

She dwells on this for a while. 'I take comfort in

knowing it was you who did this and not some unapologetic man who doesn't care.'

He takes her hand and holds it, and they stand there wordlessly but hope the same thing.

They walk out of the cemetery and sit in a quiet spot near the river. She knows this area well as it's out of the way from the hustle and bustle. They watch a young man punting. He stands at the back of the boat and gently pushes it along with a quant. He must be a student, earning extra money to pay for his books or beer, probably the latter. A gaggle of swans swims behind, and their young chicks enthusiastically follow.

'Tell me about your son.'

'What do you want to know?'

'Everything. Everything that you're prepared to tell me.'

She looks at the swans and smiles.

'He was the cutest boy you could ever meet. He had shiny brown hair, big blue eyes, and the chubbiest cheeks. I remember one time when it was my niece's birthday. We turned the lights out, and her mum came in with a cake and lit candles. She excitedly blew them out, and when we turned the lights back on, a chunk of cake was missing. We looked at the cake and then at Stephen, and he said he hadn't done it, but there was cream around his mouth, but he was adamant, and it was the funniest thing.'

He smiles at this. 'Did he like school?'

'Oh, yes. He loved school. He went to the primary school I taught at. It was just across the road from us. He was a clever boy.'

'Like his mum.'

'Yes, like me, but unlike me, he was excellent at sports, especially running. He would win sports day every year. He was exceptional at the one hundred metres. One year he won by one-hundredth of a second. I didn't show it to the other teachers or parents, but I was dancing inside.'

'Did he have a girlfriend when he...'

'When he died? No. He had one just before, though.'

Martha crosses her legs and tells him the story.

'He wanted to go to an under-eighteen disco at a local sports centre one weekend. He was sixteen, and they had groups playing there, like Take That or actors from Eastenders appearing, like Sid Owen.'

'Sid Owen?'

'Ricky from Eastenders.'

He's nonplussed and shakes his head.

'Never mind. Anyway, he came back more animated than I had ever seen him. He told me he saw this girl with her friends in the middle of the hall and he knew he would marry her one day. He just felt it, he said he had an out-of-body experience. He approached her and all her friends moved out of the way, like he was Moses parting the Red Sea. He introduced himself and she told him her name, and they talked and laughed. He forgot about his friends, and she forgot about hers. At the end of the night, they played a couple of slow songs, so he asked her to dance, and they held each other and kissed. In that second, he knew, all the electricity from him went into her, and all from her went into him. He said it was like they had levitated and only they existed. So, he came home and told me he was in love with the girl he was going to marry.'

'Why weren't they together in the end?'

'He joined the army and went away. He trained in Dartmoor and left her here. She got a job in the city and the nightlife enticed her. He was sent over there, and she called him one night after he came back from patrol. She told him she had found someone else, someone who lived close by. She said she couldn't bear being alone for weeks on end, and that was it. He cried down the phone to me. I didn't sleep that night. Afterwards, I was told he volunteered for everything, the most dangerous jobs, took risks, and wanted to get at the enemy any way he could.'

'What about you? Why don't you have a wife?'

'I was in love with a girl once upon a time.'

'Where is she now?'

'She went away.'

'You never stayed connected?'

'No,' he says with a sigh. He looks at her. 'Your son was a fine soldier.'

'Yes,' she says. 'He was.'

The swans swim gracefully. They're the most elegant of waterfowls. They glide along like a ballerina. The parents reach the edge, step on dry land, and the cygnet's webbed feet waddle behind them. She watches them. They are a family, a unit, and one for life.

Chapter Fifteen

Simon watches Olivia's lips touch the glass as she sips her wine. She has the most beautiful full lips, ones he could kiss for an eternity. He watches her closely.

'What?' she says shyly.

'Nothing...' He knows and understands the love in her eyes. It makes him feel good. It makes him feel alive. 'I'm only glad you're here in my life. I can't think of it without you.'

She places her hand on his. 'I know.'

'No one will come between us.'

'Simon, we're meant to be.'

He feels elevated, and the nerves dissipate.

'I just want you to know this.'

'You don't need to tell me. I already know.'

They leave the restaurant and walk hand in hand to Lanyon Place, near the Waterfront Hall. They look at the river sauntering through, and she rests her head on him.

'It's beautiful, isn't it?'

'Just like you,' he says.

She lets out a satisfied sound as content as the river flowing before her.

Simon puts his hands on her shoulders and stands her before him. 'Olivia, you know how much I love you, don't you?'

'Yes, I know.'

'You're the love of my life.'

'And you're the love of mine, Simon.'

He gets down on one knee, and her eyes expand. He produces a beautiful, handcrafted box and opens it. The ring takes her breath away, and her eyes become moist.

'Olivia, love of my life, will you do me the honour of being my wife?'

'Yes, I will!'

He takes the ring from the box and places it on her ring finger.

'Oh, my love, it's beautiful!'

They kiss and hold each other for a long time. They don't want to ever let go. She's too important to him, and him to her.

Craig Nowell feels disbelief and vexation at Simon's sudden announcement. His son has known this girl for under a year, yet they are already planning to get married. Simon told his mother of his intentions, and she couldn't convince him otherwise.

Elizabeth asks when he proposed, and Simon tells her it was at the weekend.

'Let's see the ring, Olivia,' she says.

Olivia holds out her hand. 'I went into shock. I'm still in a wee bit of shock, but a happy one.'

'Well, this is a surprise! Congratulations to both of

you! I'll get Lena to open a bottle of champagne.'

Nowell holds out his hand, and Simon shakes it. 'Congratulations, Son.'

'Thank you, da.'

'And to you, Olivia,' he says, kissing her on the cheek.

He looks at his son and doesn't understand what he's doing. He doesn't know how to take the news, and he feels he is being ambushed. He is calm, but inside he feels a surge of volcanic wrath.

Lena comes into the room with a tray of champagne and glasses and gives the couple her best wishes. Nowell can feel the rage erupt within him, and he excuses himself and goes to the bathroom. He locks himself in the room, splashes his face with cold water, and looks at himself in the mirror. He holds on to the basin and stands there, letting the water drip into it.

***

Michael is standing at the bar drinking a pint. It isn't one of his normal hangouts, it's too sterile and has no character. He wishes he brought a paper with him so he can do a crossword and reflects he must be getting old to think such things.

Olivia walks in, hand in hand, with Simon. She is laughing at a private joke he has just made and shakes her head in amusement.

'How are you?' Olivia asks.

'I'm grand,' Michael replies.

'How are you doing, Simon?'

'I'm good, how's yourself?'

'Not bad. Is she behaving herself?'

'Cheeky sod!'

'Do you want another one?'

'I wouldn't say no.'

Simon orders the drinks and Michael drinks his pint and looks at them together. They look besotted with each other. They constantly touch and look at each other with knowing eyes. They have a magnetic pull that no one can come between, not even Michael. He feels left out in their company and accepts his baby sister is growing up and no longer needs him like she used to.

'How are the wedding plans coming together?' he asks.

'God, there's so much to do! Hiring the car, caterers, the hall... and your page boy suit!'

'It's better than being a bridesmaid!'

Simon laughs, but Olivia ignores the retort and continues with her list.

'The church has been sorted, of course.'

'What is it going to be?'

'A non-denominational one,' she replies.

'That's the compromise. It's the only way, Michael. There's just no alternative,' Simon says.

He looks at her as Simon tells him, but she doesn't give him any discerning reaction. He just nods but knows Simon is right, they can't please everyone, and this is the only way to settle things.

'You don't need to explain. I can see your dilemma. It's the best option at the end of the day. You're happy, and that's what counts.'

'Aye, we are,' Olivia says. 'I want to ask you to do something for me on the day.'

'Being a page boy is out of the question!'

Olivia smiles. 'I want you to give me away. It would make me so happy.'

Michael gives her a knowing smile.

'Olivia, I cannot think of anything more perfect.'

2

Donnelly's cherubic features make him look more like an ageing choir boy than the cold-blooded killer Michael knows. They share a similar upbringing, but unlike Michael's, his was violent. Both their fathers were alcoholics, but Donnelly's father excelled in gambling, women, and drinking and lived to beat his wife. Donnelly also took the full brunt of his da's wrath, and this consequently made him stammer. When some boys at his school called him 'D-D-Donnelly' to his face, he became his father's son and beat one so badly he was in hospital for several weeks and was expelled.

As he grew into a confident, sturdy man, his stammer disappeared. One day when his da's fists went too far for his liking, he sent him to the hospital, and he never touched his mother or came near the family again.

Michael wants to bounce some questions off him to see if it's the right way to go. They meet in Donnelly's office, and the deafening noise he experienced before gives way to the quiet purpose of his staff going through their preparations before the rush of night.

'You still don't want a job here? You can manage this place,' Donnelly said.

'Nah, I'm too busy now, besides I wouldn't get any work done with you.'

'Aye, you're right. I'm just saying.'

'I know, and I appreciate it.'

'Good.'

'Do you remember that time when your da was too handy with your mummy one Christmas, and you knocked him into the new year?'

'And beyond.'

'Aye, well, I was just thinking about it the other day, how they can dictate our lives.'

'We were young, but we soon outgrew the bastards, yours wasn't as bad, but I get what you're saying. Why do you ask?'

'I don't know, I'm just thinking. You know Olivia's engaged.'

'Aye, great news, isn't it.'

'Well, in a way.'

'What do you mean?'

'It's his da.'

'What about him?'

'He's in the police service.'

'Fuck off!'

'And he's high up.'

'How high?'

'He's got the top job.'

'Craig Nowell! No fucking way!'

'I wish it weren't true, and I'm concerned. What happens when the media get hold of this?'

'They'll have a field day. Do you think Craig Nowell will accept the publicity? No chance!'

'Someone's bound to get hold of it, but there's nothing I can do. Olivia loves him, and I'm happy for them, but I'm just concerned that once this gets out, it will become more difficult than they think.'

Chapter Sixteen

Michael gets off the plane at Gatwick and into his hired car. He drives down the M25 and keeps right of the Dartford crossing before taking the exit onto the M2 and then the A2 towards Canterbury.

He's here to discuss a proposal made by Olivia. She is the one who is always trying to move them forward, but sometimes he doesn't know to what end. He drives to meet Martha in the cathedral city. He wants to smoke, but he gave it up in prison. He thinks about vaping, but it seems like a waste of a bad habit.

He gets there in an hour and a quarter and drives through Westgate, a mediaeval gatehouse, and into the centre. He parks up and pays the parking fee. It's a lot, he thinks, but that is English hospitality for you.

He is staying in a lodge inside the premises of the cathedral. It's serene and has the appearance of a monastery, a place of retreat and reflection, one which he thinks might do him good. He looks at the cathedral out of his bedroom window with its three stately towers and admires its gothic architecture.

He unpacks his brand-new leather holdall, which consists of a toiletry bag, jeans, socks, pants, and a pair of Adidas trainers, as he likes to wear logo designs. He brought his Kindle and is reading a biography about his hero Robert F. Kennedy. He thought about bringing a hat to keep the rain off, but this is one of the driest counties, so he thought there was no need.

Michael's phone buzzes, and he gets a text from Martha. She says she's at a café a few minutes' walk from where he is, so he collects his things and heads out to meet her.

The place is teeming with people, and he thinks it's a shame that such a beautiful place isn't as reposeful as its church. He walks over a bridge and past Huguenot's weaver's houses and sees her in the distance, flicking her hair back and watching the day go by. He walks up to her, and she gives a smile of recognition which he gets pleasure from.

'Hello, how are you?' he asks.

'I'm fine, and you?'

'Aye. I'm good.'

'Would you like something to eat?'

'Aye. I had nothing this morning.'

'I'm having a chicken salad.'

'That sounds good. I'll have the same.'

They don't wait long for their meal to be served, and Michael is the first to tuck in.

'So, what do you think?' he asks.

'It's a big thing, a BBC interview.'

'Aye. What do you think they'll ask?'

'I don't know, it's like window dressing. The media have their own agenda. It will be, *woman forgives man, who killed her son.*'

'Right.'

'But have I forgiven, or do I even want to?'

Michael picks up a piece of chicken with his fork and puts it down again. 'You think you'll be asked that?'

'Yes. I know I will. It'll be a ten-minute slot with that parley. They will say that I'm showing remission of your guilt by doing our talks, and you're accepting my forgiveness.'

'No. It should be about two people with opposing views caught up in a tragedy, but those two people are seeking something in the other.'

'Is that what you are doing, seeking something from me?' she asks.

'Yes, but I don't know what it is yet. I don't think either of us does.'

'We are still trying to come to terms with us.'

'Us?' For a moment, Michael doesn't know what she means.

'Yes. We are discovering different facets of each other, from this, our talks, and our letters.'

'I see what you mean.'

'I think Olivia has good intentions, but I'm not sure.'

A group of youths are standing near them, lining up, waiting for their teacher to lead them on. They are frenetic in their conversations, manically jabbering, like they've had six weeks' summer holiday and are catching up with what happened. Martha can tell by their accents that they are Bavarian and sound like they are from Munich.

A girl with a tight bob talks the loudest. She's wearing denim dungarees. Martha doesn't know if this is the fashion or not. The girl looks at her, then rounds to her friend and says something in German, and Martha laughs.

Michael is astonished. He hasn't heard her laugh before. 'What is it?'

She stops laughing, and her smile fades. 'She said I look like her mum.'

He doesn't know what to say and just looks at her.

Once they finish their meal, she asks him what he will do with the rest of the day. He tells her he hasn't decided. He might browse in a bookstore or look for a new pair of jeans.

'What if I show you the North Downs?'

'All right, sounds good.'

The conversation in the car runs freely. They are more relaxed in each other's presence. It doesn't bother them if there is a silence, and they feel no need to fill the tacit atmosphere with words. They have formed something they are comfortable with, and that's what matters.

They stop and take in the scenery of the chalk hills of the downs, which stretch to the white cliffs of Dover.

'What do you think?'

'It's a great view, so it is.'

'Some of the chalk is exposed because they used to be quarries.'

'Oh right.'

He watches the cool breeze blow her hair across her

face, just like it did when he first saw her, but this time her profile is restful, and she looks like what she must have done when she was younger.

They walk on a gravel path and down a hill. The shape of the hill curves up and down, each possessing a line of trees which run up to the horizon. He follows her and is happy just to watch her in her haven, she has no inhibitions here, just serenity, and he's captivated by it.

She stops and sits on the grass, and he sits beside her. She plucks a daisy from the earth and delicately puts it to her lips. It skims along them, and she brushes it down to her chin.

'It's so peaceful here.'

'What can I say? It's a grand place.'

'Yes, it's worth dying for.'

He doesn't answer because he knows how she feels. She is to her soil as he is to his.

'So, you don't think we should do this interview? What about the people who will benefit from our appearance? Where I'm from, someone personally knows someone who was killed. Three thousand seven hundred over thirty years. If it happened here, one hundred and fifty thousand would be dead. Do we not owe it to them to tell our story?

'I don't want to become a celebrity out of something so personal.'

'I don't think you will be.'

'We are helping others with our talks. Look at Claire. The talks are more important. If we do the interview, we'll lose what we have.'

He stretches his legs out and leans back. 'What do you mean?'

'We're trying to attain something. It's been so testing to get to this point, and I think the interview will be a distraction.'

'Okay. Olivia just thought it would be an extension of what we're doing now, and, like I said, it would help others in a wider context.'

'Yes, I understand your sister is a kind-hearted woman.'

'What about your family? What does your sister think?'

'My sister doesn't know. It's one of the reasons I don't want to appear on television.'

'You haven't told her anything?'

'No, I haven't. She would be mortified. Being here now with you is something she wouldn't understand.'

He knows she's right. No one can understand what the other is feeling. Only they can. He looks at her and sees someone he wouldn't normally associate with become a friend; more than that, she's become his confidante. He pulls a daisy from the ground and gives it to her, and she takes it.

Chapter Seventeen

A bullet proof car drives over the Bann Bridge in Portadown. Nowell sits in the passenger seat and reads his speech. He wrote this one himself and goes through it one more time, hoping to get the right tone and sound. He feels more important by the day, in and out of uniform. He is the conscience and torch bearer of the province. He puts his speech back in its leather binding and straightens the peak of his hat.

He gets out of his car and is greeted by a crowd of people who have turned up to see him, he waves, and they wave back. He is popular among his people, and these are his people.

He stands outside the entrance of the building and thanks everyone for the welcome.

'Ladies and gentlemen, I'm here today for the official opening of this brand-new, state-of-the-art building which is the new face of policing in our province. I welcome the officers here who will display the highest standards of professionalism and respond to the issues facing us today. They will protect you at every inch of our borders and ensure your safety at all costs. I want to say how proud I am of the men and women here, and I know they will be here for your community. Portadown has a special place in my heart as it is my wife's birthplace and where we met. I still remember when as a young officer from Armagh I drove up to see her and took her to the cinema. They were special times in a special town....'

He talks of the challenges ahead and how he will tackle them. When he's finished, he cuts the ribbon at the doorway and smiles for the pictures, not that he likes doing it, but he is a deft handler of spin and the twenty-four-hour news cycle. He goes inside to look at the premises. He is in a magnanimous mood and rallies his troops, giving a stirring oration to his officers.

They clap him as he leaves the building, and he salutes them. He walks to his car, where his driver is waiting for him. The crowd has dispersed, but not all, as an old man walking with the aid of a stick approaches him. He is with a younger man, watching him closely, ensuring he is ambulant and doesn't topple over. The lines on the old man's face are like the contours of a map, but Nowell still recognises him.

'Nowell. Remember me?'

'Yes. How are you, Ferguson?'

He is unperturbed, as he is always on show, and he doesn't let his personal animosity interfere with his public persona. Ferguson has never impressed him. He should have made a concerted effort to defeat the enemy, but instead, he was a glory hunter. The other side had conviction and a tactical advantage through their Long War policy, but his side never had that stance with the same emphasis. He looks at his pathetic condition and lets him speak.

'Oh, you know, bearing up,' he replies. 'I have type one diabetes, and my legs are shot, but I'm still here. I moved to be closer to my son and his family, and I heard you were coming, so I thought I'd say hello.'

'It was good of you.'

'Meet my son,' Ferguson says.

'Please to meet you, Chief Constable,' he says, shaking his hand. 'I'm David.'

'He owns a car dealership down the road and several others around the province,' Ferguson proudly declares.

'Do you like cars?' David asks.

'I wouldn't say I'm a car man, but my son is.'

'Well, David will take us up there, and you can have a look around.'

'I'm on a schedule, Ferguson, so I'll pass.'

'We're old pals, Nowell. We're still pals, aren't we?' Ferguson questions.

Nowell doesn't know if this is a threat or not. He gives him a look where a thousand things are running through his mind, so he walks over to his car and taps on the driver's window.

The window lowers down. 'Yes, sir.'

'Mark, I'm just going somewhere, and I'll be about twenty minutes or so.'

'Do you want me to follow, sir?'

'No, that won't be necessary.'

The forecourt is full of new and used cars of different makes. They are all in great condition and are cleaned and polished to perfection. They sparkle in the afternoon sun, and David explains that it's had a revamp, and they have incorporated an interactive area where the customer can choose the colour of their car and add other specifications.

'Where are your customers?' asks Nowell.

'It's closed for the rest of the day,' said Ferguson.

'I gave my staff a half day on full pay,' adds David.

'We closed it for you, Nowell,' Ferguson clarifies. 'We don't want people gaping at you. You know, you are famous in these parts.'

They walk around, and he stops to look at a car. He looks at its iconic prancing horse logo over a yellow background, and it has a sharp curved design with such refinement it looks like it has been carved out of Mount Rushmore.

'Do you like it?' David asks. 'She's a real beauty, isn't she. It's second hand, but it has a low mileage.' He walks animatedly up and down the vehicle. 'It has a V-12 engine, seven hundred and eighty-nine horsepower with a top speed of two hundred and eleven miles per hour.'

'It's magnificent, but it's way out of my price range.'

'It might not be,' Ferguson says.

'What do you mean?'

'Well, my son will always give a good deal to a friend of his da's.'

Nowell examines him. 'What is it you want, Ferguson?'

Ferguson ambles up to him. 'It would be a great help to my son if you could put in a good word for him and do something for me in the process.'

'In what respect?'

'He's in the running to be the mayor of Armagh, and he needs a helping hand.'

'Is that what you want?'

'Aye, that's what I want, Nowell, and you're the man to do it.'

Ferguson smiles, and his face creases so much that it's difficult to make out his eyes under their heavy lids. Nowell doesn't requite with a smile and just tips the peak of his hat in acknowledgement.

Chapter Eighteen

Rain falls hard on the village green, drumming against the ground. Michael walks briskly as it hits him, and his hair is saturated after only a few steps. He rings the doorbell, and a light comes on in the hallway, and he sees her figure in the door's frosted glass.

'Hello,' he says.

'Michael,' she says, looking at him. 'What are you doing here?'

'I haven't seen you for a few months. I just thought we could talk.'

'Talk? We've done a lot of that already.'

'Aye. I know. I just want to keep on trying. If we don't try, we might not get there, but if we do, we will.'

She looks at him in his pitiful state as rain trickles down his face.

'Come in,' she says.

He takes off his jacket and hangs it in the hall. She tells him to go into the lounge, and he walks in and stands in the centre of it. She has expensive tastes but an uncluttered approach to the décor. He looks at her fireplace. It's the focal point of the room and one he is drawn to immediately. On the mantelpiece is a picture he doesn't want to see but can't focus on anything else. It's a younger version of her, cheek to cheek with him, his eyes identical to hers, his arms wrapped around her neck, not wanting to let go. She looks ecstatic, and her eyes say to Michael that she loves her son more than anything.

She walks in, holding a towel and sees him staring. She hands him the towel, and he dries his hair. Then he hands it back and thanks her. She asks if he wants a drink and tells him she's having wine, so he agrees to have a glass. She brings in a bottle, pours out two glasses, and sits on the sofa, but he opts to stand.

'How long have you lived here?'

'Over thirty years.'

'It's a nice area.'

'Yes, it is.'

'I looked at your garden from the conservatory. It's big.'

'Yes, I spend a lot of time there.'

'I can tell. It's well maintained.'

'It's my sanctuary.'

'Well, we all need one.'

She sips her wine and gazes at the rug near the fireplace. He feels a need to stay. One where there are no talks, no people, just them together, one on one, in her sanctuary where she feels safe and protected. He tries to gauge the atmosphere, but his perception, although sound, finds this one difficult to comprehend. He looks at her from time to time, she is emotionless, and he keeps seeing the picture behind him, and he feels ill at ease.

'I saw you looking at him.'

He looks at her.

'On the mantelpiece.'

'Your son?'

'Yes, Stephen.'

She walks over to the mantelpiece and picks up the picture. 'Here, hold it.'

She hands it to him, and he reluctantly takes it from her.

'Look at it.'

He looks at it once more. Their eyes are an aquamarine colour. A colour so clear and beautiful it transfixes him.

'That's what I had, the life I wanted, and the one taken away.'

He puts the picture back on the mantelpiece. 'I'm so sorry, Martha. If I could live my life again. It would have been different. Once my girlfriend was killed...'

'Your girlfriend? Killed?' she said, surprised, and places her glass on the table. 'You never mentioned this to me?'

He sits down on the sofa, and she sits next to him.

'What was her name?'

'Sosaidh.'

'How was she killed?'

'She was working as a barmaid at a local club. It was a birthday celebration, you know, where everyone was enjoying the craic when two gunmen burst in and started shooting. I found her behind the bar, her face wasn't...' his voice breaks with emotion. 'She just didn't look the same. Not only had they taken her life, but they had taken her looks away from me. When I think of her, I picture her beauty, but then I have an image of what they did. Oh, man...' he says, shaking his head.

Martha places her hand on his. 'It's okay.'

'The gunmen were believed to be off-duty police officers, although it's never been proven.'

'They were never caught?'

'No.'

'How old was she?'

'Sixteen.'

'It's so young,' she says. 'What was she like?'

'She was kind, funny, a little bit insecure but highly capable. She was special, special to me.'

'She sounds it.'

He places his other hand on hers and holds it tightly.

'She's never left my heart.'

'I get it,' she says quietly.

'Aye.'

'You've never got over it, have you?'

'No, I haven't. My heart screams for her, but no one knows.'

'We deal with it in our own way.'

'Aye, in a way that makes sense to us.'

'Yes, precisely.'

'I miss her...' He makes a fist and knocks his knuckles on his forehead. 'every single day.'

She puts her arm around him. 'You have to make the most of your days, Michael. You're still young.'

'I don't feel it.'

'You have to stay on track because tomorrow may be derailed.'

'I'll try.'

'I suppose being in your organisation helped you cope.'

'Aye, it did.'

'So, you understand loss.'

'Yes, I do, and I want to help you with your grief.'

'I live with grief. Sure, the pain lessens, but it doesn't go away. It becomes a benign tumour, and you just don't know when it will become malignant in the form of sorrow once again.'

'I know you live with it every day. I do too. It never goes away. I have it there from when I wake up to when I sleep. I know you have it worse, and I only hope my sincere regret at what I did means something to you.'

She looks at him with sharp movements of her eyes, trying to decipher his sincerity. She wonders how a person can take another's life and live on, live with it on their conscience and get on with their life. She tries to understand how Michael can live a normal routine when his old life was far from normal. How can he live knowing he has committed the ultimate transgression? She feels a calmness knowing this, she knows he is tortured by what he has done, but she has a better understanding as to why he did it, and that hurts even more, she'd rather not know, but if she's asking him to understand her, then she must understand him.

She walks over to the table and picks up the bottle of wine. It's empty, so she gets another. She comes back and pours out two more glasses.

'When did you first see Stephen?' she asks.

'The first time I saw your son was through the lens of a rifle. The soldier in me took over, he was one, and I was one. I dehumanised him so I could make him a target. I thought of the things done to us in the name of your crown to intensify my actions, and that's when I fired.'

'How did you feel about it?' she asks with expectant eyes.

'I didn't feel anything.'

'Nothing!' she says and rolls her eyes to the ceiling.

'It was a mission, and it felt morally right. I wasn't there to question the rights and wrongs but to carry out an order.'

'So, it would sit more easily on you?'

'It never has, Martha, and that's the God's honest truth.'

'I should never have let him go. I used to wake up in the middle of the night from a dream. He would be lying there, holding out his hand...' She raises her hand. 'But I was always too far away to grasp it.'

Michael reaches for her hand and holds it.

'I never realised back then who and what I was hurting, but I do now.'

She lets go of his hand. 'Now you know the realities.'

'Aye, now I know.'

'I suppose when you were recruited, you were groomed, a gullible, malleable teenager, and they were conditioning you to commit these acts. Look at what it's done to you, Michael.'

At one time, he could see himself with Sosaidh living in a rural haven. But his circumstances changed with her death. He believed he could start again after prison, but he procrastinated and didn't realise how much his actions had affected him. Now he deems starting a family as something that lurks in a distant world, one he is not worthy of. He set himself on a path filled with punitive measures to extract himself from the compunction he feels. It is only through meeting Martha that he truly comprehends this. He looks at her and doesn't want her pity. He wants to recognise his part in her grief, recognise himself once more, and recognise the truth, not his, but *the* truth and what it means.

'Our scars aren't superficial. They're internal. They don't miraculously disappear the next day. They leave an indent.'

Michael gazes into his wine glass. 'I've ruined my life, but I don't want you to ruin yours. You deserve better than this.'

'What people deserve and what they get are two opposing forces. There is no fairness in life, we all suffer to varying degrees, some more than others, but we all suffer.'

'I don't want that for you. You deserve to be happy.'

She stands up. 'Happy? What is that?' She walks over

to the mantlepiece and picks up the picture. 'That part of me is gone.' She points at the picture. 'It's gone with him, Michael; can't you see that!'

'It doesn't have to be. You can change it.'

She places the picture back. 'We're both fatalistic, so it would be a contradiction in terms for you to believe this for me.'

'I do believe it. It can happen to you. You want it to happen. I don't. That's why you contacted me, to make it happen. You wouldn't have done it otherwise.'

She stands and holds onto the mantlepiece, looking at the picture.

'I contacted you for various reasons, but I never thought about happiness or its goal. I just wanted to know one reason, the reason why. That is why I wanted to find you.'

'It was important for both of us that you did. I've learned so much from this, so much about myself. I'm indebted to you, Martha.'

She walks away from the mantlepiece. 'Do you find life difficult?'

'Like anyone, I guess.'

'Like me, you mean?'

'Aye. We have both reached the heights of happiness and the depths of despair.'

'How do you feel about my loss and how it affects me?'

Michael stands up. 'I completely detached myself from it. I just had no idea how you feel.'

'I feel isolated. You don't know what it's like here. My

country wasn't concerned with my loss because it happened elsewhere. The conflict wasn't happening here. It was over there, and people were ambivalent.

'I never thought of it like that. It's a learning process for me. I never realised your own people would exclude you this way.'

'People didn't want to talk about it. I could see it in their demeanour. They didn't care about it or what was happening. So, I had to deal with it in a different way.'

'I'm glad people can hear you now and recognise what you have been through. This country needs to understand its victims.'

'I felt they didn't until our talks.'

He can see how she felt deserted by her own country, indifferent to a problem they created. If your nation is nonchalant to your loss, you're directionless. He had never experienced this. He was classed as a hero among his peers and not an outcast.

'Sometimes I think the only language being understood is ours, with these talks. I used to feel like I was talking in a language only linguists would understand, not my friends,' she said.

'I thought only our respective nations didn't talk to each other properly.'

'At first, we didn't communicate. We communicated like you seemed to with your peers, but now I feel we do communicate.'

'I understood you not through words, tone, and inflexions but through non-verbal intricacies like the way you looked away when describing something you didn't want to talk about or those silences when you heard something you didn't want to hear. Oh, those silences!'

'It sounds like you have done a profile on me!'

'I had to!' she replies. 'I used my cognitive reasoning to unravel the real meaning of your thoughts. I had to fully understand what you were really trying to tell me and not just go by the words.'

'Aye, I watched you too. I can see your pain.'

'I find strength in the pain. I relive his loss every day.'

'You must feel alone?'

'Yes, separate from the world.'

'I feel alone too.'

'But you have Olivia and friends to keep you busy.'

'But I still feel it. I don't feel I deserve anything, you know, like love, and I'll die like that.'

She sits down and puts her hand on his knee. 'You'll die when the last person that loves you dies.'

He looks at her and runs his hand over his hair. 'I can't say sorry enough to you, Martha. I wish I could go back to that day. I relive it every day too. I don't sleep too well... a few hours a night, that's when it hits me the most, the despair....'

'Stephen's age stopped on the day he died. Now he would be a man with a good job, a family, but all I see is a boy.'

She gets up and pours more wine into her glass, and she can feel the effects before feeling for the seat's cushion and sitting down.

'I know, but I'm here for you, to help, to help us both.'

She drops her glass on the floor, and it shatters. She gets on her knees to pick up the fragments and cuts her hand in the process. He takes her hand and stops her from picking up anymore.

'I'll do it,' he says.

He goes to the kitchen and comes back with a wet cloth. She sits with her legs sideways on the floor, and he squats down and gently dabs her cut hand. She quietly watches him pat the wound clean with each gentle touch.

'Where are your plasters?'

She bows her head down. 'It's all right. It doesn't matter.'

'It does.'

'In the first cupboard on the left.'

He returns, puts the plaster on her hand, then picks up the shards of glass around her and places it on a wet cloth.

'Are you okay?'

'Yes. I'm just exhausted.'

He takes her good hand and helps her up. 'Come on, you need to rest.'

She stands up, puts her arm around his shoulder, and he puts his around her waist. They slowly walk up the stairs, and she holds onto the bannister as she does. They step into her bedroom, and he directs her to the bed. He opens the covers, lays her down, and softly places her head on the pillow. She closes her eyes, and he touches her hair, then gently strokes it. He looks at the outline of her face, and she looks younger lying there like all her worries have faded.

'That's nice,' she says and lets out a sigh.

He moves his hand in circular motions on her temple and tenderly caresses her cheek.

She fixes her eyes on his. 'Thank you,' she says and holds up her hand to touch his face.

He places his hand over hers, and she takes it and kisses it. He leans down and gently kisses her cheek. She turns towards his lips, and they touch hers. He kisses her, and she responds by opening her mouth. They kiss, lips together, mouths open, indulging each other's needs. The kiss becomes more fervent as they impart the primary form of communication. He pulls back the covers and kisses her neck before unbuttoning her blouse. He lays on top of her, and she wraps her legs around him. They embrace more passionately, and their tongues flick in and out of each other's mouths, rolling their bodies one way then another, grasping each other's flesh with rapacity. He lifts her skirt up, kisses the inside of her thighs, and makes his way up when she suddenly pushes his head away.

'Stop! Stop! We can't, we just can't!'

He lifts his head up and moves away to the edge of the bed. She sits up, grabs a pillow, and grips it firmly over her stomach.

'How could you let this happen?'

'It just happened. I don't want to see you in any more pain.'

She hits him with the pillow. 'Just give him back to me!'

'I can't, I can't do that. I wish I could.'

She kicks out, kicking the heel of her foot into his ribs. 'You took him away! You can bring him back!'

He stands up from the bed, and she runs at him with a battery of punches, hitting him in the face and chest before collapsing to the floor.

'I need him! I need him back!'

He picks her up and holds her in his arms as tears fall from her. He holds her for a long time and lets her calm before lying her back on the bed and placing the covers over her. He sits down on her dresser chair and watches her as she falls into a deep sleep. He sits there for an hour before quietly walking down the stairs and letting himself out.

Chapter Nineteen

Olivia and Simon stroll by the river and look at the reflections of the buildings cast back from it. It ripples along and crescents beyond them, shimmering in the bright sky.

'Where do you see us in five years?'

'Together, of course.'

'With a couple of wains. One of each.'

'Each religion!'

She lets out a tender giggle and knocks her shoulder into his. 'Funny!'

'Just to be with you would be my most cherished thing.'

'Me too.'

She holds his hand and playfully swings it up and down. He doesn't mind. He likes it when she's girly because it makes him feel more gallant.

'It's not going to be easy, is it.'

He holds her. 'No, it's not, but that's life, the beauty of it.'

'What do you mean?'

'Sometimes the most difficult situations make people

closer because they have to fight for their love.'

'So, in adversity, a relationship is cemented?'

'Yes. No matter how far apart, there's still a pull, a magnetic one that draws them together when everyone else wants them apart.'

'I've read that romantic love only lasts a year, then it becomes an attachment.'

'Possibly, but you can have a connection. Obviously, you can't have the honeymoon period forever, but you can have a connection that not many people have, you can have a special place that not many people go, and you can have that pull, one which only we know.'

'Aye, I know it, and I feel it too.'

'So do I.'

'Where do you think you'd be if we hadn't met?'

'Oh, walking along the river with some other woman.'

'I bet!'

'I don't know, who knows?'

'It's strange, isn't it?'

'What is?'

'Life. How we meet the people we do. How important they are, how essential they are to you. How you can meet people, and even when they're not there, they are. You fill up your day thinking about them, imagining what they're doing at a given time, asking yourself, are they thinking of you like you are thinking of them. The mind is such a complex apparatus.'

'Especially yours!'

She pushes into him. 'Not funny!'

'I know what you mean, though.'

'Life and love are strange.'

'Yes, they certainly are.'

'How did your parents meet?'

'They met at a dance hall.'

'Dirty dancing!'

'Maybe afterwards, but not so much in those days.'

'People had sex, you know.'

'But you don't want to think of your parents having it! They were young and fell in love.'

'First loves?'

'Yes, and love at first sight, according to my mum.'

'What about your da?'

'He's hidden when it comes to matters of the heart.'

'Aye, he doesn't give a lot away.'

'He'll make a good poker player.'

'Has he said anything about me?'

'No.'

'Oh, okay.'

'What?'

'I just said okay.'

'He asks how you are and what you are doing, but apart from that, he doesn't say anything.'

'Do you think he approves of me?'

'I haven't asked.'

'You haven't asked? God, men!'

'I know my father; I don't ask because I know that he probably wouldn't answer, or he'll give a politician's one!'

'Don't you talk, like father and son?'

'Aye, but it's not a talk like a mother and a daughter would have,' he says before thinking about what he just said. 'I'm sorry I didn't think... what I meant was....'

'It's okay, I know what you mean.'

'You know how society is. It's difficult to be open with a man. I find it easier opening to a woman and easy opening up to you.'

'Aye, I know.'

'To answer your rhetorical question, why do we meet the people we meet. Maybe we're old souls from previous lives, and we haven't finished what we started.'

'So, we can meet twice?'

'Yes... well... maybe. We can meet a person twice, even twice in our life spans, and that's rare, three times even rarer, but it's all meant to be in the cycle of life.'

'If you meet someone twice in a lifespan, it's meant to be in God's plan. If it happens, then the person will become the most important person in your life. It's frightening, really, it's like it's out of your hands, and maybe it is?' Olivia says.

'It's the cycle of life, and everything has led to that point, like our meeting. Decades ago, we couldn't have been. We certainly couldn't have lived here as a couple.'

'We would have had to emigrate.'

'Definitely, but today it's not so rare.'

'That's why your da will have to accept us.'

'He'll have no choice,' Simon says.

He picks up a stone and puts his thumb over it, and before he releases it, he flicks his wrist, and it skims over the water and bounces at intervals. They watch it skate over the surface, bouncing up and down until it reaches the other side.

Chapter Twenty

He knows he shouldn't be here. All his instincts tell him not to, and when he follows them, he is always right, but his instincts don't want to acknowledge what's going on inside.

He rings her doorbell, but there's no answer. Her car is there, so he assumes she is in the house. He walks to the front window, and although the blinds are pulled, he senses she's there.

Martha is lying on the sofa, covered in a blanket. She hears the ring and lifts her head from the cushion, only for it to drop down again. Her head throbs, and her mouth is bitter. She finally sits up after the third ring and takes a gulp of water from the glass next to her. She stands up, then walks sluggishly to the door, wrapped in a blanket, and opens just as Michael contemplates on ringing again.

'What are you doing here?' she asks in a hoarse voice.

'Just to see that you're okay.'

'I'm fine.'

'You don't look it,' he replies. 'Can I come in?'

'What for?'

'Just to talk.'

'We have done enough of that, don't you think?'

'Aye, we have… Look, I just want to apologise.'

She opens the door, and he walks in. He follows her into the kitchen, where she picks up the kettle and puts water into it.

'Tea or coffee?'

'Tea would be grand.'

She settles on black coffee, which she doesn't usually drink but believes will help her head if not anything else. He sits down at her dining table, and she takes the cups over and sits with him. They don't speak, and she sits there with both hands enclosed around her cup.

'About last night…'

'Michael, please. I don't want to talk about it. We both had too much to drink, but it was no excuse, especially for me. I'm vulnerable, and I suppose you are too. It was a mistake in capital letters, and I'm too hungover to process it.'

'I'm just here to say sorry,' he says.

'We're both to blame.'

He is surprised by her admission as he believes he is the one at fault.

'It must be because we have a connection that we don't want, but it's there.'

'Connection?'

'Aye, where it comes from, I don't know, but I just feel it.'

She pushes her cup aside. 'This is too much for me to take in,' she replies, pinching the middle of her forehead.

'Then why do you think it happened? I wasn't obliterated, and I don't think you were either?'

'I wasn't,' she guiltily replies.

'It must have been a spontaneous reaction to what we've been going through.'

She looks bemused. 'In what sense?'

'It's difficult to explain. All the emotions we've been through since we met, it's for some inexplicable reason?'

'A love/hate reaction, you mean?'

'I don't know, Martha. Emotions are complicated, especially the ones we've experienced. I have never gone through this intensity before, have you?'

She gets up and pours her cup of coffee into the sink. She stands there looking vacantly out of the window looking and wishing her head would keep still.

He looks at her configuration. She has a slender figure, yet her inner strength defies her petiteness. Her blonde hair is ruffled, but for him, she has an allure.

'Why have you never married or had children?'

'It was because of Sosaidh. She was so special to me that I couldn't find anyone to replace her until I met you.'

He stands up and puts his empty cup in the sink next to hers.

He places his hand on her shoulder. 'Martha, look...'

She moves some paces away from him and raises her hand to a stop signal. 'Don't... please.'

He looks intensely at her brooding face and doesn't know what to do.

'You shouldn't have come here.'

'I came here for the same reason I did when we first met, to help you.'

'But this isn't helping. It's not helping either of us.'

'Listen to me,' he says gently.

She listens but avoids his stare.

'I will always tell you the truth. I'm here for you. I know I've made mistakes since we met, but I want and need you in my life.'

Her face is flaming, and he can't tell whether it's a reaction to him or from the alcohol last night.

She walks away from him by slowly stepping backwards. 'I can't cope with this anymore, Michael. You killed my son, for God's sake! I can't have any feelings for you. We can't be friends, let alone anything else. We can't be anything. We must accept it. We must be apart and never see each other again.'

She steps back until she reaches the wall, where she puts her arms behind her back in a V-shape and focuses on the patterns of the floor tiles, trying to disengage from him.

'Martha, we need this... to be part of each other's lives. We've only just found one another!'

'I can't!'

He pleads with her and walks towards her with his arms stretched out. 'Please!' he adjures.

Her eyes remain fixed on the floor. 'You need to go home.'

He stops as her words impale him. He feels the iciness

emanating from her and knows even the best negotiator in the world will fail to persuade her. They have reached an impasse, and he can do nothing about it. His frustration is palpable, and a lump in his throat prevents him from replying. He shakes his head, although he knows she's right, but to accept it is heartbreaking. He looks at her and tries to catch her eye, but she doesn't look up, so he walks out.

When he gets into his car, he slumps down in his seat and puts his face in his hands.

Chapter Twenty-One

When he gets home, he gets on his motorbike, a Yamaha, and revs it up. He needs to get away, run away even. He goes full throttle up the motorway in County Antrim and weaves in and out of the traffic, speeding along like he's going to the edge of nowhere. He goes at a velocity and wishes he weren't wearing a helmet. He wants to be free. Although he is free and out of prison, he never feels it.

He rides to the north coast, leans down on his bike, and easily takes corners. He wants his haste to transpose his struggles as the frenzy in his head impairs his once sound judgement until it gets to the edge of somewhere.

The Giant's Causeway.

He stops, gets off his bike, and takes off his helmet to smell the salty air. He walks along the ocean with hunched shoulders and steps on the basalt columns, and watches the waves crash into the rocks, frothing white foam and seaweed onto the land. He wants to dive off the rocks into the deepest depths of the ocean and swim down into its darkness. The waves forge and retreat, and he feels it's like a metaphor for his life. He tries to make sense of it all, he's tried to do the right thing since that horrific day, yet every positive action from him produces a negative reaction.

He wonders why people meet the people they do. Is it

predetermined, the way people are pulled together, and do they swim in a whirlpool where they come into conflict with some people and swim into the arms of others.

The most lamentable state a man can have is where he is alone. He knows what it means to live a solitary life. He has no one to share with, no one to hold and no one to convey his thoughts. His surroundings appear darker and murkier, and they have no sympathy for the unwanted. They only dismiss them, for there is only one thing worse than loneliness, and that's abandonment.

He walks over the water on a sturdy rope bridge and imagines men at the other end cutting the ropes. He wouldn't care. Such is the state of his mind. He wouldn't even hang on. He would just drop into the water and never return. As he gets to the other side, he looks out and sees the British mainland but has no intention of returning because she's there. He knows that nothing lasts forever, and this consoles him. He thinks of Sosaidh and knows Martha has taken her place.

He gets out his phone and takes a picture. He writes a message with it.

'Hi Martha. I'm here just thinking things over and thinking of you.'

He doesn't get a reply.

He rides home at speed and is lucky not to be pulled over. When he gets back, he looks at her letters on his coffee table, they are all placed neatly next to each other, and he thinks about the contents from the first letter until the last. He rubs his chin and scratches a day's growth of stubble and wallows in his predicament. He cares for her more than he knows, but it's too late, like everything else. He can't leave it like this, though, and he needs to say more because he hasn't said enough. New thoughts come into his mind, things he expunged, so he gets a piece of paper and writes to her. He puts down all his feelings, ones he can't say, lets the words fall around him, picks them up, and places them together.

He puts it in an envelope with a first-class stamp addressed to her and walks to the post box. He feels like he's walking to nowhere, and he's just a shell. He stands at the box, and before he places it in the aperture, he kisses where he sealed it and drops it in.

2

A few mornings later, he receives a reply. He reads it over and over, particularly the last line, and he puts it at the bottom of the pile in chronological order.

The door knocks, and he just sits there. It knocks again, and he doesn't move. He hears a key enter the latch, and it opens. Olivia walks into the room, and her shadowy configuration stands in the doorway.

'Michael,' she says.

He doesn't respond.

'What's happened?'

She walks over to the window and opens the curtains. The afternoon light enters the room, and he squints as it strains his eyes.

She stands at the window and observes him.

'It's Martha. She understands me, and I understand her, but it's all my fault.'

'Michael, don't do this to yourself.'

She sits down and looks at the letters.

'I sent her a letter a few days ago, and I got one back today. She doesn't want to see me anymore.'

'Why?'

'Because...' He doesn't elaborate but goes on. 'I saw her son's grave, and it changed me. I told her everything after that.'

'I'm pleased you did.'

'But the things I did to her.'

'Michael, you're the kindest man I know.'

'But...'

Olivia stands up. 'Michael! I know what happened, but we can't change it. It's just part of our lives!'

'I know, but I can't see her now.'

'You can.'

'No, the pain is too severe, the depth of our feelings is too deep and because we...'

He stops himself from saying it. It is crazy to even think about it let alone make it a public declaration.

'Because what?' she asks.

He looks at her hesitantly, but he still refuses to say.

'I think you'll regret it,' she adds.

'I will, until my final day, but I must do it, for her and for me. We have gone as far as we can go. She needs to move on with her life, and I'll have to exist in mine.'

'I want you to live a happy life.'

'I don't know what that is. I don't know what my life is anymore?'

'It's here with me.' She walks over and sits next to him. 'I need you here with me. You and Simon.'

He looks at her, but it's a look that is indicative of sadness, as there is no joy in his eyes. She sees this, and it worries her.

CHAPTER TWENTY-TWO

Olivia makes her way back home from a conference in the west of the province. She goes through the sprawling uplands of County Tyrone's Sperrin Mountains. The late afternoon sun is disappearing into the soon-to-be night sky. It's been a hectic day, and she wants to relax. She played Adele on the way there but just wants to chill to some great eighties tunes on the way back. The first track is A-ha's *Take on me.*

'Oh, I love this!'

She sings along to Morten Harket's soaring vocals and tries unsuccessfully to hit his falsetto in the chorus. She sings at the top of her voice until the song fades out and another one starts. This time it's Depeche Mode's *Personal Jesus.*

The shadows from the clouds rapidly change the appearance of the mountain range. The green hues shaded with black give the landscape an autumnal feel, even though it's late summer. She marvels at the landscape and believes Ireland has the best in the world. Its mystical beauty is as inviting as any vista in the world. It has a harshness and beauty in equal measure. Any person seeking shelter from the dark realities of life could do no better than to come here.

Dusk falls upon the horizon, and she believes it is

where everything and everyone belongs. She thinks of these things, her man, her world, her life, and she feels this is her world, this is her safe place.

She hears and feels a loud thump from behind her. The car judders, and her heart seems to jump out of her mouth with panic. She looks into her rearview mirror and sees a black SUV. Its headlights are on full beam, and it hinders her vision. The windows are tinted, so she can't decipher its driver.

It smashes into her again, and she lets out a yelp and shunts forward. The SUV now seeks its advantage and moves parallel to her. It hits the front side of her car. The fenders crush and a hub cap breaks off. It jumps forward, and she jerks the steering wheel. It slams into her again, and she can't maintain it, loses control, and comes off the road. The SUV screeches off, and she slumps forward in her seat. Her head drops to the side, and she closes her eyes.

***

Michael is in his apartment. He percolates the coffee in his expresso machine—an expensive gift from his sister. He has dark circles around his eyes, and his stubble has grown into a short beard. He had a shower this morning, his first in three days, he had forced himself to, and when the water soaked his hair, he felt better for it, if he feels better at all.

He hears his mobile phone going off and goes into the lounge to answer it. It's on the table with Martha's letters which remain neatly placed next to each other.

'Hello.'

'Michael, it's Simon,' he says with urgency.

'How are you doing?'

'It's Olivia. She's been in an accident, but she's okay. She's in Altnagelvin hospital.'

Michael sits down and doesn't say anything.

'Michael... Michael? Are you there?'

'Aye.'

'Where are you?'

'At home,' he slowly replies. 'I'm driving there now.'

2

Michael and Simon walk into a cubicle as the police officers finish their questioning. One of them tells her he will return after speaking to the doctor.

Simon goes to her first and gently puts his arms around her and kisses her. Michael walks round to the other side, and she holds out her hand for him, and he puts it in his.

Michael smiles. 'How are you doing?'

'I'm okay. Just cuts and bruises. My knee is a bit bashed up, so I had some scans. I'm just waiting for the results.'

'What happened?' he asks.

'I was driving along, and suddenly this black SUV smashed into the back of me.'

'Deliberately?'

'Aye. I thought it was an accident at first, but then it was side by side, and it smashed into me again.'

'Did you get a look at them?'

'No. The windows were tinted.'

'What about the registration?' Simon asks.

'No. It was an SUV with a front safety guard. That's all I know.'

A doctor walks into the cubicle with a clipboard.

'How are you, Olivia?'

'I feel okay. Do you have the scan results yet?'

'Yes, we have all the results. Your CT scan is fine and doesn't show any internal injuries to the brain. There are no fractures from the X-ray results, and your blood results are fine. You have a concussion, though, so I've requested that we keep you in overnight just to monitor you, and all being well, you can go home tomorrow morning.'

'That's fine,' Olivia says.

'Good. I'll just contact the ward and let them know you're coming.'

'Thank you so much, Doctor.'

'That's no problem, Olivia.'

'Thank you,' Michael and Simon say in unison.

She looks at them both with a smile to assuage their concern. 'You see, I'm fine.'

'Thank God,' Simon says. 'I'm going to call my da and see what he can do about this.'

'What do you think he can do?' Michael asks.

'He can speed the process up and get the force here to go through everything with a fine-tooth comb.'

'As long as the media don't get any of this.'

'Michael, I assure you my da won't let them.'

'Look, the main thing is I'm okay,' Olivia says.

'Yeah, that's the main thing,' Michael agrees.

Olivia is admitted to the ward an hour later and tells them to go home, but they protest and say they will book a hotel nearby for the night.

Michael and Simon sit in the hotel bar and have a nightcap. It's one of those cheap, ubiquitous hotels that businesspeople usually use, or couples go to if they're having an extramarital affair.

'What do you think your da can do?'

'I think he can do a lot. He's the chief constable. He has people who can investigate this.'

'How long has your da been in the force?'

'Since the eighties. It's what he always wanted to do.'

'Did you ever think about joining?'

'No. Although he did say, I'll be good at it. He said it because he wanted me to follow in his footsteps.'

'But you've never changed your mind.'

'No. I've found my vocation and my wife.'

'You certainly have,' Michael replies, knowing Simon means it. Michael raises his glass, and Simon follows, and they clink them together. 'Well, she can't ask for any more than that.'

Olivia lies in a bed of starched sheets, and flashbacks begin to appear. She hears metal twisting, and the sound is amplified, and the twists repeat. The smell of burning tyres enters her nostrils and makes her nauseous. She sits up and feels a stinging sensation in her knee. Her physical pain, amalgamated with her mental one, assures her that she won't get much sleep tonight.

3

Nowell signals his son to come into his office. It is a busy day for him as he must make a speech later, and he's going through the last details of it with his media adviser.

'Yes, I think that part's relevant,' Nowell says. He crosses some sentences out and writes a line on the side of the paper. 'I think this will have more resonance.'

The adviser looks at it and nods.

'If you could just give me a minute.'

Simon sits down as the adviser leaves.

'It's great to see you, son. Are you and Olivia coming for dinner this weekend?'

'Da, there's something I want to talk to you about.'

'By all means, go ahead.'

'Olivia was involved in an accident.'

'What? What happened?'

'It wasn't an accident, though. Someone purposely crashed into her.'

'Why?'

'That's why I'm here. I need your help.'

'Anything I can do to help, son, I will. Where did it happen?'

'Tyrone, she was at a conference there.'

'All right, I'll contact their HQ and see how the investigation is going.'

Simon stands up. 'There is one more thing, something I need to tell you.'

'Yes?'

'It's about Olivia's brother. He was in the Republican movement. He was operational, a sniper. He served time for murder.'

He thinks for a moment. 'Who did he kill?'

'A soldier.'

He looks at his son but doesn't show any emotion.

'How long have you known this?'

'Well, from the start. Olivia has been open about it.'

'Have you met him?'

'Yes, several times.'

'Do you trust him?'

'I haven't really thought about it. He's always fine with me and he accepts my relationship with Olivia.'

'Does he know about me?'

'Yes.'

He stands up.

'Simon, you're my only child. I want you to be careful. It could be a Republican feud that he hasn't told you about.'

Simon looks at him and thinks. 'He wouldn't harm us, I know that.'

'But it's who he associates with.'

'He has left that behind.'

He stops walking. 'Has he? You can't be sure of that? They still have enemies inside their own ranks. Maybe they know, maybe they have found out who his sister is dating, and, for that, they will never let it go.'

'They'll have to.'

'Simon, you have to think things over.'

'I will, and I appreciate your concern, but I'm determined to live my life.'

'I'm here to support you in whatever you do.'

Chapter Twenty-Three

The phone rings at a quarter to midnight. Michael is still awake; he's been watching a classic movie for the past hour. It's about a Vietnam rookie who is torn between following two sergeants into the hell of combat. He makes up his mind after one of the sergeants oversees a massacre in a village, and, although he is only a grunt, he decides to follow the good sergeant over the bad one.

He pauses to answer the phone. 'Donnelly. What's up?'

'I don't know how they know, but they do.'

'Who does?'

'Frank O'Daniels.'

'What does he know?'

'They know about Nowell.'

'How?'

'I'm not sure, but they know the whole thing. They must have someone in the force working for them.'

'Got to, surely.'

'They want to talk to you about it.'

'You don't know anything?'

'No, they're not telling me much.'

'What can I do? Olivia's made up her mind, and she won't change it. I know her.'

'Aye, I know, but they want you to come in and see them all the same.'

'To do what?'

'I don't know, but you have to come in.'

Michael scratches his face. 'Right. I'll see you tomorrow.'

'Aye, no bother.'

The cottage blends in perfectly with the landscape. It's built of stone, clay, and sods and painted in distinctive whitewash renowned for this land. The steeply sloped thatched roof is made up of straw and sedge, among others giving it a traditional look that hasn't changed for centuries.

Several men are outside the cottage, and some are smoking in a huddle. Donnelly shakes one of the men's hands and talks to him for a while, asking after his family. Michael stands with his hands in his pockets and feels out of sorts. He hasn't been part of this for a long time now and feels no part of it, whereas Donnelly still associates with them like he never left.

They enter a small, compact room with low wooden beams and a damp aura. It has an earthy smell; an odour of peat and smoke rises to the roof. The kindle smoulders, and a man with a grey quiff stands by the hearth, sticking a poker into it before resting it next to the grate.

''bout ye, Frank,' Donnelly says.

'Sit down, lads.'

Donnelly does, but Michael chooses to stand.

'It's been a long time, Michael, a long time. How have you been keeping?'

'I'm grand, Frank, and yourself?'

'I can't complain, Michael. I've got a younger wife, so I can't complain.'

'Fair dos.'

'Donnelly introduced me to her, so I have him to thank.'

'You gave her the chat, Frank, so it was all down to you.'

'I suppose you're right there, but now she gives me all the chat, so what can I do?'

'Well, it's all swings and roundabouts,' Donnelly says.

'Too true, boy!'

Donnelly hates being called a boy, his father had a habit of using this epithet, and he hates it, but he lets it go over his head at this instant, for he knows not to cross Frank. He is the leader, after all.

'Look, lads, we're not happy with this situation you've got yourself into, Michael. First, why didn't you do something? Why didn't you change her mind? She's a young girl, and there are plenty more fish in the sea.'

'I can't, she's got her own mind, and she's made it. Anyway, he's a nice fella. There's nothing I can do about it.'

'We'll sort it out,' Donnelly says.

Michael looks at him with consternation.

'You can't sort it out to our satisfaction not once the press gets hold of it, and they will.'

'It's a family matter,' Michael says.

'A family matter, you say. No, it's not, it's a public one, and it looks bad from where I'm standing!'

'I don't know what to say. They're going to get married.'

'Oh, for fuck's sake! Why didn't you put a stop to this in the beginning? She's your sister.'

'I had the same reaction as you, but once I met him and saw how happy they were, I knew I had to let them get on with it.'

'We want a political compromise.'

'What do you mean?' Michael asks.

'Nowell to stand down and a new man to take his place. Our man, a man we can shape in our own image. We want Flaherty.'

'Nowell will never stand down,' Michael says.

'He'll have to. We'll put it out to the press who his daughter-in-law will be. It's embarrassing for us too, but he'll have no alternative if you can't persuade her.'

'Frank, Olivia has nothing to do with this. Please leave her out of this.'

'We can't. If you can't persuade her, we have no choice. We can't have him in the top job and his son as your brother-in-law.'

'We'll see what we can do, Frank,' Donnelly says.

'You better.' Frank walks over to Michael and pats him on the shoulder. 'It's for the best, boy!'

2

Donnelly drops Michael off at his flat. They talk, but he doesn't want to give away too much. He wants to talk about Olivia first. He gets out of his car, tells him he'll see him later, and then wanders the neighbourhood. He contemplates what will happen to his sister and knows he needs to speak to her before things escalate. He takes out his phone from his pocket and calls her.

'Are you in?'

'Aye, what's up?'

'Nothing, just coming up for a coffee. Is that okay? Are you alone?'

'Yeah, Simon's away at a conference.'

Driving up there, he thinks of what to say, how to start the conversation, and even how to end it. He knows this will be the most important conversation they have.

When he gets there, she is already making a latte, so he sits down and looks at some notes she's been making on her laptop.

'You've been busy.'

'Aye, I've got a conference on Monday, and I'm just making some notes!' she shouts from the kitchen and over the noise of the barista coffee machine.

A few minutes later, she walks in with two cups.

'When's Simon back?'

'Tomorrow night.'

'That's not too bad.'

'No, and it gives me an opportunity to do this. Anyway, how have you been?'

'I'm okay.'

'Have you heard from…'

He interjects before she can say her name. 'No, I haven't heard.'

'Okay. I'll have to contact her, but I've been too busy.' She looks at him sympathetically. 'Things will work out.'

He doesn't say anything and quickly changes the subject.

'How's the wedding arrangements going?'

'Great! Did you get the email about the venue?'

'Aye. It looks spectacular.'

'It costs spectacular!'

'It's your special day.'

'Aye. It's funny because I don't feel nervous, not now anyway. Just excited.'

'I'm glad. How's Simon?'

'You know him. He just takes it in his stride. He doesn't suffer from nerves.'

'How's the in-laws?'

'They're fine.'

'His dad? How's he been with all this?'

'He's fine. He doesn't say too much.'

'He hasn't talked to you about it?'

'No, not even that much to Simon.'

'What about when this gets out?'

'We'll cross that bridge when it comes to it.'

'You love him, don't you?'

'Aye, to my very bones, even through the trials and tribulations, it won't part us.'

'You know it'll be difficult for you both. It'll test your relationship to the core.'

'I know we've spoken about it, and we're ready for it.'

'Ready for what it'll be.'

'Aye. Ready for anything.'

'You'll need to be because you'll have things coming at you from all sides.'

'We know. It'll come from my community and his. People may even betray us. People close to us, but we're prepared for that.'

'You know I won't.'

'I know.'

He knows he can't change her mind, but somehow, he doesn't want to. He needs her to convince him they're doing the right thing. He isn't there to change her mind. He decided he was just there to protect her at the cottage, and now he must establish a way to do it.

3

Simon and Olivia sit on the sofa with her head resting on his lap. Her eyes are closed but she isn't dropping off to sleep as she has a multitude of things running in her mind.

'We need to get away.'

She opens her eyes and looks up at him. 'Away?'

'Yeah, we can book online and go somewhere.'

She sits up and turns to him. 'Go where? What is it? What's wrong?'

'It's many things. We can wait a few weeks until your knee is better, but once it is, let's just go.'

'Many things?'

'I'm just got so many thoughts in my mind right now. I just trying to understand why this accident happened?'

'We don't know why, Simon.'

'That's what I'm trying to get my head around. My da is helping us with the investigation, but there are no leads.'

'I don't know why it happened either. I was thinking about my line of work last night. A lot of people don't want integration. They want us to stay within our own communities, our own schools, our own places of work, and live separate lives.'

'It could be that, but we just don't know.'

'Where do you want to go?'

'Anywhere,' he replies.

****

They saunter up to the lighthouse in Rethymno, Crete, taking in the turquoise water and sand hills that slant and disappear into the sea. A white fishing boat passes by, and an old man next to them calls out to it. He shouts something in Greek, and one of the fishermen holds up a tuna fish. The old man shouts something else, and the fisherman laughs.

'That was some fish,' Simon says.

'It could feed you for a week,' Olivia replies.

The old man looks at them and measures with his hands. 'Big.'

'Yes, it's a big fish!' Olivia replies.

The old man laughs. 'Big, big!'

They all laugh.

He whistles to his dog, who is about the same age as him in canine years. The dog dawdles up to him, and Olivia makes a fuss of it. Its sad old face likes the attention as it lifts its head, and she ruffles its neck.

'I love dogs,' she says. 'But I could never have one because of my job.'

The old man gives her the dog's lead.

'He wants you to have it!' Simon says.

'No. I can't!' Olivia shouts, thinking the volume of her speech will make him understand.

The old man laughs, and she gives the dog one more fuss before it goes off.

They walk back, following the dog, who looks back at them and doesn't know whether it wants to be followed or not.

'Shall we get a wee bite to eat?' she asks.

'Aye, that fish has made me hungry.'

They find a café table near the gold sandy beach with a hundred blue umbrellas and loungers neatly distributed. They order, and there's some confusion in what they want.

The waiter tells them in his broken English that the dish of the day is crab. Crab meat, mayonnaise, lemon juice, white wine, aromatic herbs, and a salad with olive oil. Simon likes the sound of it and orders. Olivia tries to explain that she doesn't eat seafood, and the waiter tells her it isn't seafood. It's crab! They go back and forth for a few minutes until she eventually orders dakos—a dish of barley rusks, tomatoes, and feta cheese.

'You seem more relaxed,' she says.

'I am, and it's more than just the sunshine.'

'What is it then?'

'There are no flags and no borders.'

'Do you ever want to move?'

'To somewhere else?'

'Aye.'

'No. It's my country, and I belong here.'

'That's what I like to hear.'

'Anyway, how's your crab?'

She lets out a delicious laugh that he finds so captivating. He enjoys it the most when they are in bed together after they have made love and are having banter. He could listen to it all day and not tire of it, just as he could be with her all day and not tire of it.

The olive trees blanket the hills. The higher they go, the more there are. They are green and grey, and some of the tree trunks have a perimeter of twelve metres. They go to an area and watch three generations of production, from one run by a donkey, one by a diesel machine, and one that uses the latest technology.

The family who owns the establishment are from all generations. There is a toddler up to an old woman. The old woman sits in the corner and pours the oil for customers to try. The mature people seem to be the most revered, and it isn't as youth-obsessed as other Western countries. The old lady has a face like a walnut with a sun-dried complexion. She is quite content and smiles more than talks. She talks quietly to the toddler, and the child seems to obey. They seem to like each other's company, and the many years between them do not have any concern for it.

The old lady lets the toddler pour out some extra virgin oil for Olivia to try. She dips bread into the oil and gives her the thumbs up. The young girl asks the old lady for some, and she obliges. The toddler dips her finger in it and doesn't flinch from the taste. Olivia smiles at her, and she returns it.

'I'm going to buy a couple of bottles,' she tells Simon.

'Aye, they look grand.'

She takes out some euros and pays at the counter. She waves to the old woman and the toddler. The little girl runs up to her and gives her a cuddle, which surprises Olivia but brings joy to her heart.

They step out into the burning sun, and Olivia is glad she's wearing factor 50 sun cream. The sun beats down on them with no reluctance to stop, so they get in their car, drive down the arid hills, and park near the beach.

They walk along the paved promenade and onto the sand, and as they get to the water, Olivia takes off her flip-flops and lets the water splash onto her feet. It's cool, clear, and refreshing to the touch, and it washes away the sand between her toes. Simon takes his flip-flops off, too, and kicks water at her, and she laughs and kicks some back.

They stop and look out at the ocean and the surface waves of white and blue.

'Look,' she says.

Simon looks at a boat going by. 'It's the old guy.'

'Where's the dog?'

'I'm sure it's there somewhere.'

'He must have been a fisherman once upon a time,' she says.

'Aye, I would have thought so,' he replies. 'I wonder if he's catching crab?'

'I wonder!' she says, then kicks some water at him.

They get back to the apartment, and she texts Michael and attaches some pictures of her day. She gets in the shower, and he gets in behind her, and they make love in and out of it.

The following day they go to a beach some miles away for a camel ride.

A man leads them to a Dromedary camel, and it stands there casually chewing on dry grass. Its long thin neck swallows, and the man gives it some more grass. It has a single hump, and Simon pats its straw-like hair as it continues to chew in an unconcerned way.

The man taps it with a stick, and it sits, folding its front legs in and its back ones out.

'Ladies first,' Simon says.

'Okay,' Olivia replies.

The man leads her, and she approaches it diagonally, stepping on the stirrup and propelling her leg over the hump. Simon follows and hurls his leg over and sits behind her. They are told to lean back and hold onto a handle at the front of the saddle. The camel stands with its back legs first, and they are thrust forward and counteract with its movement as it stands.

They are high up as it stands over seven feet. The man takes the reins and leads the camel, traversing across the sand. They mimic its irregular movements as its big hooves tread the sandhills. Two camels are ahead of them, and two more are behind.

The ride lasts for about half an hour, and they both enjoy it.

When they disembark, Olivia asks Simon to stand next to it.

'Take off your cap and shades then!'

He takes off his Levi shades and Boston Red Sox baseball cap and smiles. She takes the picture and sends it to Michael, saying Simon's got the hump.

They get back to their apartment and decide to go out for a meal. They shower together. Simon wears a lightweight linen shirt and slacks, and Olivia wears a strappy white print dress for the occasion.

They eat at a restaurant by the ocean. It's still warm,

but there is a relaxing breeze to temper it. He slices his sea bass, and she eats creamy tagliatelle with mushrooms and tomatoes.

'The camel reminded me of someone I went out with,' he said as he put some fish into his mouth.

'She must have looked bad!'

He chews and then swallows. 'She had frangible hair, but it was the eyes. Almond shaped with long lashes and a haughty expression.'

'Well, I don't think I'm haughty!'

'You're not, anyway, she went to a fee-paying school, and they all have that expression!'

They clink their wine glasses together. 'I love you,' she says.

'I love you more,' he replies.

'I could stay here forever,' she says.

'Me too. It's such a beautiful island.'

'We could retire here,' she says.

'That's a thought.'

'Where would you retire to?' she asks.

'Outside of our place?'

'Aye.'

'New Zealand.'

'Wow! That's far.'

'I just like the look of it.'

'We'll have to go there one day, taking in Australia, of course. I have cousins there.'

'Of course. You do know it's over a thousand miles away from there.'

'Really, that far? I only thought it was a few hundred.'

'No, it just looks like it on a globe,' he explains. 'Where would you go?'

'I'd stay in Ireland. There is nowhere else I'd rather be.'

'I would stay with you.'

She leans over to him, and they kiss. An older couple at the next table smiles at them, and she hopes when she's older, they'll be like them.

The next morning the sun is at its hottest, so they decide to stay around the pool under the shade. Olivia flicks through a magazine, looking at the latest fashions as Simon lies back and closes his eyes.

She puts down the magazine, looks at her phone, and sits up from her lounger.

'I'm worried.'

'Why?' he asks.

'Michael hasn't contacted me, and this is the third day. I asked him if he was all right, but there was still no answer.'

'He may have lost his phone?'

'He may not have, though. I've already left two voice messages.'

He sits up from his lounger and takes the phone from her. He taps it and rings Michael. It goes to voicemail.

'Hi Michael, it's Simon. Can you ring Olivia? She hasn't heard from you. Just give her a call. Thanks, bye.'

He hands it back to her. 'Don't worry. He'll probably give you a call today.'

'I hope so.'

Chapter Twenty-Four

Michael drives alone and tells no one of his journey. The bustling life he's used to is far away as a gap opens and takes him into a different world, one full of hills, hedges, and cattle grazing on the lush grass. He doesn't go to its centre as someone will recognise him and that someone will tell someone else, and soon everyone will know he's here, like the return of the prodigal son.

He looks at skeletal trees where the branches look like arthritic fingers and brittle leaves dance onto the edge of the road. He twists round mounds of horse manure and tyre tracks of mud left by a tractor. He thought about coming here yesterday, then changed his mind before his head hit the pillow, only for him to have a deep and hounding need to return when he woke.

He drives to a place overlooking its centre, a place he has not been to since his twentieth year, but it has been waiting for him and knows his secrets. He drives a mile away from any kind of civilisation, and the track, once full of potholes, is now smooth.

He parks and gets out.

The church stands there sanctimoniously like Mount Sinai, commanding the habitat where its spire remains the same, its sharp point looking like a blade stabbing the sky. He scents the air, and it produces the ordure of old.

It is the smell of his youth, running errands, playing in the fields, and being innocent.

He looks over at the graves and lets out an involuntary shudder. There are many Celtic cross headstones, but he immediately pinpoints the one he used, although its gleaming newness has been replaced by drab greyness. He is in his forties, and all that's gone before feels unreal and committed by a stranger he has never met. He walks over to the headstone and forces himself to touch it and make it real. Tear drops fall unremittently, and the drops become a stream as he holds firmly onto the headstone. He lets all his emotions surge out of him, all the anger and all the hate.

He stands there for a long time, brushes away the tears on the sleeve of his jacket, and looks at the stone brick cottage adjacent to the church. Father McKenzie is long gone. He was once the lord of the manor, packing a lot into his sixty years, not all of it good, for he renounced God by going against his sacred vows. The priest is not here to let him in this time, so he turns the round handle himself and opens it. There is an eerie silence that all old churches have, and only his footsteps can be heard as he walks up the aisle. The last time he was here, his mission was to purge an oppressor as he succumbed to hate. He doesn't feel that now and it's as if he is standing on a mountaintop, looking down, surveying his life. The anger isn't there anymore as the rational part of his mind has taken over and given him the perception to understand. He had no comprehension of his actions then, only implementation, but now comes wisdom through the awful grace of God.

He walks to the transept of the building and stands beside one of the pews, making a sign of the cross. He kneels on a kneeler and joins his hands together in prayer.

'Father, forgive me for my sins. Let the suffering she has for her son go away and give her the strength to live. Take her hand and lead her to a place of safety, a place she can call home. Do this in your name, Amen.'

He opens his eyes and looks at the unchanged altar knowing only he has changed. The door creaks open, and he stands up. A man with salt and pepper hair walks in, walks hand in hand with a woman of around twenty and assumes they are father and daughter. They bless themselves, and he walks her up the aisle and gives Michael a friendly smile. Michael can tell by the way he leads her that she is blind. They stop at the organ in the corner, and she sits down, and her father sits on the front pew.

She puts her foot on the pedal and, with dexterous application, moves her fingers up and down on the ebony and ivory. She starts to sing to the music, and out of her comes this ethereal harmony of such divine tones it pierces his heart. She sings the chorus of Amazing Grace in Gaelic with such undiluted passion that he cannot take his eyes off her. God has taken away one sensory and has gifted her with another. He is spellbound and beholds this woman to be more than just mortal. She is eternal. He watches her head rise and fall, and she seems to be searching and probing with each note. He feels it and wants to go on the journey with her, she leads him there, and he feels a spirit enter him. She finishes the last line, translated in English, 'was blind, but now I see.' She raises her head for these final words, then drops it and stops playing. He gazes at her and stands there for a moment, a moment in time.

Chapter Twenty-Five

Michael is parked across the street from the main entrance of the Northern Ireland police headquarters. He watches Nowell drive out of the barrier, stop at a junction, and turn right. He follows him, and Nowell drives for half an hour with Michael stealthily in pursuit until he stops at a row of garages and gets out of his car. Michael parks nearby at a safe distance where he thinks he won't be detected.

He gets out of his car and watches Nowell open his garage door electronically. The door opens, and a black SUV with tinted windows is parked there. Ferguson's son had provided it for him, and it was put to effective use. Michael can clearly make out the damage on its fenders as he surreptitiously but resolutely walks towards the garage. The door begins to close, so he swiftly ducks down under it.

Nowell is alarmed by this and swiftly steps back. Michael looks at him, and they stand face to face for the first time, surveying each other like lions in the wild.

'Who are you, and what are you doing here?'

'You know who I am.'

'Do I?'

'Aye.'

Nowell is unforthcoming, and there's a hush before he answers. 'And who are you, Michael Doherty?'

'I'm here to see who you really are.'

'You? The face of a terrorist?' Nowell says disdainfully.

'You're the bigger one. You colluded your way to power on the pretext of respectability.'

'And you? Killing young boys barely out of school.'

Michael gives him an intense look and points a finger at him. 'I want you to leave Olivia alone. If you don't, I'll kill you without hesitation.'

'You! You are defunct. Do you think you mean anything to people today? Do you think you're admired? You don't represent anything; you have no identity!'

'My past is gone; it doesn't belong to anyone.'

'It belongs to me because your sister will never marry my son!'

'Never, you say! They love one another. Why can't you just let them live their lives? They have nothing to do with our past.'

'Because I don't want my son associated with Republican scum.'

'You'll have no choice.'

'I'll give them no choice.'

'They will be together, and there's nothing you can do. I've accepted it. Why won't you?'

Nowell lunges at him and grabs his head, and he thumps it against the wall. Michael knees him in the groin, and he tumbles back and drops down. He then punches him, and Nowell crashes into a tool cabinet.

Michael grabs him by the throat and begins to choke him. Nowell tries to push him off but can't, and then for some inexplicable reason, Michael lets go. Nowell is surprised by this and reaches for a hammer and hits him on the side of his head, letting out an adventitious sound. Michael stumbles back, and Nowell seizes the opportunity and, with all the force he can muster, hits him again with a hoarse crackling pitch. Michael drops down against the wall as scarlet bleeds and streams down his face, and the blueness of his eyes magnifies as they become bloodshot. He wants to let go, let go from all that's been before. By letting go, he is extinguishing his past. He now accepts that he has no future without her in his life. She is gone, and now he must go too. He feels at ease as he places himself into a new existence, wherever it may be.

Nowell coughs and splutters. He drops the hammer and stands back to watch Michael with a combination of confusion and awe. He can't understand why he let him go as he watches him drift in and out of consciousness.

Michael can see a path before him and stands there facing it. Walking down the path are two figures. They're silhouettes at first but become clearer as they approach. It is the figure of a young woman, and as she walks closer, he sees her beautiful blue-green eyes. It is Sosaidh. She is holding the hand of a young boy. The boy on the mantlepiece. They stand there looking at him. Michael's blue eyes widen and gleam. The blue becomes pellucid and otherworldly, seeking, gaining, perceiving, and concluding.

Stephen holds his hand out, and Michael takes it, and the boy looks at him and smiles. Sosaidh takes his other hand, and he feels its softness. He is untroubled, and all his dark and sinful actions have been seized and extenuated. They walk together as a triumvirate of forgiveness and disappear.

Nowell watches him hold out his hand to an unknown entity. He holds up his hand as far as it will go before it drops, and then there's no movement, only stillness.

2

Nowell stops his car in a quiet deserted place off the road, adjacent to a forest. He knows the area well, and it's a safe spot to do what he needs to. He reverses his car along a small tarmac road on the edge of the forest and gets out. He looks around, but no one is there. It's just him and the body.

He is dressed in a boiler suit, gloves, and a sports cap. He opens the boot of the car and pulls Michael's tarpaulin-wrapped body out and onto the ground. He judges it weighs one hundred and seventy pounds, one, Nowell thinks his six-two, two-hundred-pound frame can manage.

The deciduous forest is full of oak, elm, and sycamore trees. He exhales condensation into the icy air and knows he must get the body to the right place before the soil becomes too hard.

He drags the body over a tussock pile of deadwood, bracken and moss and realises it isn't going to be as easy as he first thought. The waterproof cloth scrapes along the surface, hitting various objects like a dead tree branch. He heaves it at short intervals and grunts with every haul. He can't stop. He must get there. He tugs again but falls backwards over a log and lies there, breathing out more condensation. He gets up, drags it again, and feels the pull in his biceps. Still, he's determined to keep going until he finally reaches the place, drops to the ground, and sucks in the chilly air.

He walks back to his car, takes out a heavy bag, and carries it into the forest. When he gets there, he unzips it, takes out several flasks, and sets them in various locations around the body. He pours the hot water from the flasks onto the soil to soften it, and steam rises. He takes out a shovel and pickaxe. He picks up the pickaxe, hits the ground's surface, and begins to make a rectangular shape. He huffs with each strike until he gets the outline he needs; he picks up the shovel, and with his large right foot, he digs. It takes him an hour to get to the depths he wants, and when he's finished, he sits on a log, takes one of the flasks he hasn't emptied and pours out a cup of tea.

He looks at the body and wonders why he gave himself up like a sacrificial lamb. He knows what he did and knows about his talks with a woman called Martha. He has been there from the start; from the time Michael took Stephen's life until his last moments when he sought forgiveness. He thinks this man wanted to die, so he doesn't feel responsible for his death. He interprets it as a form of suicide and probably a slow one due to not wanting to live with the guilt of what he did.

Nowell thinks Catholics want to obtain this. It dictates their psyche and resolves to find punishment in the end. He stands there feeling exonerated. How can he be responsible when he is dealing with a relatively young man with a death wish.

He is glad that his son doesn't have to deal with such a man or feels obliged to form a relationship with someone diametrically opposed to his family. He believes his son isn't as liberal as he thinks. But it's water under the bridge because he has unchained him from any inclination to merge with a man such as this one.

He's heard snippets of Michael's life and how he was seeking redemption by participating in talks with the mother of a slain son. He believes it was a false exercise because he was only doing it for himself and not his victim. If he did it with the right intention, why would he make it so public? He just saw Michael as a man who prophesied his journey from lost to found, and he believes this man's repertoire was to consciously tell the story of his people's suffering.

In mediaeval Ireland, the origins of this torment were written in stone in the form of the Senchas Mar, the Irish civil code. It consisted of beliefs such as Troscad (fasting against a person) and Cealachan (achieving justice by starvation), so if a person had done injustice against you, it was your right to fast outside their abode until they admitted the injustice and penance.

He muses that Michael's self-sacrifice was the culmination of overcoming the literal restraints of his physical self and seeking a final form of control by the tragic beauty of death. He rebuffs his aesthetic demise because he only sees self-destruction and he doesn't believe in it.

He thinks they have the upper hand because of their victimisation. The culture he was brought up in had the belief they were the chosen people and had a sterile hold over the land. He knows he is fighting against a system that wants to overthrow his hitherto majority and replace it with martyrdom, but he wants to seal his presence and produce a hermetic hold on the six counties. He understands the external powers are trying to dilute his beliefs, but he wants the top job, that of the First Minister, and defend his people, and this is his primary ambition.

He looks at his fingers. They are large and strong, mainly through the weights he lifts in the gym. He rubs some dirt off his palm and thinks if only the hand of Ulster had the strength of his hand, then it would be impenetrable. He puts his hand into a fist, looks at the veins bulging, and picks up the shovel and digs some more.

He sits back on the log and hangs in repose before pulling the body to its final resting place. He gives it one more heave, unties it from its cover, and rolls it into the hole. He looks at the lifeless body, takes one of the flasks, and pours lime on it to disguise any odour as it decomposes. He then digs the mound of dirt and shovels it back into the hole, throwing soil upon soil onto Michael.

Chapter Twenty-Six

Olivia sits in Michael's flat. The curtains are still drawn, and his half-empty cup of coffee is left untouched. There has been no contact for four days, and she reported it to the police on the first day she got back from her holiday. They normally contact each other every day, sometimes several times, so it isn't like him. There have been no phone calls, texts, or emails. Nothing. She drove around the city, around South Armagh, anywhere, to find him. She knows the situation with Simon's family hasn't been easy for him, but he's handled it well, a lot better than she thought he would.

She sits on the sofa and thinks of the antecedents leading up to his disappearance. The crash. The talks. His past. She knows it is not in his nature to leave without telling her. He was always in contact, wherever he was and whatever he was doing. He has never left her side.

She thinks of all these things, and her chest tightens, giving her palpitations, and she tries to get her breathing together. She enters the kitchen, runs the cold tap, and fills a cup with water. She drinks it readily and stands there for a while until she feels the pulsation subside.

It is her second night here. She must be here, just in case he might open the door at any minute and walk-in or phone to say he's okay and don't be worrying. She just wants to be here when he does.

She walks into his bedroom, undresses, and puts on a t-shirt. She phones Simon and tells him she's fine, although she knows she's not, and they talk about her brother. She says goodnight and lifts Michael's duvet at the top and gets inside. She can smell his aftershave on the pillow and closes her eyes.

When their mother died, he and the late Auntie Bernie became the sole carer and provider. Their feckless da had his own issues with drink, so Michael was the one who took the reins. He had to. She was his sister. They were more than siblings. They were like twins, with similar looks, blue eyes, high cheekbones, and a similar disposition. They liked and disliked the same things. They telepathically knew what the other was thinking. He understood her, she understood him, they wanted the same things for each other and were fiercely protective.

She tosses and turns in the bed, unable to sleep, so she sits up and puts the bedside lamp on. She puts her legs out of the bed and her feet on the floor. She looks at the cabinet and opens the door. Inside are a neat pile of letters sitting on top of each other. She always wanted to ask about them, but he never really told her.

She picks up an envelope from the top of the pile and opens it. It is Martha's distinctive handwriting. She recognises it because it is not a scrawl; her style is beautifully crafted, full of long sloping letters, especially with the capitalisation. Judging by the perfect grammar and punctuation, she can tell she is educated. The font is written in the black ink of a fountain pen, consisting of no smudges. She reads the first paragraph.

'Mr. Doherty, you may wonder why I have written

this letter given the circumstances. Well, to tell the truth, I have asked myself the same question a thousand times. I have seen your face, and you mine, but what lies in your make-up is open to conjecture…'

Michael's words are a scrawl, but she can read it. She is used to his illegible handwriting and can translate it where others cannot.

The letters consist of them trying to establish a relationship from different perspectives. Michael is initially full of conviction, whereas Martha is bursting with emotive language. Her descriptions have a humanised approach, and she is really trying to humanise her son and not make him a statistic or a victim. She wants to bring him to life and make his life mean something, not just to her but to the world.

Michael uses a more measured approach in his principles. He isn't preaching, but he wants to get the sentiment over. The history, the justification, and the hypocrisy of the British. Olivia reads Martha's letter and then Michael's to see his reply. His responses are formal, but as she reads on, they become less so, mainly due to her frustration at them, where she implores him to be more open. He is equally exasperated when he senses his beliefs are being misconstrued and taken out of context.

There is a lot of this in the first quarter pile of their letters. It's like the start of an early relationship when a couple presses a button to elicit a reaction. If the reaction is negative, they don't normally take the risk again, but some do, like in this case, a negative response is exactly what is wanted so they can establish a dialogue, whether it's good or bad because that's what the need is, to talk, to gain something, something positive from the pain. And pain is all they have in common.

The letters go on in this vein until she reaches the middle, where they deviate from denunciation to a consideration of each other's plight. He acknowledges her suffering, and she heeds his convictions.

It is something that doesn't come naturally to their dispositions. She is a woman who deconstructs everything that is said and deduces reasoning from it. He is a man of such complexities that his words could be interpreted as passive and uninterested to the untrained eye, but once he lets go, he reveals things that hit the person in their direct profoundness.

As she continues, this understanding appears to produce a friendship and an unusual alliance form, that is both fascinating and bittersweet.

She knows they met for a reason. She brought them together, so is part of that reason. She saw how Michael had changed from an insular character to someone who discarded his chains and became lucid about his transgressions.

Martha appears to have eloquently given a semblance of forgiveness, even if she thinks this is abhorrent to her sensibilities. Olivia can only applaud her bravery after all the tribulations for her to cede this form of forgiveness. She wonders if she could have done it if she lost a child. She would only know if she went through it, experienced it, and not in a hypothetical way. She cannot comprehend the agony Martha experienced. No one could, and to live your life after would be virtually impossible. She would have hidden away, hidden in her grief like Queen Victoria and not had a life. She wouldn't have socialised, walked the streets, or gone to restaurants or concerts. She would have just hidden in her work, much to her own detriment.

Martha confronted her fears and pursued the things she knew would make her happy. Her stoicism led her to a greater understanding of her capabilities. She has intrinsic values that have benefitted not just her but Michael too. He didn't understand what he had done or who he had hurt. He was brought up to be self-reliant. He was predisposed to take risks that were not just deleterious to him but to others.

He was damaging himself psychologically. His silences were synonymous with a reluctance to show weakness, and this would manifest itself in the form of depression. He would tell Olivia that he felt 'down,' but he would not elaborate as to why. She thought this would only manifest itself in several ways, mainly through an unwillingness to admit failure through his tough exterior.

Olivia thought she was the only one who could extract any meaningful communication from him, but from the contents of these letters, she believes Martha has succeeded in that too. She achieves this in subtle ways. At first, she opens him up through refined manipulation, through her use of language, and gently entices him out of his dormant emotionless existence and through patience, she leads him out into the world again. But in the world of their letters, only they exist. She cocoons them in a place where they can speak one-on-one, where what they think is what they write. There are no inhibitions, no fallings out. They just read, evaluate, contemplate, and reply without prejudice. They say what they can't always say in a face-to-face meeting. If their words hurt, then it's fine. They are meant to. It's good that they empathise with each other's pain. That's part of the process. Michael must come to terms with this; if he doesn't, he knows he's finished in her eyes.

As the letters go on, the contents transfigure into a scope Olivia never saw when they were together. What she reads surprises her. It is something she had never thought about before. The words reveal an affection for each other. They overcome distrust and hurt to develop a relationship that is essential to their lives, whether they want it or not.

She thinks it was inevitable from all the exposed emotions from their first meeting that there would be a reaction to it. All the components are here, and they are primed to explode. It comes in stages, but as each one is conquered, they move on and start to get to the core of what matters. The disguises they present to the world are dismantled, and they clarify what has been mystified. They know it is more than a sea that divides their nations, but they have built a bridge to join each other's hearts.

Michael writes: *'If I lose this relationship, I'll be in no place. No place of significance. I'll be here, and you'll be there with no one to pick up the wreckage left behind. We need each other in our lives. We can get through this together and help find who we are…'*

Martha replies: *'We have a bond, one I don't understand nor, at times, want, but it's left an indelible mark on me. I never wanted to form a relationship with you. I just wanted to know why? But by finding out what happened, we have formed a connection, and this is what it's led to… I do have feelings for you, but they can't be acted upon…'*

Olivia now realises their connection is more profound than she could ever have imagined. She can perceive more from these letters than she could ever have when they were all together. The words are not oblique. They are candid and unequivocal in their meaning.

She wonders whether they are lovers and is shocked at the thought, but it could be a possibility. She just can't comprehend it, and it would be inexplicable for her to comprehend, but there is a chance.

The next letter from Martha confirms it.

'Our embrace was a mistake. We must never let it happen again. We were inebriated, and our emotions were running high. Although, that is not an excuse, I needed someone, but I don't want to admit it was you...'

Michael replies: 'Martha, what we have is something extraordinary, out of something so tragic. I want to tell you how much you mean to me, without saying it. I know what I feel. We could be together. It is possible. We could move to another country, and no one would know. I would love you and take away your pain. That's what I'm here to do.'

She ends: 'Michael, you know it's impossible. Why would you ever believe it would be! I'm sorry, but I don't want you to contact me anymore. I will speak to Olivia and say I've reached the end, and I am satisfied in my own mind that I have an explanation for my son's death. I now feel it's time to say goodbye, and I will think of my son and take pride at what he achieved in his life.'

I think a lot of you, as crazy as it sounds, but I can't love you the way you want me to. I want you to live a happy life, it would be hateful of me not to, but I want you to do it without me. I'm going to live my life on my own terms, and that's why we must part.

I want you to stay on your road, and I will stay on mine.'

Goodbye,

Martha.

Olivia sits back in shock, but she's exhilarated at the same time. She feels so much happiness for him. She has never seen him in love. Ever.

She knows it is one that can never take place, not in a conventional way, at least for they would be condemned by the mores of society. The discrimination and oppression Michael suffers would pale in comparison to this, and Martha's status and privileges would be eradicated overnight, and she would be ostracised forever.

What society forbids and what is considered legitimate is of no consequence to Olivia. Her relationship with Simon holds cultural bias, but being a forceful woman, she merely dismisses those prejudices. She can only see love, and if it comes in the most unusual way, then so be it.

She brought them together. Without her, none of this would have taken place. Was it fate? Yes, she thinks it is. The world has an omniscient force that brings people together, and she believes she is part of it. She wants Michael to finally accept what he did and free himself from its turmoil. She wants that for Martha, too and now this is what has come of it. It's a form of love, a love that has a host of enemies and even more distractors, a love only they can contemplate.

Is this the reason for his disappearance? There can be no other, she thinks. He cannot understand the privileges of love within himself, so he does the only thing he knows best, and that is to escape. He knows they can never be and relocates, not just geographically but psychologically. She can see him musing and trying to determine what future there is for them and what he should do to change his.

The doorbell rings, and she lets Simon in. She wraps her arms around him, and he holds her.

'He'll turn up.'

'I hope you're right.'

'He just needs time away from things. He will contact you when he's ready. He knows you worry, and he won't want you to.'

'I'm just trying to understand his mind. So many things have happened. It must have been too much for him to take. I blame myself for a lot of it.'

'Why?'

'Just forcing him to get involved with Martha and not letting him make his own decision.'

'You did not. You knew he needed to. He couldn't go on properly without confronting it.'

She rests her head on his chest but still doesn't feel any solace in it.

He looks at the contents of the table. 'There are a lot of letters.'

She lifts her head. 'Aye, there is. They're letters from Martha and copies of Michael's replies. He kept them all.'

'It must make for interesting reading.'

'Aye, it does. It tells me why he's gone.'

'What do you mean?'

'They seem to be more than just good friends...' She delays herself from saying it. 'I think they're lovers.'

'No, that can't be!' he said in disbelief. 'Do they explicitly say that?'

'Aye, they do, close enough anyway.'

'I wasn't expecting that when I came here.'

'Neither was I. I just hope he hasn't done anything to himself.'

'Like what?'

'Hurt himself.'

'I don't think he'll do anything like that, Olivia. He's not the type.'

'What is the type?'

2

Nowell puts on a pair of goggles, latex gloves, and a white polypropylene coverall. He wipes the walls with wet paper towels and squeezes the blood into a washing-up bowl. He gets into every crevice and every minute part of the wall. The distribution of blood varies. There is blood spatter and smaller drops on the wall and floor. When he has cleaned all the blood the eye can see, he puts on a mask, picks up a hose, and steam cleans the wall and floor. The vapour steams up his goggles, and he stops to wipe them before starting again.

The blood has also radiated onto the car when it is cast off from the hammer, so he points the hose and cleans it, starting with the outside and then onto the seats and boot.

He steams down the tarpaulin used for the body and disposes it along with the paper towels, washing bowl and hammer and puts them into refuse sacks. He removes his protective clothing, bags them up, and steps back to see that everything is as it should be.

Once he has disposed of the sacks, he calls Ferguson's son and asks him to come to the garage.

David Ferguson puts his phone on charge and looks up the address on his sat nav. He taps on to directions and a woman with a clear well-spoken voice tells him to take the first right. He wears a suit, as he was just finishing a meeting when he got the call. He stops and parks at a place almost identical to the one Michael did.

He walks up to the garage and knocks. The torsion springs lifts the door up and David enters, and the door closes behind him.

'David, thanks for coming,' Nowell says.

'It's no problem.'

He looks at the car and sees the damage on the fender.

'I see you've been in the wars.'

'Yes, I had a slight accident.'

'Oh, well, it can be rectified.'

'I'm afraid it will need to be destroyed.'

'It's about fifteen hundred to two thousand pounds worth of damage. It'll be as good as new once my lads pick it up.'

'They can't pick it up, David. You need to get rid of it. They'll be implications if you don't.'

He looks at him and sees him as transparent as an icefish and the coldness inside the man. He feels tense from Nowell's deep modulation and doesn't say anything.

'You're the mayor-elect now, much of it with my help. I'll be first minister in the future, so you need to help me now.'

'I could sell it abroad,' he said, although, as the words come out of his mouth he knows it's a foolish move.

'No,' Nowell says. 'Look, I know you'll be losing money on this, but I'm interested in another vehicle, and if you give me a good deal on it, then we are even.'

David thinks about it. 'All right, we're even.'

CHAPTER TWENTY-SEVEN

Donnelly stares at the screen in his office and watches his cleaner vacuum. She is quick and efficient, and he's happy with her but distracted. Michael has been missing for nine days now, and his instincts say he's dead. Ever since they were wains, they never went a week without seeing or talking to each other. When he spoke to Olivia, he could hear the anguish in her voice and tried to mollify it.

He walks to the bar and watches the cleaner busily work away. She wipes the tables down in a circular motion, swiftly cleaning each one. He's impressed by her work rate and thinks she would win a gold medal if it were an Olympic event. As he watches her, he thinks of the fun times with Michael, especially the teenage years, the times when they got into scrapes with all kinds of ructions. They never got into the drug scene. It wasn't for them, alcohol was their poison, and it was enough to give them the fun they wanted. Those days are long gone, but it's never left him.

One night they got so drunk they both went off with other girls. Donnelly thought Michael was a goner because he went off with the girl from a notoriously violent family named the Daltons. Donnelly thought she possessed their temperament and tried to dissuade Michael from pursuing her, but the more he interfered, the more Michael wanted her.

He watched them go off together and thought Michael would not only have to cope with her highly strung disposition but that of her brothers. After he got what he wanted from his girl, he slept off his stupor and by mid-morning had wondered how Michael had got on. He called him a few times until finally, a few hours later, Michael picked up the phone. He could tell from the coarseness in his voice that he had a hard night. Michael told him she got so drunk she fell over and broke her nose. When her brothers turned up, he explained to them that he just saw her lying in the road and went to her aid. Luckily, they shook his hand and thanked him, saying if there's anything he needs in the future, don't hesitate to ask. Michael tells him that never seeing them again would be the best help.

He always thought of the good times, even in the bad times, like the loss of Michael's secret girlfriend, Sosaidh. Michael didn't express it in so many words, but his friend knew the agony was there. He would pray for him at night, sinking to his knees, hoping God would give his friend dispensation.

Michael knew she was gone yet remained. She would be there in his sleep, haunting him with her presence. He wanted to let go, but in doing so, she might disappear from his life, and he always wanted her to stay through the pain because somewhere in those thorns is comfort.

He watches the cleaner's head go back and forth as she clears a cobweb from the ceiling like she's a cat watching a piece of string above its head.

A man around his age comes in, and they shake hands.

'Anna, there's some pasties in the fridge. Go and rest yourself,' Donnelly says.

'Aye, no problem,' she replies.

The man sits down next to him. He looks like a Neanderthal with his thick eyebrows and full beard which compensates for his receding hairline.

'Thanks for coming, Tommy.'

'It's no bother,' he says as he plays with the top button of his shirt.

'You know why I called you here?'

'Aye.'

'So, what can you tell me?'

'I can tell you he was part of us.'

'In what way? Was he involved in operations? Was he directly involved?'

'No, not completely.'

'Then how?'

'He would get intel, mainly from an informer he had, and pass it on to us.'

'The Joiner, you mean?'

He stops playing with his button. 'Aye, that's him. He gave you up, didn't he?

'Aye, the bastard. He was working for the Brits, and he was the one who betrayed us.'

'Well, he had him in his pocket.'

'How many did Nowell kill?'

'He didn't kill anyone. He let us do it.

'Did he shoot anyone?'

'The only time he came close was with youse two.'

'Michael and me?'

'Aye. The attack at O'Neil's.'

'He was behind it?'

'Aye, but it went wrong. He was going to finish you off, but the ambulances got there before him, and that's the reason you're still here,' he said without dubiety.

Donnelly strokes his chin. He doesn't stroke a stubble because, unlike Michael, he has a soft, smooth complexion, but he strokes it, nonetheless.

'And now he's the most powerful enforcer in the land,' Donnelly reflects.

'And it's not just you who wants him out.'

'Aye,' he says, ruminating. He looks at him. 'Are you still in the narcotics business?'

'Aye, and he's cracking down on it too. No one is happy with him. That's why I'm here.'

'I'll speak to my people and see what can be done.'

'I hope you do, for all our sakes.'

'Thanks for telling me all of this. I know you don't have to.'

'Well, do with it what you will.'

'Understood.'

Tommy walks out, and Donnelly thinks of his best friend. Nine days, he thinks, nine days too long.

2

Donnelly reaches the cottage in the early evening. The lights are on, and the front door opens before he gets out of his car. A young man stands there and walks forward a few feet, kicking some stones as he does. Donnelly walks past him and into the cottage where Frank is sitting by the smouldering fire.

'Donnelly!'

''bout ye, Frank.'

'I'm not too bad now.'

He pours a pot of tea into cups. 'Here, have a wee cup of tea. When the boys make it, it tastes like cat's piss, but this is a grand one.'

'They don't know their arse from their elbows these days.'

Frank laughs. 'Too true, boy, too true!'

Donnelly takes a cup and sits down near the fire. Frank puts more turf onto the fire, and it slowly burns, giving the flames a hypnotic quality.

'I got your call, so what brings you here.'

'You know about Michael?'

'Aye, we do. Still no word?'

'No, none.'

'It's not us, you know that. He's one of our own.'

'I know. He's like a brother to me.'

'Aye, he is, surely.'

'And I don't think it's them.'

'I haven't heard anything from their side.'

'So that's why I think it's something higher.'

'The authorities?'

'Aye.'

'Why the feck is Olivia involved with Nowell's son?'

'Because she loves him.'

'But it's his son!'

'I know, but Michael says it's the real thing.'

'Jesus, but it's his sister! She's a good-looking girl. Surely, she can find someone better.'

'Well, she hasn't, so this is where we're at.'

'So, what do you want from me?'

'I think Nowell has something to do with Michael's disappearance.'

'Christ, he wouldn't be that bold!'

'He could be. He might want him out of the way, so his family don't have to deal with him.'

'I see what you mean. He wouldn't want that either.'

'Nowell's an arrogant bastard. All that he cares about is his reputation.'

'I agree, he's a charming fecker, too smooth for my liking, but a killer?'

'Lots of killers are charming. He's just one from a lengthy list.'

'So how can we help?'

'I just need one thing from you.'

'Anything, anything you need.'

Donnelly puts his cup down, and Frank listens.

3

Nowell stands behind a two-way mirror with his arms folded. Two detectives are in an interview room sitting opposite Frank O'Daniels and his lawyer. One of the detectives unwraps two new discs and puts one of them into the machine. Nowell thinks the PACE (Police and Criminal Evidence Act) law hinders the police, as up until that time, police could interview suspects without recording them. He feels they could be more aggressive in their approach, which is lost somewhat with this disposition.

The detective presses the record button and warns O'Daniels that an alarm will sound when the recording commences.

'The time is eight minutes past nine am on Monday 8th November 2017. The interview is taking place at the Police Service of Northern Ireland Headquarters in Belfast. My name is Detective Sergeant Andrew Bishop, and my colleague is Detective Nick Hammond. We are here to interview Mr Frank O'Daniels in the presence of his solicitor Mr Patrick O'Kane. This interview is being audio recorded,' he explained. 'Mr O'Daniels, can you please tell me your full name, address, and date of birth?'

Detective Hammond takes notes as his superior talks.

'Francis Eugene O'Daniels. 15 Ardstraw, Crossmaglen, South Armagh. Born on the third of June, nineteen fifty-five.'

'At the conclusion of this recording, I will explain the interview procedure and how you can access it,' the detective says. 'You do not have to say anything, but I must caution you that if you do not mention when questioned something which you may later rely on in court, it may harm your defence. If you do say anything, it may be given in evidence. Do you understand Mr O'Daniels?'

Frank slumps back in his chair. 'Aye.'

'Mr O'Daniels, were you the quartermaster general of the Provisional IRA from nineteen eighty-five to ninety-eight?'

'No comment.'

'You weren't?'

'No comment.'

'Are you saying you weren't the quartermaster general in those years?'

'No comment.'

'I don't think you have to harass my client,' O'Kane says.

'Mr O'Daniels, are you the leader of the dissident group 'The Real IRA'?'

'No comment.'

'Are you saying you have never been the leader of 'The Real IRA?'

'No comment.'

'Mr O'Daniels, do you know Michael Doherty? Michael Doherty was in the Provisionals and was convicted of killing a British soldier. Mr O'Daniels, Michael Doherty has been missing for two weeks. He's missing, his car is missing, and there is no trace of him. Mr O'Daniels, do you know what happened to him? Are you in any way responsible for his disappearance?'

'No comment.'

'Mr O'Daniels, do you know John Donnelly? He was also a member of the Provisionals. When did you last see him?'

The questioning continues for another hour, and Frank defies them with the same repetitive answer. Bishop is starting to tire of it and feels like he's talking to a ventriloquist's dummy.

'We are going to have a break from this interview for refreshments. I am turning off the recording now.'

The alarm buzzes, and the detectives step out of the room, where they are approached by Nowell.

'I commend you for putting up with his antics.'

'Thank you, Chief Constable,' Bishop says.

'It's good you mentioned John Donnelly. When are you going to question him?'

'Tomorrow, Chief Constable.'

'Good,' he says. 'And well done.'

The two detectives grab some tea and biscuits. They offer Frank and O'Kane a drink, and they ask for tea. Frank isn't impressed when he gets one, and he thinks his boy's cat's piss tastes better.

They sit down again, and Nowell watches from the next room.

'May I and my client have a private consultation.'

The detectives leave and return after twenty minutes.

'My client has prepared a written statement, which I shall read,' O'Kane says.

Nowell leaves the room as he doesn't want to hear it.

'I, Mr Francis Eugene O'Daniels, refute the allegations against me. I know Mr Michael Doherty as an acquaintance, but I do not know anything of his disappearance. On the day of his disappearance, I was at my holiday cottage, and I was there with my family. At no time did I leave the cottage on the said day...'

The two detectives know there isn't any further reason they can question him. They will interview his wife to verify his alibi, but they'll get no more than another prepared statement from her once she confirms it. The detectives will get the same from Donnelly as they are blocked at all quarters.

Frank stands up and shakes his solicitor's hand. 'Well done, boy!'

Chapter Twenty-Eight

Nowell is looking forward to seeing him. He doesn't see him as often as he would like, but he tolerates it. He doesn't know how to convince his son to renounce her. He mused over subtle ways, but when they announced their engagement, he sought to get rid of her. When it failed, he realised he had to volte-face to pacify him, but he wonders if he can change it.

Simon walks into the lounge where his father is waiting.

'Hello, son, how are you keeping?'

'I'm okay. Is there any news you can tell me about?'

Nowell gives him a serious look. 'We're looking into Michael's Republican activities and what his Provisional associates are doing now.'

'Have you found anything?'

He motions him with his hand. 'You better sit down.'

Simon takes a seat.

'There are some men who have come to the forefront.'

'Do they still live here?'

'Yes, and these men are very dangerous and haven't taken too kindly to your relationship with his sister.'

'But it has nothing to do with them.'

'I'm just stating how people feel, and I'm sorry, son, but I had to put Michael under surveillance.'

'Why?'

'Do you know John Donnelly?'

'Yes, Olivia has told me about him.'

He hands him a couple of photographs. 'The man Michael and John Donnelly are talking to is Frank O'Daniels. He is the leader of one of the top dissident groups.'

'What?' he says, looking perplexed. 'Why are they meeting him?'

'Because they are still involved.'

'Involved? In what capacity?'

'In every capacity.'

Simon stands up, holding the photos. 'No, that can't be.'

'I'm afraid it is. Michael is a killer, son, however, you look at it. I know he has seemingly accepted you, but has he really?'

'He says he has, and I believe him.'

'Well, I don't, and our family is at risk, Simon. I need to take this seriously, so I'm going to step up our security.'

'Is that necessary?'

'Yes, especially to me. I know what Michael is capable of.'

'He'd never harm me. He knows how important I am to Olivia.'

'That's another thing I want to talk to you about.'

Simon places the pictures on the table. 'Go on.'

'Have you heard of honey traps?'

'Vaguely?'

'On the tenth of March, nineteen seventy-one, three off-duty Scottish soldiers were lured out of a pub by a woman who promised them a good time at a party. Two of the soldiers were brothers. When they urinated at the side of the road on their way there, they were shot dead. Two in the back of the head. It was a theme at the time, and I think it's one now.'

'I don't really know what you are trying to say?'

'Olivia, son. She could be working for dissidents, and she's seduced you to get to me.'

'No. No way! Do you know how crazy that sounds! We met by chance. She didn't lure me into anything!'

'What about your relationship? Look how quickly it took off. Doesn't it seem unusual to you?'

'A lot of relationships can be like that. It's common.'

'Son, I'm talking about our family's safety. I'm here to protect it, and I won't let anything get in the way.'

'I'm not giving her up!'

He picks up the photographs and looks at them. 'Son, I only want what's best for you. You and your mother are my life. Simon, please postpone the wedding until I can ensure your safety.'

'No, we're going to get married. I know you are looking out for me, but I can look out for myself.'

He walks over and touches his son's shoulder and

squeezes it hard. Simon can feel his strong grip. He knows his father isn't demonstrative in his affection, but this is more than enough to indicate how he feels.

'I have something to show you.'

'Show me what?'

'Come with me, son.'

He follows his dad to the front door, and his dad opens it and looks back at his reaction.

A Ferrari 812 GTS is parked in the driveway. Ferguson's son gave him a good deal as a thank-you for getting him the job as mayor.

Simon looks at it and then at his dad.

'I know you've always liked them. 'Here,' he throws him the key. 'It's yours.'

'Dad, I can't accept this.'

'You can and you will.' He walks up to him. 'And we'll sort out all your troubles.'

'Dad, as I've said, Olivia and I will be together.'

Nowell walks towards the car and gestures. 'Come on, let's go for a spin.'

Simon stands there.

'Son,' he says and gives him a broad smile.

Simon looks at his smile and likes seeing him happy, so he relents and presses the fob.

A swoosh of metal debris and fragmented, shattered glass hits his father at high velocity. Compressed air travels outwards and throws him forward like a crash test dummy, unable to save himself. Simon falls back and sees everything in slow motion. He sees himself propelled through the open door and his father being ejected into the air from the fireball and falling like a rag doll onto the ground. Simon's ear drums burst and bleed from the canal. He can hear nothing. Like an unnatural silence has fallen. He can smell the odour of gasoline as thick black smoke bellows up from the twisted body of the car. Debris falls on and around his father's body like a meteor shower. Simon lies dazed, in and out of consciousness. It's the weakest he's ever felt in his life, and he tries to get up, but he drops back down again, unable to move. He sees his mum's face, and she's bawling mutely. He sees the fear in her eyes and the absolute despair that can't be quantified. She runs out to the driveway and runs back in. He sees her, and then he doesn't. She runs back and stands over him with a phone to her ear. He looks up and sees the frantic flaying of her arms and falls unconscious.

Chapter Twenty-Nine

Simon looks at the tubes surrounding his father's body, the ventilation machine bleeps like a ticking clock, and his vital signs show a low pulse rate and saturation reading. He walks over to his mother, who is holding a bedside ritual. Her complexion is pale, and her face is drawn, but she continues to tend to her husband's hair by keeping it clean and neatly combed.

He stands beside her and offers her a cup of tea, but she doesn't respond and continues combing his hair, so he gently takes the comb from her and makes her stop. He asks her to sit down, but she doesn't, so he leads her to the chair.

'Drink, Mum, you haven't drunk anything today,' he tells her as he holds the cup to her lips while she takes a sip. 'That's good.'

She stares blankly at him.

'Here, take some more.'

He looks at her in a dependent state, one he hasn't seen before, and his heart aches like it's never done. He looks at her, then over to his father and the ventilation machine trying to maintain his life and feels defenceless.

There is a soft knock on the door, and it opens, and a consultant walks in with a nurse.

'Hello, Simon,' he said.

He looks sympathetically at his mother. 'How are you, Mrs Nowell?'

She doesn't reply, and Simon squeezes her hand.

The consultant looks at the vital signs on the machine and looks back at the nurse.

'No change,' he says.

'No, doctor, the same as an hour ago,' she replies.

'How do you think he is, doctor?'

'Well, the primary concern is the blast lung injury he sustained from the impact of the bomb and the respiratory distress inflicted by the tissue damage. The alveoli are a vital component of this and are the endpoint of the respiratory system. It consists of minute, balloon-shaped air sacs which distribute oxygen and carbon dioxide molecules into and out of his bloodstream. The damage to this has caused it to rupture and has led to a consolidation where the part of the lung normally filled with air is now being filled with blood,' he explains.

'What can be done?' Simon asks.

'He is on airway pressure release ventilation, offering him the best chance, and we're hoping this will work.'

He looks at his father, the chief constable, a once powerful force, lying helplessly in a hospital bed, and he can do nothing to alleviate it.

He squeezes his mother's hand, but she just stares into space.

He remembers a time when he was at school, and he was being bullied. The bully didn't like him. He called him a 'pretty boy' and a rich one to boot. Simon didn't agree with the latter assumption, and he couldn't do anything about his looks.

One day when he came home with a black eye and finally told his da what was happening. He sat him down and gave him a talk, not a father-to-son but a man-to-man one. He told him that he needed to face his fears, not give up, and if he did, he wouldn't amount to much. Simon was taken aback but understood that there was no sinking into oblivion in his father's eyes. Whatever it throws at you, you must keep going. Life stops for no man. He then taught his son how to fight. The techniques used to defend himself and the offensive ones to defeat his opponent.

When he was bullied again, he felt the fists of his father's pounding the face of this kid, and he didn't stop until he was lying on the floor in submission. He knew then what his father expected, and it has always stayed with him. Now he is the one who wants his father to fight, but he has no techniques of how to help him, only hope, and he hopes he has the will to pull through.

As the hours pass into days, he and his mother keep a vigil and sit by the bedside day and night, taking the burden off each other by being there on a shift pattern basis. They alternate. Sometimes Simon is there in the morning and his mother in the afternoon, but they are always there, never leaving his side.

On the third day, the consultant comes in with a nurse. It is after nine o'clock, eight minutes past, according to Simon's phone. The consultant says his pleasantries and looks at the patient. He then refers to his notes. Simon looks at him, searching, waiting, preparing to hold on to his every word until he can't wait no more.

'Doctor?'

'Nurse Kelly, may I have a chair.'

'Certainly, doctor.'

She comes back with a chair, and the doctor takes it from her and sits.

'Mrs Nowell. Mr Nowell. We are keeping his organs working, but as for the whole man, we don't know whether he will regain consciousness or not. We might succeed in getting some form of consciousness.'

Elizabeth looks bewildered. 'Might? What do you mean by some form?'

'Minimal consciousness.'

'What does that mean?' Simon asks.

'His quality of life will be impaired.'

'How much?' Simon queries.

'A lot. He won't be your father as you know him, mentally or physically. He will be impaired in every way, and that's even after regaining full consciousness.'

'What is the alternative?'

'We have endeavoured to save him, but even with further aggressive treatment, we cannot meet the goal of saving his life. I'm so sorry to tell you this, but we recommend and are asking for your permission to turn off the ventilator.'

Elizabeth winces with pain.

'There's nothing more you can do?' Simon asks.

'No, I'm afraid not.'

'Thank you, doctor.'

'I'll leave you for a while.'

Simon turns his chair closely to face hers and

delicately breaches the question. 'Mum, what do you want to do?'

'He wouldn't want it, not that type of life,' she answers as a tear drops on his lap.

'I agree, he wouldn't. So, is that what you want?'

'Yes,' she whispers.

He holds her, and she cries on him until he can't take it anymore and cries too.

There is no drama, no fuss. The endotracheal tube is removed as the withdrawal protocol is conducted. He looks at his father as the nurse turns off the machine, and his arduous breaths come, each more laboured than the last, until the final one, and he's gone.

2

Craig Nowell receives a funeral befitting of a chief constable. It is like a state funeral, and the full regalia of the police service are there to pay their respects.

Simon stands behind the hearse and holds hands with his mother to his right and Olivia to his left. He looks at the Union Jack draped casket and knows today will be a great tribute to the man he is proud to call his father. His mother looks shell-shocked, and today will be unbearable for her. She has been up most of the night pacing the floor. He had to discourage her from going for a walk at three in the morning, so she just paced like she was trying to walk off the trauma.

They get into a black limousine, and he sits next to his mother and clasps his hand over hers. She doesn't make a sound and just looks ahead. He looks over to Olivia, and she gives him a consoling smile. He tries to return it, but his expression barely moves. He never told her about the last conversation he had with his father, not about her anyway, it's too preposterous to believe, and he'll never tell her because some things are best left unsaid. He grasps her hand, and she feels his warmth. He knows he must be strong for his mother, but internally he is suffering a deluge of sorrow.

The hearse begins to move away, and their limousine follows with other cars following behind them as it slowly meanders its way through the city.

Thousands of people have turned out to pay their last respects, clapping the hearse as it goes by, some throw flowers onto the bonnet, some land and stay on, others just fall off to the ground. Simon is moved by this and feels goose bumps forming on his neck, he feels weak, and his hand begins to shake, and Olivia can feel the vibration.

He never risked a full confrontation with his father until his love for a woman who didn't fit his family's conventional expectations entered his life. He knew a fissure would try to cut into their prism, but he was roused into defending her and defying him. He didn't have his father's natural propensity to pick fights, but he knew it came to the surface when needed, as with dealing with a bully who tormented him.

He knows that flame is now extinguished, and he must be the yardstick for his father's courage. He doesn't particularly want it, nor does he see it, but publicly at least he must demonstrate it.

Olivia holds his shaking hand still as he looks out at the mourners with stoicism, even though he feels the weeping heart within. He knows he isn't his father's mirror opposite, yet he doesn't want to be heir apparent to his father's community. He wants to build bridges, not breach them. He isn't impressed by public relations in the political sense as he sees it as a false declaration of his own beliefs. Public relations are tantamount to denying what you really are for the sake of the majority. He is too independent for that, a man with his own mind who is pliable to no one.

He looks out at these mourners. Most look like they are from the working-class east of the city, with proud yet world-weary faces. They look angry and alone, fearful of the future and clinging to lost times. He doesn't pity them but tries to understand their lives from his privileged perspective. He can never come close because the only way to understand would be to walk in their shoes, and his ones don't fit.

The funeral mass is full of mourners. Thousands more stand outside, most of them watch the large screen from inside the church as it is being televised live. In the days after his father's death, he spent excessive time staring into space, stuck in his own grief, but now that grief is public, he must be the bearer of it.

He walks to the lectern and looks at his father's Union Jack-draped caisson. He would rather be alone at this point, say things inwardly, only his private thoughts, not a speech he has to give to the world.

He looks past his father at the lectern and out into the congregation. He tells himself that his father is with him, and he must take on his persona for the minutes he stands here. It will get him through and appease any doubters of his community.

He looks down at his speech, doubled spaced, and reads:

'I would like to address the people today and tell you what my father means to me and our family. I stand here today to mourn as you do, but my sadness is tempered by a strong belief that my father did his best to follow his strict moral code. He lived and died by this code, for better or worse, but he stuck by his principles, and no one can say he did not. He was a man who tried to take the changing world with him, who tried to maintain the status quo, who tried for the love of one thing, his country...'

He goes on to say what a decent father he was to him and a loving husband he was to his mother. His voice never quavers, but it isn't monotone, either. It is crisp and clear in its delivery.

'...my father raised me to be a good and decent man,

and with that, I'm eternally grateful. He was an honest observer of my failings yet a great mentor of my strengths. Without him, I would not have been half as successful. He drove me, criticised me, but his advice was second to none.'

He feels unflappable saying these words, akin to his father. He can feel him breathing on his neck. He can hear him with every syllable. He has his strength and fears no one.

'...my father's love for his country was only superseded by his love for his family, even though it is intertwined, family is country, and country is family, and he would never want it any other way. I love you, Dad; may you watch over us and may you rest in peace.'

The people inside the church begin to clap, and he stands back from the lectern, surprised yet appreciative of their gesture. The sentiment echoes to the outside mourners as they clap and cheer. He feels he has done his job. His father will be gratified that he is so highly respected, and his son now understands how much his father means to them.

Chapter Thirty

Olivia looks around the place. Her clubbing days are over. She enjoys a party but prefers to go to a restaurant or the cinema. She is disinclined to rave now as she has different priorities and the life she wants.

She walks to the office door and knocks.

'Come in!'

She walks in, and he looks surprised.

'Olivia?'

'Hello, Johnny.'

'What brings you here?'

'I've just come to ask a few things.'

'Right? Take a seat.'

She takes the arm of the chair and sits.

'Michael told me you met Frank O'Daniels.'

She omits to tell him it was Simon who told her. Her lover has taken the place of her sibling as the man she feels most protective of, and she will never forsake him.

'Is that what he told you?' he asks.

'Aye, it is. Why did you meet him, Johnny?'

He goes over to the fridge, opens a bottle of beer with

a magnetic opener, takes a swig, and then turns to her. 'Michael was worried about you. We met Frank to straighten things out.'

'What things?'

'About your boyfriend's da.'

'Did they know about Simon and me?'

He rubs his nose. 'No, not that I know of.'

'What did he want to know?'

'He wanted to know if we could get anything on him.'

'Like what?'

'Did he collaborate with Loyalists.'

'And did he?'

'We couldn't find out anything.'

'Why did they want to know this?'

'They didn't want him there. They wanted him to be replaced, so they needed information to use against him, to oust him if you like.'

'And you and Michael didn't tell them anything?'

'We had nothing to tell.'

'How's the investigation going into his da's death?'

'It's going nowhere. Everyone is silent.' She stands up and looks him squarely in the eye. 'They killed him, didn't they?'

'Jesus, no!'

'Give me the truth!'

'Okay, okay. They wanted him replaced but by political, peaceful means, not like this. Frank is a political being, and he won't do anything to impede it. He could never do what he did twenty or thirty years ago today.'

'Jim Flaherty has taken over; does he know anything?'

'God no! Olivia, you're clutching at straws.'

She jabs a finger at him. 'Simon and I are this island's future, people from different backgrounds living together, accepting things and striving for tomorrow.' She looks at him directly in the eyes. 'What are you?'

She walks out, and Donnelly picks up his bottle and downs it.

Chapter Thirty-One

Martha hands a spade to Olivia, and she holds one herself. It's her idea to do this. She wants to plant an apple tree in memory of her son and wants Olivia to be here, just the two of them, no family members, no friends, just them.

Martha digs to the right and Olivia to the left. Once the hole is sufficient, Martha takes the sapling from its pot and places it in it. Olivia holds it upright as she pours the soil before patting it down. They step back and stand for a minute in their own silence.

Martha hands her a glass of red wine and has one herself. She is stopping the night and might have more if she's in the mood, but she's still undecided. They sit in the gazebo, and Olivia watches her look at the tree.

'Are you all right,' Olivia asks.

'Yes. How are you bearing up?'

'I'm worried,' she replies wistfully.

'You must be beside yourself with worry.'

'Aye, I am.'

'What is the latest news?'

'There's still no change, no new clues or evidence into his disappearance. There's nothing...' There's a pause as her voice cracks with emotion. 'Sorry.'

'It's okay, I understand.'

'It's just he's not here. He's always been here whenever I needed him, and now, he's gone.'

'I know how you feel.'

She says it before she can retract it. She thinks of Michael too. She doesn't like her thoughts, thoughts she shouldn't be having, but she can't help the sensation. They don't rationalise because nothing that derives from the heart does.

'If there's anything I can do to help…'

'Thank you, Martha.'

'Anything.'

'You're such a good friend. Michael and I think so much of you.'

'I know.'

'Martha.'

'Yes.'

'I read your letters.'

Martha looks at her.

'I hope you don't mind. Michael left them there.'

She stays composed. 'Maybe he wanted you to see them?'

'Do you think so?'

'Maybe? It's a possibility.'

Martha isn't surprised by Olivia's confession. She even feels a sense of relief that someone apart from her knows.

She doesn't feel solely responsible, nor does she feel shame, much to her chagrin, and she knows Olivia won't let this go any further.

'They read like a letter from a soldier to his sweetheart.'

'Olivia, it's not what you think.'

'It is Martha. It is what I think. I'm in love, and I recognise those words. I recognise what they mean, directly and indirectly.' Lowering her voice. 'I read all of them, and my interpretation is that they are letters of love.'

'Olivia, I don't want you to think that. I didn't write it in that way.'

'You both wrote from the heart, and it shows. It's magnified and lit in shining lights. I'm the only person who has read them apart from you. I'm impartial, and still, it shows. The letters are beautiful. It shows two people struggling with their feelings but at the same time letting them out.'

'I care for your brother, but so much damage was done. It just made our emotions even more acute. I, nor he, could really understand what the other felt, but we came to understand our own emotions, and it was scary.'

'He loved you.'

'Olivia...'

'He did! He's never been in love since your son died, but he loved you. I'm glad he found it. Discovered what it is, before he...' She stops herself from saying it. 'Before this.'

'Olivia, my feelings confuse me. I have so much

tumult. I did have feelings for him, ones I didn't want to contemplate, but we couldn't pursue them because it would have been inconceivable to do so. That's why we must be apart.'

'The pull was too strong, you mean?'

'Whatever it was, it was too strong.'

'I know what it was.'

'Why are you delving into this?'

Her voice cracks with emotion again. 'Because I have to!'

'Are you all right?'

The pause endures.

Martha holds her hand. 'Olivia?'

In a quiet voice, she replies. 'I'm okay. It's just if there's a chance he may be found. He may have gone somewhere to find himself. He's a searcher, constantly looking for meaning, even when it isn't there. I can see him now... searching....'

'You're looking for meaning, but life doesn't always have the answers we want. It's as if we're spinning around in the universe, and it just does that—spins—and we spin with it, searching but never finding.'

'I brought you together, so I feel responsible.'

'You don't need to. What happened has happened. We can't change it.'

'You seem detached from it?'

'I must look at it this way. Michael and I both have our wants, and the desire to combat our pain was even more intense. In a way, Michael is my pain, he's the sole cause of it, and in combating him, I was combating the hurt.'

'He loves you, though,' she replies, trying to regain her self-control.

'And I have feelings for him too, but I can't express them, Olivia. You do understand that don't you?'

'Yes, I understand.'

'Our feelings, in the sense you mean, are elusive. I must dissociate myself from them. It would destroy me if I didn't. I must survive. Either I switch the light on, or I switch it off.'

'I know. I'm sorry, Martha. Now that he's gone, I want the things he wants or is searching for, he's never been genuinely happy, and that's all I want for him.'

'Happiness is a state of mind. A person can be happy alone, walking in nature, or they can be happy with others in a social setting, but in the end, it's all in the mind.'

'You know, I saw you as his rescuer, someone who would save him from himself.'

'How do you save a man from himself?'

'Well, I couldn't, and the answer I found was you. You were the only one.'

'I don't know if I did or if I gave him the answer. The answer may or may not have been the one he was looking for.'

'But he confided in you more than me. What he wrote I was never privy to. I don't know everything you talked about, but some of it was between you and not me.'

'I think as time has gone on, he opened up more. Before that, he was closed, but I gave him time to talk. I'm an open book, and with patience, I opened him.'

'You did, surely. I saw his face lighten and your face calm. You did extraordinary things for each other; a semblance of peace came over you, and the chance to heal gradually took place. It was moving to watch.'

'That's what I wanted—to heal. It takes time to do it, but I could feel it. The anxiety slipped away, and I could breathe again.'

'It's all I ever wanted for both of you. I brought you together to heal.'

'And you achieved that for your brother. He'll be indebted to you. You saved him just as much as me and tended to the cuts inflicted by the traumatic torture of fate.'

'That's beautiful.'

'I hope so. I don't think my education has gone to waste,' she said in jest to ease the atmosphere. 'Look, Olivia, we were just trying to find our way back home again. We were lost until we met, and then we found the directions which led us to the place we wanted to be.'

'Your Garden of Eden?'

'Yes, if you like. We defeated all the obstacles first, and this led us to our special place.'

'So, surely, it was inevitable that this would happen, that you had to part ways.'

'Yes. Looking at it objectively, it was the only way we could continue in life. It had to be a transformation. We were adrift. Michael couldn't talk easily, so my grasp of the English language fitted his curious mind. He is highly intelligent, more than he makes out, but his virility hinders it. I knew it was there, but I had to prize it out of him. We both have a love of language, and this gradually brought us together.'

'I know. He wrote such fitting words, and you brought out that side of him. He left his tough side at the door and walked into your world. You saw his weakness, his sensitivity, and you opened the door for him.'

'He may have done it for himself. I saw it in him from our first meeting even when he was a closed book. I knew I could open his pages.'

'And you did, surely. You gave him the willingness to face what was troubling him the most, to show a side of himself that I always wanted him to show, and you did it with the same emotion—love.'

'Sui generis.'

'What does it mean?'

'It means of its own kind, and that's what we had.'

She holds Olivia's hand tightly and doesn't say anymore. Olivia tries to stop herself from crying and fails, so Martha consoles her and looks back at what they planted.

2

The last attendance of summer is gone as Martha explores the woods. The air is cold against her face and sharpens her sensibility. There is a chill in the atmosphere and a smell of autumn dew. Leaves are falling, clouds are prevalent, and the sun is no longer conspicuous.

Flora and fauna fight to survive, but they only have a certain life span to do it. The seasons dictate whether they will or not, not their survival instincts but by the passage of time.

Her boots squelch in the mud as she goes along, and she looks back at her footprints. Every season has its beauty, and every orbit has a new meaning, something to see that she missed before. The colours of the foliage are radiant, even in the bleakness of winter.

The cold air whispers to her, and she hears its voice. Some of those voices stay with her like the sun in the Sahara, while others fade like the melting snow. They are voices she understands, voices she has heard many times before. A voice with which she is comfortable. Is it her voice telling her things she wants to hear or one that means something to her? She doesn't want it to disappear because if it did vanish, she couldn't continue. She wouldn't have the strength to. She would fight, but it is worth it when it is only a pyrrhic victory.

She takes in the red, orange, and yellow colours of the leaves. A crisp breeze blows some of the leaves off their branches, and she wraps her arms around herself and feels snug in her fleece jacket.

A robin moves from branch to branch, eagerly marking its territory. It perches itself on one of the branches and swiftly tilts its head from side to side, then flies down and catches a worm before flying back to a branch to readily eat it.

She looks at it and knows it will soon find a mate, soon build a nest, and soon lay eggs. Her body has relinquished those things. She can never start a family again; biology has put an end to it, but she can still move forward into a new dawn if she tries.

The surface of the Downs consists of chalk grasslands. Orchids thrive in the lowland calcareous grassland. In mid-summer, they flower beautifully with pink sepals that look like wings with furry brown markings akin to a bee. In this season, there is a different beauty. The orbital axis brings birth, death, and renewal. She thinks of him in these moments as the seasons pass by, each bringing a distinct perspective of her feelings for him. Can she see a renewal in herself now. She has isolated herself for far too long, and she wants to change it and walk in the beauty of nature and feel alive again. She feels that meeting Michael has torn down her emotional barricades, and they aren't returning. She isn't all cried out, she has times of utter despair, normally in the dark of night, but she feels she has the mechanisms to cope.

She thinks her life is like the seasons of the year, from spring to winter. It comes and goes in stages. All the joy and belief are in their initial stages, and all the tragedies are at the end. But in the end, comes wisdom and an acknowledgement of what her life has been, not what it could have been but what it is.

She thinks of the tree she planted with Olivia, the tree of what should have been his life and wants him to be her little boy again. She phoned Olivia this morning to see if she got back home safely and feels strangely maternal towards her. No one can go through what they've been through and not be. She doesn't want to admit it, not to Olivia, but she feels relieved that Michael is gone. If he is still in the world, she would think of him, he would dominate her thoughts, and that's something she doesn't want. If he's dead, then the shackles can be lifted and banished forever. He won't exist because he doesn't exist, and she does, and she's alive.

She continues a well-trod path that leads to a gate. She opens the latch and steps onto an elevated part. She progresses further onto a pathway with wired fencing on both sides, and this leads to a farmer's field. The field is fallow from the harvest, and the churned patterns from the tractor plough are fading. She looks at the horizon, and two bright arches of a double rainbow are in the distance. She gazes at them in wonder, taking in their semi-circular aura and glorious colours, which make her feel part of this world. She thinks about what's best for her and her future. Yes, she thinks, my future, and draws in the air deeply and walks towards the rainbows.

3

Olivia walks hand in hand with Simon, and love radiates from her rosy cheeks.

'It's so quiet here, isn't it. It's such a beautiful place to rest, and she's resting all right. I just hope he's resting with her too?'

'I'm sure he is my love.'

They are man and wife now; they had a humanist wedding, not to assuage family and friends but to get as far away as possible from their denominations. They agreed on one thing, to let their identities be channelled with love.

Olivia had an Irish harpist play as she walked up the aisle of rose petals. She walked up the aisle alone as no one can take her brother's place. Simon wore his father's red silk handkerchief in his blazer pocket and wondered if he would be proud? He knew his mother was proud because she told him so. She took Olivia at face value and welcomed her. They would walk around his mother's vast estate, two women deep in conversation, conversations only women can have, and he knew she was accepted.

Olivia said she is nearly as close to his mother as she is to Martha. Martha came to the wedding, she was the one who placed the rose petals in the aisle, some of those petals were from her garden. When Olivia walked over those roses Martha had tears in her eyes, they were not just for Olivia though, they were also for Michael. She knew he loved her, but she couldn't allow him to. She only hoped if there is another world that he would find love again.

Olivia lets go of Simon's hand, and she picks up a

bunch of wilted sunflowers Michael had placed there and replaces them with new ones. Simon takes the wilted ones and goes off to dispose them. She makes the sign of the cross and steps back and rubs her stomach; her bump is beginning to show as a new life grows inside her. A seed of hope that breathes a new sense of purpose in her.

She prays for her brother too, wherever he is. She feels he will never meet her child but sees him from a distant shore, he gives her that look of his, and she is encapsulated by his love, but now they are apart.

She knows that being apart from someone, whom you feel is a part of you, is like being in a different dimension. You are here, and they are there, and you will never see them or hear their voice again, although it speaks to you every day. You will never be able to touch them, and only in your dreams will you ever get close. It is something that lives with you, day in and day out. Some days it's like a waterfall of emotion, such is the pain. On other days you fight it off, and a victory has been achieved, only for it to return and hit your weakest point once more.

She realises this and knows she will have to come to accept he is missing from her life, like a limb that's been lost and not sewn back together. She looks up at the nimbostratus clouds dominating the sky around her and holds her stomach.

'It's going to be a boy, Michael, and we're naming it after you because you are my hero. You always looked after me. You deserved more than this life threw at you. I hope all the hurt is gone now and the angels catch you when you fall.'

She says this knowing she could never have saved him, but what she can do is reconcile all the chapters of his life, collated into one with meaning. His life did have meaning, and like all life, it tells the story of our existence. It tells it truthfully, whether it causes joy or anguish, but it tells it, and it echoes with our frailties, our decisions, our mistakes and who we are.

It begins to rain.

About the Author

Shaun Francis was born in Dartford, Kent. He has a HND in Professional Writing from North West Kent College and a BA (Hons) degree in Humanities from the University of Greenwich.

9 781967 441426